A Cowboy and his Christmas Crush

A Johnson Brothers Novel, Chestnut Ranch Romance, Book 3

Emmy Eugene

Copyright © 2020 by Emmy Eugene

All rights reserved.

No part of this book may be reproduced in any form or by any electronic or mechanical means, including information storage and retrieval systems, without written permission from the author, except for the use of brief quotations in a book review.

ISBN-13: 978-1659748239

Chapter 1

Russ Johnson stood outside, the faint music from the wedding dance behind him. He couldn't go back inside, not with his chest as deflated as it was. He was thrilled for Seth and Jenna, who'd been friends for a very long time. And he owed his last two months of dating the beautiful Janelle Stokes to Seth, who'd encouraged him to get out there and meet someone.

And he had. He and Janelle may not have seen each other every day for the past two months. Some people would call their relationship slow.

Russ didn't mind either of those things. When something awesome happened, he wanted to tell Janelle. When she had something to celebrate, he wanted to be the one who showed up with a cake.

And he'd thought they'd been getting along really well since the speed dating event in October. *Slow and steady wins the race*, he'd told himself.

Except he was losing. Big time.

Janelle had called him on Tuesday, and Russ had known from the moment she said his name that he wouldn't like what she was about to say.

And he hadn't. Because she'd broken up with him, citing her daughters as the reason why. He'd wanted to meet them. She'd freaked out.

It's fine, he'd texted her after she'd told him she didn't want to see him anymore. *I don't have to meet them until you're ready.*

He hadn't heard from her since.

He took a big breath and looked up into the starry sky. Behind him, the music stopped, and the door opened. People began piling outside, and Russ wanted to disappear again. But he joined the crowd instead, stepping over to Griffin and Rex while he scanned the crowd for Travis. He didn't see his brother, and Rex stepped out to help their parents get out of the fray.

The photographer came out and raised both of his hands. "Okay, everyone," he yelled. "Sparklers for everyone. Don't light them until I say, and you're going to hold them up like this." He held the sparkler right up above his head. "And wave them in short bursts. We only get one shot at this."

He started passing out sparklers, as did his assistant. Russ had no way to light the sparklers, but the photographer and his assistant started handing out matches too. He backed up to the doors and opened them a couple of inches. "Are the bride and groom ready?"

He must've gotten the go-ahead, because he turned back to the crowd outside. "All right, light 'em up."

The buzzing and fizzing of sparklers started, and the photographer called for Seth to bring Jenna outside. He did, and Russ could feel his brother's joy all the way at the back of the crowd. A cheer went up, and everyone lifted their sparklers and started waving them as taught.

The camera went *click, click, click* as the photographer walked backward, capturing the sparkler sendoff. He turned and took several pictures of the car, which Rex and Griffin had decorated. The décor was barely appropriate, but Seth and Jenna laughed at the cookies stuck to their car and ducked inside.

With them gone, the event concluded, and the vibrant atmosphere fizzled along with the sparklers. Russ watched his burn all the way down, and then he put it in the pile with all the other burnt-out fireworks. He and his brothers still had an hour of clean-up to do, and he still didn't know where Travis had gotten to. *Probably with Millie*, Russ told himself, as he'd been the one to tell his brother to go ask her to dance.

Russ found him inside, alone, folding up chairs. "You didn't come out for the sparkler thing?"

Travis shook his head, looking a bit dazed. Russ didn't have time to wonder what that was about, because they had to be out of the posh castle where Seth and Jenna had gotten married in exactly one hour.

He started helping with the chairs too, while others pulled down decorations, picked up centerpieces, and loaded everything into boxes to be taken outside. When everything was finally done, he got in the truck with Travis and started back to Chestnut Ranch.

Neither of them spoke, and Russ was grateful Travis wasn't the kind of brother who needed to know every detail of everything the moment it happened. He alone knew that Janelle had broken up with Russ—well, until that disastrous dinner conversation. Now everyone knew, and Russ was actually surprised his mother hadn't cornered him during the dancing to find out what had happened and then offered advice for how to fix it.

His momma meant well, he knew that. But she didn't understand that Janelle was as stubborn as the day was long.

She was smart too, and beautiful, with a wit that spoke right to Russ's sense of humor. She outclassed him in every way, and he told himself he should be grateful he'd had two months with her. But he couldn't help wanting more time. Wanting forever.

"How was the dance with Millie?" he asked when he went through the gate and onto the ranch.

"Good," Travis said.

"You gonna call her?"

His brother sighed and looked over at Russ. "Yeah. How do I do that?"

Russ grinned at Travis, who was a couple of years younger than him. "You just put in the numbers, and when she answers, you ask her to dinner. Easy."

"Easy," Travis said, scoffing afterward. He got out of the truck when Russ parked, but Russ stayed in the cab for another moment. Could he just tap a few times to pull up Janelle's contact info, call, and ask her to dinner?

"Yeah," he said to himself darkly. "If you want another slash on your heart." And he didn't. It was already hanging in shreds as it was, and Russ rather needed it to keep breathing.

* * *

Russ survived Saturday and Sunday, because Travis was there. They did minimal chores on the ranch on the weekends, and he and his brother could get the animals fed and watered in a couple of hours. He'd napped, and he'd stared at his phone, almost willing it to ring and have Janelle on the other end of the line.

Monday morning, Travis loaded up with the ranch hands that lived in the cabins along the entrance road, and they left to go move the cattle closer to the epicenter of the ranch.

Russ was glad he hadn't drawn that chore this time, but his loneliness reached a new high in a matter of hours. Griffin and Rex worked somewhere on the ranch, but Russ wasn't as close with them as he was Seth and Travis. He certainly didn't want to talk about Janelle with Rex, who thought it was fun to go out with one woman on Friday night and a different one the next evening.

Dusk found Russ standing on the back edge of the lawn, looking out over the wilder pastures of the ranch. In the distance, dogs barked and barked and barked. Russ normally loved dogs, but the increase of them on the ranch over the course of the last month had been too much.

With Seth gone for the next couple of weeks, Russ didn't even find the puppies cute anymore. Winner barked, as if she was the mother hen and was telling the other dogs to settle down. They didn't, and she ran along the grass line, barking every few feet.

"Enough," Russ told her. Eventually, he turned back to the house. He ate dinner, showered, slept. Then the next morning, he got up and did everything all over again. Travis returned that afternoon, and Rex ran to town for pizza and their mother's homemade root beer.

"To a successful relocation," Rex said, his voice so loud that it echoed through the kitchen.

Travis just grinned at him and took a bite of his supreme pizza. Russ was just glad there were more people in the homestead that night. It was a giant house, and he didn't like being in it alone.

"I'm goin' to shower," Travis said, and Russ picked up another piece of pizza. Griffin started telling a story about something Darren had said, and Russ was content to listen and laugh. A few minutes later, Travis came thundering down the stairs, his cowboy boots loud on the wood.

Rex was practically standing in the doorway already, and he ducked out to see what Travis was doing. He whistled and said, "Hoo boy, where are you off to?"

Russ exchanged a glance with Griffin, and said, "He's so loud."

"Try living with him," Griffin muttered, and they both

moved into the living room, where Travis was putting on one of his nicest dress hats. He turned toward everyone and said, "I'm goin' out with Millie."

A smile crossed Russ's face. So he'd called her.

"Good for you, bro," Rex said.

"You look like you're going to throw up," Griffin said.

"Go," Russ said, stepping in front of the younger brothers. "Don't listen to them. Have fun." He smiled at Travis and nodded, because his brother needed to go out, and he needed the encouragement.

"What if—?"

"Nope," Russ said. "Now where are your keys?"

Travis patted his pockets, panic filling his face. "Shoot. I must've left them upstairs." He bolted back that way, and Russ shook his head.

"Don't give him grief over this," he said to the other two brothers. Rex held up both hands as if surrendering, and Griffin wandered back into the kitchen. Travis came back downstairs, his keys in his hand, and Russ said, "Have fun."

Travis said nothing as he left, and Russ chuckled and turned around. "I hope he calms down and has fun."

"He will," Rex said. "Travis gets along great with Millie. They'll be fine."

Russ nodded, wishing he was the one going out tonight. He didn't realize Rex had left until he brought him a piece of pizza from the kitchen. How much time did he lose thinking about Janelle?

"What about you and Janelle?" Rex asked, lifting his new piece of pizza to his lips. His eyes were sparkling, like he wanted all the dirt on the painful break-up. His half-smile said he'd definitely tease Russ, who wasn't in the mood.

"There's nothing about me and Janelle," Russ said.

"You like her though, right?"

"Of course I like her," Russ said, his voice growing as loud as Rex's. "I like her a whole lot. But what am I supposed to do? Drive over to her house and beg her to go out with me? She won't talk to me, Rex. She doesn't want me in her life. So liking her is irrelevant, isn't it?"

Rex lowered the pizza and stared. "I'm sorry, bro," he said, really quiet.

All the fight left Russ, and his shoulders slumped as the air whooshed out of his lungs. "Me too. Sorry, none of that was fair."

"I get it," Rex said. "No explanation needed." He fell back a step. "But if you like her as much as you say you do, she probably likes you too."

"Knock, knock?" a woman said, and Russ spun toward the front door. It started to open, which meant it hadn't been latched all the way.

How much had Janelle heard?

Humiliation filled Russ, and he turned back to Rex, but he was gone. At least his brother had done one thing right that night. He'd brought dinner too, so Russ would give him two points.

"Janelle," he said, her name scratching in his throat. "What are you doing here?"

Chapter 2

Janelle couldn't believe she had the courage to be standing on Russ's front porch. She also couldn't believe she'd heard his entire conversation with his brother.

"Janelle?" Russ said again, and she blinked.

"Yeah—yes," she said, clearing her throat. Her heart had been pounding for a solid hour, and she just wanted to calm down.

He came closer, and it was so unfair that he was so tall, with such broad shoulders, and that caring glint in his dark eyes. Janelle had always loved his eyes, from the very first moment she'd sat down across from him at the speed dating event during Chestnut Springs' Octoberfest.

"You have another dog with you," he said, looking down at the mutt panting at her feet.

"Yeah, uh…" She'd maybe used the dog to get herself out to the ranch. Somehow, she could deal with cheating husbands and angry wives as they became exes. She could argue for the rights of one of those parents in court until she got what she wanted. She owned and ran the biggest family law practice in the country.

And Russ Johnson made her heart flutter and her nerves fray. He could also make her laugh faster than anyone else, and the man kissed her like she was worth something, and Janelle had been miserable for almost a week now.

"Look," she said, brushing her loose hair out of her eyes. "Someone brought the dog over, and they brought him to me, because they thought we were together."

Russ started nodding, the pain etched right on his face. He ducked his head, that dark gray cowboy hat hiding his eyes. She hadn't meant to hurt him, and she wanted to tell him she was miserable too. "And I brought him over here, because I want us to be together."

I like her a whole lot.

Janelle knew Russ liked her. When she'd called him to say she wanted to take a break, he'd gone silent. He accepted what she said, and she liked that he didn't argue back. Her ex would've argued back. In fact, she'd taken Henry back three times because of his excellent argumentative skills.

She never should've married another lawyer.

"You want us to be together," Russ said, lifting his eyes to hers. "You know what you're saying, right?"

"Yes," Janelle said. "And I told you last week, I just wanted a break. It wasn't a full break-*up*."

"No, what you said was that you didn't want me to meet

your daughters." He held up one hand. "Which I'm fine with, sweetheart. Honest."

"It's not fair for you to call me sweetheart," she said, teasing him now. And he knew it.

"It's just me," he said, saying what he'd always said. "And when you meet my momma—"

"I know, I know," Janelle said, smiling. "She'll call me baby and sugar and sweetheart too."

Russ bent down and picked up the leash Janelle had put around the dog's neck. "I'll take him out to the enclosure, but I don't know where we're going to put him. We've got at least eight more dogs than we can house."

Janelle saw another opportunity zooming toward her, and she snatched at it. "I could take some," she said.

Russ's eyebrows went up, and she desperately wanted to swipe that cowboy hat from his head and kiss him. She licked her lips instead, her fantasies going down a path she couldn't follow. At least right now.

"You could take some?" Russ repeated. "Where are you going to put them?" He leaned in the doorway, easily the sexiest man alive in that moment.

"I have an old stable in my backyard," she said. "Maybe you could come help me fix it up, and I could probably put six or seven dogs back there."

Russ considered her, the corners of his mouth twitching up.

"What?" she asked, smiling at him.

"Do you know what to feed a dog?" he asked. "Or how often they need to go out? Or any of that?"

"No," she said. "That's why my awesome, handsome cowboy boyfriend will come help me...and the girls."

Russ's eyebrows went all the way up, and he folded his arms. She loved that he stayed silent during key moments, because the mystery of what he was thinking was hot.

"I get to meet the girls?" he asked.

"That's what you want, isn't it?" Janelle wanted that too. She was just overprotective of Kelly and Kadence.

"No, Janelle," he said, oh so soft and oh so sexy. "I don't know what you did or didn't hear. But I'm pretty sure it's obvious that what I want...is you."

The air left Janelle's lungs, because Russ Johnson always knew what to say and how to say it. Her fingers twitched toward his cowboy hat, and Russ chuckled.

"I saw that." His eyes twinkled like stars, and he took off his own cowboy hat this time. Janelle slipped one hand along the waistband of his jeans, his body heat so welcome. He enveloped her in an embrace, pressing his cowboy hat to her back.

"Russ," she whispered. "I like you a whole lot too."

"So you heard everything."

"I need to go slow," she said, closing her eyes and tipping her head back, an open invitation for him to kiss her.

"I know that, baby," he said, sliding his fingers around the back of her neck and into her hair. His lips touched hers in the next moment, and kissing Russ was like coming home. He took his time like he'd really missed her, and Janelle knew that he had. She hoped he could feel that she'd missed him too, and that she was sorry she'd freaked out about him meeting her kids.

THE FOLLOWING AFTERNOON, she picked the girls up from school and said, "Okay, we have a new project."

"Another one?" Kelly asked, adjusting her backpack between her feet. "Mama, we're still making the brownies tonight, right?"

"Yes, yes," Janelle said, smiling at her oldest. "Chocolate and caramel swirl."

Kelly smiled. "So what's the new project?"

"It has to do with that dog someone brought over last night." Janelle made the left turn out of the school pick-up lane.

"You took it over to the ranch," Kelly said. "And then brought it back."

"They don't have room over there, and I told Russ we could put a few dogs in our stable. So we need to get it cleaned up for them." Janelle knew seven was more than "a few," but she didn't want to think too long about it. Otherwise, she'd wonder how she was going to keep them all happy and fed.

But it couldn't be that hard. The girls could help her put out fresh food and water morning and night. She had a fenced backyard they could romp around in while she went to work and the girls went to school. And then she wouldn't have a canine sleeping in her bed, like she'd had last night.

She turned onto their street while the latest and greatest song came on. "Mama, turn it up," Kadence said from the back seat. Janelle smiled as she did, so glad she'd been pulling her hours back at the firm so that she could be there to pick up her girls in the afternoons.

She'd had a nanny for the past three years—since Henry had moved out—but she didn't want Mallory to be the one who knew her daughters. She didn't need to work as much as she did, and she wanted to be as good of a mother as everyone believed she was as a lawyer.

So she put up with the tween pop song her daughters knew every word to. Even Janelle could sing along, because the song was completely overplayed. She pulled into the garage and waited for the song to finish before turning off the car and getting out.

"Everyone in," she said. "Wash your hands and change your clothes. We'll work for an hour in the stables, and then it's brownie-making time."

Kelly cheered, and Janelle smiled at her. She'd taken off a huge bite this holiday season, but her ten-year-old loved baking and cooking, and Janelle had said they could put up a post every Sunday, asking all the clients and followers of the Bird Family Law social media to suggest the things they should make that week. And they'd make at least three of them.

The fun had only been going for a week, and since there hadn't been school last Wednesday, Thursday, or Friday, they'd made five of the dozens and dozens of suggestions.

This week, they'd chosen caramel swirl brownies, carrot

cake muffins, and mini cheesecakes. They'd already made the carrot cake muffins last night, and Janelle wouldn't be surprised if they made five additional desserts that week.

The employees at the firm enjoyed the leftovers, and now that Janelle had gotten Russ to forgive her, she'd have another reason to pay the sixteen-year-old next door ten dollars to sit with her sleeping kids while she ran out to the ranch after dark.

She felt giddy at the idea of seeing him again that night, and she told herself that a woman her age shouldn't be sneaking off to see her boyfriend. But she wasn't *sneaking off*. She'd go out to his ranch for a few minutes, and then she'd bring him back here to see her shed and eat brownies.

As if on cue, her phone chimed and it was Audrey from next door, asking if she was still coming over that night.

Yep, Janelle sent. *Thank you so much.*

She got a smiley face and a thumbs up in return, and she put the step-stool in front of the sink so Kadence could reach to wash her hands. "Kel, did you wash?"

"Yes," her daughter called as she ran down the hall, and Janelle had the suspicion that her daughter had not washed her hands. Janelle was a bit of a germaphobe, as she worked with a lot of people. Always in and out of her building, with their kids, and their babies, and her daughters went to school with a plethora of kids who could have anything.

Her rule to wash hands after school eased her mind, though it probably didn't do anything to actually eliminate the germs she could be exposed to.

"Snacks?" she asked.

"That white popcorn," Kadence said, soaping up really good.

Janelle pumped some soap into her hands too and shared the running water with her daughter. "White popcorn comin' up." She washed, dried, and got down the bag of white popcorn before Kelly came back down the hall. She now wore an old pair of plaid pajama pants and a T-shirt that had been bleached at some point. "What do you want for a snack?"

"Cheese quesadillas," Kelly said.

"That's a meal," Janelle said. "We'll eat dinner while the brownies bake." She didn't have time for cheese quesadillas either.

"Granola bar," Kelly said.

"Great," Janelle said, giving her daughter the side-eye. "Wash your hands and get the box down. Let's go change, Kade." She gave Kelly a *don't even try to lie to me again* look as she guided Kadence out of the kitchen. "Pick something that can get dirty, okay?"

Kadence skipped into her room, and Janelle went into hers to change out of her pencil skirt and silky blouse. She kicked off her shoes, missing the cute heels she used to wear. But she had bunions now from all those adorable shoes she'd worn in her twenties. She'd been wearing orthopedic flats for over a decade now, and she actually really liked them.

Several minutes later, she and her daughters went outside, where the dog that had been dropped off last night came over to greet them. He jumped away when Kelly reached for him, and Janelle said, "Go on back to the stable, girls." She herded them out of the gate, because Russ had warned her that stray dogs were unpredictable.

"What should we name the dog?" Kadence asked.

"Name him?" Janelle stepped through the gate too.

"Yeah, if we're gonna keep him, he should have a name."

"Oh." Janelle took her daughter's hand. "I don't know how long we're going to keep him, baby. But what do you want to name him?"

Kadence thought while they walked back to the stable. "King."

"King it is," Janelle said, smiling. She wished she could bottle up seven-year-olds, because they seemed to have the magic of the world inside them. Kadence skipped everywhere, and even mundane things like dandelions intrigued her.

Janelle reached the stable and opened the door, the smell of something old and dusty coming out. "Oh, boy," she said, looking at the wreck that existed inside the stable. Her first thought was to call Russ and invite him over right now. But that wouldn't be fair, because he had a ton of work to do at his own ranch. With his brother gone, Russ was working more than usual, and she'd agreed to go consult with him about taking on half a dozen dogs that night, after the girls were down for the night. He'd said he'd then come look at her stables for a couple of minutes.

Janelle turned back to her kids. "Kelly, go grab the broom from the garage. Kadence, see if you can get the garbage can we use for weeds."

The girls turned to go do the things she wanted, and

Janelle reached for a pair of gloves on the shelf by the door. She could do this for one hour, just to be able to tell Russ that she hadn't done nothing that day. She didn't want him to think she was using him, and though he'd kissed her last night and said they were good, Janelle knew he didn't trust her completely.

She also knew trust was built one brick at a time. One day at a time. One good experience at a time. So she'd put the girls to bed, drive out to the ranch, and hope she could have another amazing night with Russ Johnson.

Her phone blitzed out a high-pitched noise, and her heartbeat leapt over itself. She'd assigned that chime to Russ, and while she could hear Kadence pulling the garbage can across the cement, she hurried to pull out her phone.

I have something to show you tonight.

Great, she tapped out. *Can't wait.*

Oh, and how does hot chocolate sound?

"Amazing," she whispered, a smile crossing her face.

Can I take you to dinner too? he asked next. *You could come out to the ranch at say, five-thirty or six instead of eight.*

Janelle very much wanted to go to dinner with him, and her thumbs flew as she texted Audrey to see if she could come earlier.

Sure can.

"Great," Janelle said under her breath. She texted Russ that dinner would be lovely, and she added, "Can't wait," out loud and via text.

"What, Mama?" Kadence said, arriving behind her out of breath.

"Nothing." Janelle pocketed her phone and reached for the garbage can. "Nice job, Kade. Now, we're going to fill this thing up."

She'd work, and she'd bake with the girls, because there would be nothing better for dessert than hot chocolate and caramel swirl brownies.

Chapter 3

Russ's excitement over the new dog enclosure was probably ridiculous, but he leaned over the blueprint paper Travis had left on the kitchen counter. He'd gone to shower, and he'd be down soon enough. Russ needed to make hot chocolate, as he planned to keep warm a couple of different ways while he and Janelle examined the stables she had to keep dogs in.

His brother came into the kitchen, and Russ cleared his throat as if Travis could see what he'd been thinking. "I don't see why it has to be lesser than the one we have," Travis said, tapping and swiping on his phone. "And we have those plans right here."

"You want to build the exact same thing?" Russ looked at him incredulously. Travis was a master carpenter, having spent years working with some of the best cabinetmakers in the business. He could build entire homes with his bare hands, with custom kitchens, baseboards, linen closets, exposed wood beams in the ceiling, all of it.

Why would he want to build something he'd already designed?

"No, because the orientation would be wrong." Travis glanced up at Russ as he opened the fridge and got out cream and milk. "But we need the kennels. The outside doors. The shelving in the pen and the pantry near the front door. We need the outside entrances."

He picked up a pencil, and Russ set a pot on the stove and then watched. Travis had a unique ability to pull his thoughts out of his head and make them appear on paper, and it was beautiful to watch. "How many can we get in the space we have?" he asked.

Travis paused for a moment, his pencil hanging in midair. "Eight."

"Only eight?"

"Wait, I have an idea." He erased and redrew, pulling the bottom lines longer. "We don't need twenty feet to get to the enclosure if we do it this way."

Russ leaned over, and Travis looked up at him. "You better go shower before Janelle shows up," he said, smirking.

Russ got up, realizing how late it was getting. "I want to see that when I'm done." He showered and shaved, trying not to let his nerves get the best of him. Rex and Griffin had gone for the day. Darren had invited Russ over to his cabin to play cards, but Janelle was coming to the ranch, and he'd declined.

He didn't have to say why, not to Darren. Millie was

coming over that night to set up a Christmas tree with Travis, and Russ had promised not to be underfoot. He felt bad making Janelle drive all the way out to the ranch, but their relationship had never been one where he picked her up at her place. If he did that, he might meet her girls.

And Janelle didn't want him to meet them yet.

Twenty minutes later, Russ returned to the kitchen and his hot chocolate. Travis had sat at the bar, and he leaned away from the blueprints, shaking out his fingers. "Sixteen," he said. "We can do them in a double stack, with a door out the front leading to the range. The pens can be left open for a double-long area or closed so dogs can be isolated."

Russ studied the blueprint, taking in all the details Travis had been able to capture. Seth would love this, and more enthusiasm built inside him. It was insane. He was insane. He had plenty to do around the ranch, especially with Seth gone for the next two weeks.

And Russ loved it. He loved getting up early in the morning, before the sun. He loved watching the golden light transform the flat, gray landscape of the Texas Hill Country. He loved the goats, the chickens, the hay fields. He loved all of it, and he couldn't imagine doing anything but running a ranch.

This ranch.

He loved Chestnut Ranch, and while Seth was the oldest and loved the ranch too, Russ was the foreman. Russ ran things, and Seth worked the land alongside him.

"Entrance on the side. Brilliant." Russ looked at Travis, a

smile appearing on his face. "This holds more than the one Seth currently has."

"But not even all the dogs we have right now," Travis said, a bit of misery in his eyes. "And it'll take at least a month to build."

"Let's call Seth." Russ picked up his phone and started tapping on the screen.

"We can't call Seth," Travis said, reaching for Russ's phone. He bobbled it and ended up setting it on the counter. "He said not to call unless something was on fire or one of us was in the hospital."

"We need to get started on this," Russ said. If they wanted to have something ready for their brother before he got back, supplies needed to be ordered. Equipment rented. Russ would gladly pass off other chores so he could work on this building, and he wanted to clear things with Seth.

"Yeah," Travis said. He got up and retrieved a notebook out of a nearby drawer. "And we don't need Seth's permission. He knows we need another building. Let's just start on it. It'll be his Christmas gift."

Travis started making a list of the things they'd need to order and have delivered to the ranch. While he did that, Russ turned to the stove and turned the knob to light the flame. He poured water into the pan and added sugar, cocoa powder, and vanilla.

Whisking, he hummed, bringing the mixture to a boil and then adding the cream and milk. He loved working in the kitchen and around the ranch. He loved seeing things come together, and he loved making other people smile with a simple meal—or a hot mug of liquid chocolate.

The doorbell rang, and Russ jerked his head toward the front door.

"What time is it?" Travis asked, a bit of shock in his voice.

Russ glanced at the clock on the stove. "Five-thirty," he said. "Holy cow, Janelle is going to be here soon."

Travis abandoned the blueprints on the counter. "That means that's probably Millie."

Russ practically jumped in front of him, a smile on his face. "I'll get it."

His brother glared at him, and Russ could see how much he liked Millie. He couldn't hide it, even if he'd tried. "No, you will not."

Russ held up both hands and faded back to the stovetop.

"Feed Winner, Cloudy, and Thunder. I'll bring Millie to meet you." Travis nodded and slicked his palms down the front of his jeans.

Russ chuckled as his brother went to answer the door. He did need to feed the dogs, and he set about doing that while voices came from the front room. Russ wouldn't want Travis up in his business either, so he didn't go intrude. Rex would have, and Russ was glad his brother had chosen to live in town instead of out here at the ranch.

Seth had moved next door already, and Travis didn't love ranch work. Russ had thought about suggesting Travis do something else, but he didn't want to bring it up. And Travis never had, so the conversation had never happened.

He stirred the hot chocolate on the stove, his stomach grumbling for something more than just sweets. Janelle should be here soon, and they'd go to dinner. He was hoping for some good old fashioned Texas barbecue, but Janelle loved to eat at more…adventurous places. Russ had tried more foods in the past couple of months since starting a relationship with her than he had in his entire life.

He didn't hate everything he tried, and in fact, he'd grown to sort of love the bento box at Ramen Nation. Maybe he'd suggest there, because Janelle loved soup as a meal, though Russ couldn't understand such a thing.

If he made soup for dinner, there was always bread and salad and maybe even a sandwich to go with it.

He flipped off the burner and the flame went out underneath the pot of hot chocolate. He got two thermoses down from the cabinet above the refrigerator and turned to get a ladle. It was almost December, and once the sun went down, the temperatures could take a nosedive. He filled the thermoses, and a feminine laugh filled the front room.

Russ ladled some hot chocolate into a mug and moved over to the doorway. Travis and Millie were laughing in the living room, Travis leaning over one of the boxes they'd hauled inside. Russ cleared his throat, and they both looked at him.

"Oh," Travis said, straightening out his smile. "Millie, this is my older brother, Russ. Russ, Millie Hepworth."

"So great to meet you." Millie strode forward and shook his free hand. "I mean, I've probably met you before, but not for a while."

"True," Russ said. "Your brother is Chris, right?"

"One of 'em," she said, smiling. "Are you going to help us with the decorations?"

"No, ma'am." He chuckled. "I'm pretty useless with that stuff." He took a sip of the hot chocolate and *wow*. If this didn't win over Janelle, nothing would. "But I wanted to let you two know I made hot chocolate if you want some."

He glanced at Travis, who knocked into the end table on the other side of the couch. The lamp fell to the floor with an earsplitting crash, and Travis looked like he might topple over. Russ smothered a laugh and a smile while Travis found his footing.

"I'm okay," Travis said, and Russ couldn't hold back his laughter for another moment. It burst out of his throat before he could silence it. The doorbell rang, and everyone turned toward the front door.

His laughter cutoff mid-ha, and he spun back to the kitchen to get the blueprints and the thermoses. He wasn't finished with his hot chocolate, but he had plenty to enjoy—with Janelle. "Don't you dare answer that!"

He rolled up the blueprint quickly and tucked it under his arm before grabbing the thermoses. Hurrying back into the living room, he told himself to calm down. Take a breath.

"Are you guys going to be here?" Travis asked. "You could help with the tree."

"No, we're going to her place, remember?"

"Oh, right," Travis said. "You're showing her the blueprints?"

Russ paused with his hand on the doorknob. He hadn't even thought Travis wouldn't want Janelle to see it. But he had drawn the new dog enclosure, and it wasn't Russ's to share. "Is that okay?"

"It's fine," Travis said, but Russ should've talked to him about it. Before Russ could say he didn't need to show anyone, the doorbell rang again.

Russ pulled open the door. He could deal with Travis later. "Janelle, hi," he said, stepping outside as he spoke. He handed her one of the thermoses and pulled the door closed behind him. "Hot chocolate for later. It should stay plenty warm during dinner."

Janelle took a step back, but she didn't leave much space between them. She smelled like flowers and peaches, and Russ couldn't help grinning at her like she was his best friend. In many ways, she was.

She grinned back at him. "Hi, yourself, cowboy."

Oh, so she was going to be the flirty single mom tonight. Russ sure did like that, and he ducked his head to conceal how much he liked it. The air had a bite to it, and he started for the steps. "How does Ramen Nation sound tonight?"

"Amazing," she said. "I haven't been there in a while." She linked her arm through his elbow, dislodging the blueprint. "Oh. What's that?"

The rolled up paper bounced its way down the steps, and Russ went after it. "Travis and I are going to build Seth a new dog enclosure."

"Oh, that's right," she said. She stooped to pick up the blueprint. "Maybe you don't need my stable."

"We do," Russ said quickly. He arrived at his truck and took the thermos from her, setting both of them on the front seat. He turned back to her and took the blueprint, spreading it out on the hood of the truck. "It's going to take at least a month to build this. I'm hoping to have it done by Christmas, but honestly that will take a miracle."

"A Christmas miracle," Janelle said, a playful edge in her voice.

"Better start praying," he said, glancing at her.

She smiled again, and with the sun almost down for the day, and the last of the golden light haloing her, she looked like an angel straight from heaven.

He cleared his throat and ran his hands over the blueprint again. "Okay, so this one will hold sixteen dogs." He went on to show her the entrances, the double-stacking of the dogs, the gates between them. "And we're going to start tomorrow."

"You'll get to drive the excavator," she said, leaning against his bicep.

"You know what I like," he said, chuckling.

"Yeah, the big machines."

"They're fun to drive," he said, leaning against her and pressing his lips to the top of her head.

"This looks intense," she said. "You're going to be busier than normal."

"Probably," he said. "I'll get everyone around here on board."

Janelle's feet scuffed against the ground, making a

scraping sound. "What if...what if the girls and I came to help this weekend?"

Russ whipped his attention toward her, his eyes searching her face. Was she serious?

She looked serious as she gazed back at him. She finally asked, "What?"

"You and the girls?" he asked.

"Yeah." She shrugged, but everything about this was important. "I'd like you to meet them."

"This weekend," Russ said.

"Yeah." Janelle leaned into him and ran one hand down the side of his face. It was very, very hard for Russ not to press into that delightful, feminine touch. "This weekend."

Chapter 4

Janelle couldn't believe she'd volunteered to bring the girls out to the ranch. But it was time.

It is, she told herself again as Russ walked with her over to the passenger side of his truck and helped her up. He seemed a bit more guarded with her. A week ago, before she'd broken up with him, when she'd touched his face and traced her fingers down the side of his face, he'd have kissed her.

Tonight, he hadn't even moved in that direction. Janelle wished with everything inside her that she hadn't freaked out when he'd suggested that it might be time for him to meet her girls.

Janelle didn't mean to be overly protective of them. She simply was. Henry could be an absolute nightmare sometimes, and sometimes Kadence and Kelly paid the price during one of his bad moods.

And until recently, Janelle had been more concerned

with her work than her family too. The moment she'd realized she sometimes acted exactly like Henry, she'd decided to cut back on her hours and let the law firm run like the well-oiled machine she'd set it up to be.

Being a more involved mother was harder than she'd thought it would be. Preparing a case? That she could do. Interviewing a client? Easy. Working sixteen hours a day? No problem.

Dealing with homework, making dinner, or listening to Kelly cry after she didn't get picked for the right part in her class reader's theater had been much harder than Janelle had anticipated.

If she were being honest with herself, she didn't know what she was doing, trying to raise two girls by herself. Things weren't neat or pretty, and facts didn't line up the way they did in legal briefs. Sure, she'd seen plenty of custody fights over the years, and she was very good at winning them. But she honestly had no idea how to win her own, or how to make sure the girls had all of their needs met.

Her anxiety over being a good mother had bled into other parts of her life—including her new relationship with Russ—and that had led to her slight overprotectiveness.

"Hey, are you okay?"

Janelle turned and looked at Russ, who had gotten in the truck and started driving toward town. "Sorry," she said. "Yes, I'm okay." She put a smile on her face, because she'd been looking forward to seeing him all day long. She couldn't get lost inside her head again, especially because she'd been through all of these thoughts dozens of times before.

"What are you thinking?" he asked.

Janelle turned away and looked out the window. Darkness was falling fast, and the trees crowded so close to the road anyway that she couldn't see much of anything. She and Russ had started this game on their first date, and she'd found it cute then. She'd loved learning more about him and sharing more about herself with him.

But now that they were a little deeper into their relationship, her confessions weren't about the fact that she liked pistachio ice cream or watched Saturday morning cartoons with her daughters. If she told him, he'd see real fears and concerns. He'd know she wasn't perfect.

"Are we not doing that anymore?" he asked, and Janelle knew he was trying so very hard.

"I was just thinking about how hard it is for me to be a good mom." She tried on a grin, but it felt a little watery.

"You are a good mom." Russ glanced at Janelle, and she looked at him. The same connection that had formed between them the moment she'd sat down in front of him at the speed dating event materialized again.

She reached over and slipped her hand into his. "You don't even know that."

"Sure, I do," he said. "You're a good person, so you have to be a good mom."

"You think I'm a good person?"

Russ looked at her for so long, Janelle thought he'd drive them right off the road. "Tell me what you're thinking."

He looked back out the windshield. "Janelle, I wouldn't go out with you if I didn't think you were a good woman." He squeezed her hand. "I want a good woman in my life."

Janelle had no idea what to say. She really wanted to be the woman he wanted in his life, and a slip of anxiety moved through her. What if she couldn't be good enough for him? He'd never been married. He didn't understand how messy marriages were. How disgusting her house was ninety percent of the time.

She'd given up the housekeepers at the same time she'd stopped working afternoons. She could wipe down a counter and put in a load of laundry when she wasn't working eighty hours a week. And she did, but she liked making piles of papers, art projects, bills, ID cards, and anything else that came into her hands that she might want later.

She held onto all the girls' ceramics, drawings, and notes from school. She had a bin in the laundry room for school things and a bin for the after-school clubs Kelly and Kadence attended. Everything else got piled on the built-in desk in the kitchen or a box in the pantry when the desk got too full.

No wonder she'd never invited Russ to her house. He'd run screaming, and she was glad she'd only be taking him out to the stables that evening.

"Do you want to get the food and eat under the stars?" Russ asked, and the husky quality of his voice was the most romantic thing in the world. "Maybe it's too cold for that."

"Do you still have that blanket in the back of your truck?"

Russ glanced at her, and that was an affirmative.

"Let's get it to go," Janelle said.

Russ joined the drive-through line, and Ramen Nation was one of the fastest restaurants in the county, and before Janelle knew it, he passed her a bag with two bowls of soup and an order of edamame. She balanced it on her lap while Russ drove out of the parking lot and headed away from the main square in Chestnut Springs.

Janelle didn't have to ask where he was headed. They'd gone to Bridal Veil Falls several times in the past few months, and after a short ten-minute walk, the entire sky opened up above them. With the sound of rushing water nearby, and the universe winking to life overhead, and the delicious soup... It was the best date Janelle had ever been on.

The light pollution from the town disappeared behind them, and a minute later, he made a right turn into the parking lot. Only a couple of cars sat there, and Russ pulled all the way to the end of the lot, nearest to the trailhead.

"You've got the food?"

"Mm hm." Janelle collected it and slid out of the truck, glad she'd put a jacket on. She'd take Russ's arm around her too, though, and she hoped that would happen.

Russ joined her at the hood of the truck, a blanket in his arms. He reached for her hand, and she easily put hers in his. The hike didn't last long, and neither of them spoke. Janelle liked that everything about Russ was about ten times slower than the rest of her life, all aspects of it. She liked that she didn't have to call for an assistant or wonder where the file she needed was.

Russ went past the last stand of trees and said, "Here?"

"Yes," she said. The short walk had gotten her blood moving, and she settled onto the bench next to Russ and he draped the blanket over their legs.

"Okay?" He lifted his arm, and Janelle leaned into him.

"Now it's okay." She snuggled right into him, and she loved the affection he showed for her by tucking her right into his side and pressing his lips to her forehead again. She really wanted him to kiss her that night, but she didn't think it was going to happen.

Number one, she'd told him that she needed to go slow. Number two, he didn't trust her. So tonight, they'd eat soup, and she'd take him to her house for the first time. Her nerves flew through her, and she straightened as he handed her a plastic to-go bowl of soup.

He removed his arm from her shoulders and handed her a spoon. "You sure you can handle several dogs, sweetheart?"

"If you show me what to do."

"We'll see how your facilities are."

Janelle suddenly wished she'd hired someone to come work all afternoon and evening, only to deftly clean up quickly only moments before she and Russ arrived at her home. She realized in that moment that she desperately wanted to impress Russ for some reason. She wanted to win him back. She wanted to earn his trust.

"This is so good," Russ said, stirring his soft-boiled egg into the soup.

Janelle smiled, because the first time she'd suggested Ramen Nation, he'd looked like she'd asked him to eat poison and enjoy it too. To his credit, he'd tried everything she'd suggested, even though he didn't like some of it.

"I'm glad you like it," she said. "Kelly gets the same thing as you."

"She does?" Russ looked at her, but it was dark enough that she couldn't see a whole lot in his eyes.

"Oh, yeah. Pork broth. No bean sprouts. Chicken, not pork." She nodded as she wound up another forkful of noodles. "She's going to love you."

"You think so?" A hint of true nerves ran through his question, and Janelle thought it was really cute.

"I think so, yes," Janelle said. "And you want to know what I'm thinking?"

"Always," he said.

"I'm scared to introduce you to them," she said. "Not because they won't love you, but because it's a lot to take at once."

Russ took another bite, and Janelle knew he was thinking about what she'd said. "I'm going to like them," he said.

"I didn't say you wouldn't."

"But that's what you're worried about," Russ said. "When you say it's a lot, you mean you think I'm not going to like them, or I'm not going to be able to handle them."

"They're a lot to handle," she said.

"Well," he said, calm as ever. "I still can't wait to meet them."

Janelle's stomach quivered slightly, and she took another bite of noodles to calm it. That didn't really work, and she put her spoon back in her bowl. She took a deep breath of the crisp, clean air, toying with the idea of introducing him to the girls that night. But she'd asked Audrey to put them to bed by eight, and with her drive to the ranch and back, they wouldn't make it to her house before eight.

Which is fine, she told herself. The thought of introducing him to her daughters on Saturday was nerve-wracking enough. Saturday. She sucked in a breath and held it for a moment.

She could do this. She liked Russ a whole lot, and she didn't want to lose him. The several days where he hadn't called or texted and she hadn't seen him had been terrible. She didn't want to go back to that.

Russ was a patient man. He could wait to meet the girls, and she knew he would. But she'd have to introduce him to Kelly and Kadence at some point, and it might as well be Saturday. Then she'd get to see him on the weekend too.

"Janelle," Russ said, taking her bowl and setting it on the bench beside him along with his. She had no choice but to look at him. "If you don't want to—"

"I do," she said.

He just looked at her steadily for what seemed like a long time. "All right," he said. "But all you have to do is say something, and I'll...you know. Do what you're comfortable with."

"I know," Janelle said, and that was exactly why he was too good for her. Too good for her messy, always-late, sometimes smelly life. "We'll be there on Saturday morning," she said. "But I hope that's not the next time I see you."

Russ's lips twitched into an upward slant. "Come on, baby. Let's see if we can see the Milky Way tonight." He put the soup bowls on the ground and leaned back against the arm of the bench.

Janelle leaned back into him, and the two of them gazed up into the sky. Janelle let go of her worries, her fears that Russ wouldn't like her kids or the fact that she came with two little girls, and just enjoyed stargazing with the handsome, warm cowboy.

Chapter 5

Russ loved holding Janelle. He knew she'd drawn distinct boxes in her life, and she'd kept him in the ones she liked. She didn't let him come to her house, meet her kids, or show up at work with a chocolate cupcake on her birthday.

She wanted to see him on the ranch, and she really liked to be taken to dinner, to movies, to symphonies, to State Parks to experience nature and look at constellations.

She'd basically hidden all the most personal parts of herself, and Russ really wanted to crack her open and see what was inside. At the same time, a twinge of fear accompanied the idea, because what if what she was worried about was right? What if he didn't like her girls? What if they didn't like him? What if the idea of an instant family of four did become too much for him?

He didn't allow the thoughts to stay for very long. The scent of Janelle's sweet perfume helped chase away some of the doubt, and he reminded himself that she was the first woman in five years to catch his eye and stoke his interest. He'd imagined her on the ranch with him, and she seemed to fit there, especially when she wore jeans and T-shirts, though he liked her power skirts and silky blouses too.

She fit perfectly in his arms, and in his life, and Russ just needed to figure out how to keep her there. He wondered if he was really the type of man she wanted, but he was who he was.

A shiver ran through her, making her tremble against his chest, and Russ ran his fingers down her arm. "Should we go?"

"I love the stars," she said, her voice awed. She made no move to get up, and Russ was content to stay with her under the blanket of stars for as long as she wanted. He might be exhausted the next day but spending time with her was worth it.

"I do too," he said.

"I thought you were a fan of the moon."

"That too," he said, not daring to speak too loudly out here. For some reason, he felt like loud noises would scare away the stars. "But there's no moon tonight."

"I think it just comes up later," she said.

"No, I think it's the new moon, baby." He caressed her upper arm. "We should go. It's getting cold and late."

"Let's have hot chocolate before we head to my house," she said.

"All right, but we still have to get back to the truck."

Janelle sat up with a groan, and that made Russ feel

better about the ache radiating through his back too. He stood up and bent to get the bowls. "Can you handle the blanket?"

"Got it," she said, folding it neatly and tucking it over her arm with a smile. Russ reached for her hand and secured it in his. He remembered the first time he'd held her hand. Their second date in as many days after the speed dating event. She'd taken him to a fast-fire pizza joint, and then they'd walked up to Chestnut Springs. On the way back, he'd held her hand, pure electricity flowing through him.

Those same sparks moved through him now, and he really liked them.

"Are you going to be extra-busy around the ranch with this new enclosure?"

"Yes," he said simply, thinking telling the truth was the best idea here. "You can come out any time you want. And I always have time for a dinner I didn't make."

"Oh, I know," she said with a giggle. "The way to your heart is definitely through your stomach." She sucked in a breath. "Oh, no. I left the brownies in my car."

"It's stupid you came out to the ranch," he said. "I should've just come and picked you up for dinner." He watched the ground, so he didn't trip over something. He'd never pegged Travis as a clumsy man, but he'd nearly fallen down in the living room. "I'll take you back now, and you can lead me to your house."

"That adds thirty minutes to our trip," she said.

"Either now or later," he said. Russ didn't push very many issues with Janelle, but he felt like pushing this one.

"So we'll go now, and then you can just go inside with your girls when we're done in the stable."

Surprisingly, Janelle didn't argue with him, and Russ let go of her hand to dig in his pocket for his keys. He clicked a couple of times, and the truck's engine fired up.

"Always showing off," she said, a grin in her voice.

"I'm actually chilled," he said.

Janelle burst out laughing, just as Russ had hoped she would. He joined her, going all the way to her door chuckling. She stepped in front of him and turned around. The interior light from the truck illuminated her face, and she looked at him with a coy smile on her lips. "I'll keep you warm, cowboy."

"Yeah?" Russ liked the sound of that, but he still made no move to kiss her. He felt like they were starting back at square one—maybe two—and he needed to learn more about Janelle before he took things to the next level in their relationship.

So he ducked his head, practically tasting the disappointment on his tongue, and fell back a step. "Let's get going," he said. "I'm not convinced you have somewhere for these dogs to live."

They drove back to the ranch, which only took ten minutes, as they were already outside of town a mile or two, while Janelle poured hot chocolate for them. "Let me grab the brownies." She slid from the truck before he could protest, hurrying to her car and returning quickly. The scent of chocolate came back with her, along with something salty.

"Caramel swirl brownies," she said. "Kelly and I made them this afternoon."

"I didn't realize you baked," he said, eyeing the square plastic container as she plucked a brownie from it.

"Kelly loves to bake," Janelle said. "And we're sort of doing this challenge with the firm."

"Oh?" He accepted the brownie and took a bite, hoping she'd talk for a few minutes. Because brownies were invented to eat with hot chocolate.

"Yeah," she said. "Every Sunday night, we post on the firm's social media and ask people to give us desserts to make during the week. We've committed to making three each week, but we made five last week, and this is the second this week already."

"Wow," Russ said, polishing off his brownie. "You and your ten-year-old made these?"

"She does most of it," Janelle admitted. "I mostly supervise around the hot stuff." She took a bite of a brownie, and Russ watched her for an extra moment before looking away.

"What's on the agenda for later this week?" he asked.

"Mini cheesecakes for sure," she said. "But we can bring something sweet to breakfast, too. I think someone suggested cinnamon rolls on one of the social media streams."

Russ would love cinnamon rolls on Saturday morning, delivered by her daughters. "Would you make those on Friday night?"

"Sure," she said. "I can't get up that early on a weekend." She grinned at him, clearly flirting with him.

"So we won't be going out on Friday night." Russ reached for another brownie, the container holding them much too close to him now. He could literally eat the whole lot of them if they remained within such easy reach.

"Are you asking me out?" Janelle asked.

"Yeah, that's right," he said. "Can you get a sitter for Friday night?"

"Yes," she said without hesitation.

Russ nodded, the smile on his face pure and wide. "So it's Tuesday," he said. "And we have way too many dogs here. So let's go see what your stable looks like. And maybe I'll be back at your place tomorrow night too."

He wanted to see Janelle every day, and they'd gotten to that point in their relationship after about six weeks. Those had been a couple of great weeks—until the break-up had come out of nowhere.

Not nowhere, he told himself. She'd been afraid of him meeting her daughters. Russ really hoped he wasn't setting himself up for another massive fall come Saturday morning.

Twenty minutes later, he pulled into the driveway of a house with white siding above gray, marbled brick.

He peered through the windshield at the house, somehow expecting it to be different. It was utterly normal, with a light over the porch and motion lights that had kicked on as Janelle pulled into the garage. It was a two-car garage, and the other half held bicycles and a lawn mower, boxes, and a bag of dog food.

"Well, she has something to feed the dogs," Russ

muttered to himself, wondering if involving Janelle in their dog rescue operation was a mistake.

He got out of the truck when he realized Janelle was standing at the corner of the garage, next to her black garbage barrel. They held hands as they snuck around the house and into the backyard. Russ didn't want to admit that he felt like he was sixteen-years-old again and sneaking off with a girlfriend his parents didn't approve of.

Janelle's yard was in decent shape, and she led him to an outbuilding that had obviously had someone looking after it recently. "The girls and I cleaned up a little this afternoon."

"Yeah?" Russ stepped over to the door and peered inside. "Does it have lights?"

"Yes, and they work." She reached past him and flipped a switch.

Russ stepped inside the stable, seeing all kinds of flaws. But there was potential here too. The stalls had been swept out, and they could easily house a canine in each one. Six stalls, with waist-high doors lined one side of the stable. On the other side, hooks stuck out of the wall, and there was space right by the door for bags of food and a few supplies.

"This is great, Janelle," he said, her name rolling off his tongue easily. He hardly ever called her by her name, and it felt good to do so.

"You think so?"

"Does this window open down here?" He walked all the way down the aisle. "The dogs will need some air flow," he said. He tried the window, but it didn't budge. "And are you planning on letting them into the yard during the day?"

"Yes," she said. "That's okay, right?"

"It might be kind of messy," he said. "Honestly."

"We can handle it," she said. "I want to help you guys." She put her hand lightly on his back, and sparks shot up to his shoulders.

"I think if we can get this open, we can move dogs here tomorrow." He looked down at her. "Are you ready for that? I can bring the food they need too. Then it's just feeding in the morning and evening, fresh water at those times too. Monitoring them to make sure they're not fighting or injured or sick." Russ's mind began to move through possibilities. "I can bring the tamest, nicest dogs we have right now. I'd hate it if something happened to your girls." In fact, he'd never be able to live with himself if she or her kids got hurt by one of the rescue dogs they were housing.

"They named the one we already have King." Janelle leaned into Russ, and he did like how much she touched him. "And you'll notice that he's not out here. I probably won't be able to get rid of him now."

"Definitely not," Russ said, chuckling. "Once you start naming them, it's all over."

"Your rescue dogs don't have names?"

"Oh, they do," Russ said. "But we don't let them all in the house." He turned around and took a couple of steps away from her. "I'm going to check this window from the outside."

"I'm not sure it ever opened," she said as he walked away.

"We'll figure it out," he said over his shoulder, and he meant more than the window. Janelle was definitely giving him all the signs he'd normally need to kiss her goodnight and make sure they saw each other the next night.

And for some reason, despite kissing her last night, Russ wasn't ready to do it again.

The window didn't open from the outside either, and he determined he'd bring some tools with him tomorrow night to get it unstuck. A yawn pulled through his whole body, and he rounded the corner to see Janelle talking to a teenage girl.

They laughed together, and Janelle said something else. Russ watched them interact, and everything seemed so easy for her. He wondered what he'd even say to the girl, so he stayed in the shadows.

Once she left, headed back toward the house, Janelle turned to see where he'd gotten to. He moved then, coming out of the darkness beside the stables and asking, "Is she your sitter?"

"Yeah, she had to leave," Janelle said. "But she can take the girls to get ice cream tomorrow when you bring the dogs."

Russ nodded, his jaw suddenly tight. He wasn't sure why he couldn't just meet her kids the following evening. What was so special about Saturday?

Doesn't matter, he told himself. He'd always said he'd do what she wanted, and they were her kids.

So he'd wait until Saturday. Simple as that.

Chapter 6

Janelle clicked through her email, seeing three messages from clients that she needed to answer quickly. She also had a meeting in twenty minutes, and she reached for the phone. She loved the feeling of accomplishing many little tasks in a short amount of time, and she'd spoken to two clients, reassured them of the progress of their cases, and responded to the third via email before gathering the two file folders she needed for her client meeting.

She'd barely reached the door when Libby Hawker came through it. "Oh," the brunette said, giggling. "Sorry." She carried a to-go cup of coffee in one hand and a stack of folders in the other. "I pulled all those files you wanted. Shall I just put them on your desk?"

"Yes, please," Janelle said, smiling at her personal secretary and best friend at the office. Libby stepped past her, and she was young enough to still wear the cute high heels. Today, they were pink to go with her black pencil skirt and white blouse with pale pink pinstripes. She put the folders on Janelle's desk and turned back to her.

"What?" Libby asked.

"Do I have time for lunch today?" she asked.

A huge smile filled Libby's face, along with a knowing glint in her dark, hazel eyes. "I think you do," she said. "Tell me what's going on so I can prepare myself."

"I got back together with Russ." Janelle braced herself for Libby's squeal, which came a moment later. Janelle laughed, shaking her head. She loved Libby, who'd been with her for eight years now. She had been the one to tell Janelle to pull the trigger on her own divorce, after Henry had been unfaithful to her for the fifth time.

And yet, that had been so hard. But once it had been filed and things started moving, the peace had come to Janelle's heart.

"I can't wait," Libby said as the phone started ringing. "You have a meeting. Go. I'll get the phone."

Janelle left her office first, and Libby followed her, stopping at her desk to answer the phone. She ducked into the conference room, Lilly already sitting at the table, her eyes on her phone.

"Morning, Lilly," Janelle said with a professional bite to her tone. "How are the kids?"

Lilly looked up, and she looked tired. Exhausted, really. Redness rimmed her eyes, and Janelle recognized the pure helplessness in the woman's eyes. She'd seen it in her own before, while she was going through her own separation and divorce.

She didn't miss those sleepless nights, nor the constant ball of worry in her gut about what might happen that day. She smiled at Lilly and sat down, covering both of Lilly's hands with hers.

"Talk to me," Janelle said. She ran the best and busiest family law firm in the county, but she knew it was the personal touch that set her apart from the others. She called back within hours, she answered texts and emails as quickly as she could, and she took time to make a real connection with her clients.

That was why her social media accounts were full of followers and fans, and why when she sponsored the pool day in Chestnut Springs, hundreds of past clients and their families attended.

"Bruce called again last night." Lilly sighed, but she wasn't frustrated or angry. Only tired. "I just can't keep having the same conversation over and over."

"I understand. Is he still arguing for shared custody?"

Lilly nodded. "But I don't see how he can do that. Bruce works graveyards, and there's no way he can have Tina half the time. He'd have to have someone sleep with the kids, and someone to take Tina during the day too, while he sleeps." Lilly shook her head. "It's fine. Whatever. Just tell me what to do."

"So we'll fight the shared custody," Janelle said, flipping open her folder. "The best he can do is weekends, when he's not working. Now, the judge might give him every weekend, not every other." Janelle glanced at Lilly, who seemed so worn down that she'd accept anything at this point.

And that was why Janelle was there. She wouldn't accept just anything, and certainly not anything that would make life harder for Lilly, or for her two girls, Emily and Tina.

She remembered well her worries over Kadence, who'd only been four years old when Janelle had filed for the divorce. The difference was, Henry hadn't fought her for anything except a few weeks in the summer, one of the major winter holidays, and the chance to communicate about other times he might want to see the girls.

Someone knocked on the door, and Janelle glanced over to see Libby poke her head in. She wore a look on her face that was made of pure concern, and Janelle's heartbeat bumped over itself painfully.

Without saying anything, Libby pulled the door closed, and Janelle looked back at Lilly. She didn't appear to even know the door had opened. "Okay," Janelle said with a long exhale. "I think you were going to bring me paystubs from the last three months today, so we could prove that you can support the girls, but that your request for child support is warranted."

"Yes." Lilly started digging in her purse, and the door opened again.

This time, a man stood there, and Janelle stood up, her pulse stopping completely. "Excuse me a moment," she said to Lilly, already moving toward Henry. "What are you doing here?" she hissed, pressing against him so he'd back out of the conference room.

"I'm sorry, ma'am," Libby said. "I told him he had to wait."

"I need to talk to you," he said. "I called and texted."

"I'm in a meeting," Janelle snapped. Henry was a lawyer; he knew not all calls and texts could be answered instantly. "My office. Now." She marched away from him, avoiding Libby's anxious eyes as she passed. Libby knew the drill. If Janelle went to the door and opened it a crack, she was to call security.

Janelle rented the whole building for the law firm, and she paid two security guards. One circled the building outside, drove around the parking lot, that kind of thing. The other watched the front entrance and walked the two floors periodically. They'd both come the moment they were paged, and Janelle closed the door behind her ex-husband.

"You can't just show up here anytime you want," she said crisply, walking away from him. "I don't take my phone into meetings, and you can't have called more than ten minutes ago."

"I was driving by," he said. "I thought it might be easier just to stop by rather than wait." He groaned as he lowered his tall frame into one of the chairs in front of her desk.

Janelle stayed standing behind the desk, glaring at him. "Well, let's hear what was so important. You have five minutes."

Henry simply looked at her, and Janelle had seen that glint in his eye before. She saw her December plans blowing up right in front of her face. The three desserts each week. The Saturday morning breakfast at the ranch, and then helping Russ with the dog enclosure. The holiday gift shopping. The visit to her parents down in Hondo.

She sighed and folded her arms. "You're not saying anything."

"I want to come home," he said.

"No," she said before he'd even stopped speaking. "Henry, *no*. I've moved on, and I'm seeing someone else. I'm introducing him to the girls this weekend." She shook her head, already frustrated with herself that she'd told him all of that. Henry could take the most innocent of statements and twist them to his advantage. "No."

"You're seeing someone?"

Janelle just sighed. She'd told him she was seeing someone almost a month ago, when they'd worked out their holiday plans. He'd taken the girls from Wednesday to Sunday for Thanksgiving, and Janelle hadn't expected to hear from him again until at least January. Maybe even February.

She needed to get him out of the building. Out of her life for good. For some reason, she had a weakness for this man, and if he was nice to her at all, she might give him what he wanted.

Her phone brightened, and she glanced down at it. Russ's name flashed across the top of the screen. Her emotions had been belted into a roller coaster, and she was glad she hadn't eaten anything for breakfast. Not that she ever did. Only coffee for her, and usually as she ran out the door to get the girls to school on time.

"You need to leave, Henry." Janelle rounded the desk and headed for the door. She opened it all the way, though Henry hadn't even gotten up yet.

He sighed as he did, buttoning his suit coat as he turned toward her. "You look good, Janelle."

She said nothing as he approached, and Janelle wasn't afraid of him. He wouldn't hurt her physically. He'd only reach right into her chest and squeeze the life out of her heart. He'd already done it three times, and Janelle was ready to move past him completely.

And she felt *this close* to achieving that milestone. Maybe this Saturday, when she finally involved another man in her children's lives. Janelle's nerves vibrated in her chest, both about the huge step she was about to take with Russ, and the nearness of her ex.

She felt nothing for the man, but he was the father of her children, and Janelle believed families were better together than they were apart. But Henry was all wrong for Janelle, and no matter how hard she tried, she couldn't make a relationship with him work.

She wondered if she could make any relationship work, as Henry had implied that their marriage would've worked if Janelle had made some changes.

She reminded herself that she wasn't the one sneaking out with someone else several times a week. She hadn't lied about where she was. She hadn't been unfaithful to him, not even once. Not even remotely.

He stepped past her without another word, and relief filled Janelle. She gave Libby a look that said *add Henry to the list of lunch topics* and stepped back into the conference room. "Lilly," she said diplomatically. "I'm so sorry for the interruption. Did you find those paystubs?"

* * *

A couple of hours later, Janelle finally sat down behind her desk while Libby passed out a soup and salad combo from the local deli. "Ham and cheese with pesto," Libby said. "Tomato basil."

"You're a lifesaver, Libs," Janelle said, giving her friend a grateful smile. "Which do you want to hear about first?"

"Henry," Libby said, opening her own bowl of soup. She always ordered vegetable chowder and started stirring in a spoonful of cheese. She didn't look at Janelle, which was a tactic to get Janelle to talk more freely.

Which she usually did. "He just wanted to come home. Those were the words he used."

"And you said…?"

"No," Janelle said. "Emphatically. I mean, I have Russ now, and I'm not going to give him up for a fourth chance at Henry. There's no way he's going to remain faithful to me for longer than a week."

Last time, he'd been home for eight days before she'd learned he'd driven an hour south to meet up with a former female client. And it wasn't for a business meeting, no matter what Henry had claimed.

"You have Russ now? I thought you didn't want him to meet the girls and you broke up."

"Technically, what I said was I needed a break, but I don't think I communicated it very well." Everyone thought Janelle had wanted to break up with Russ. Everyone but her. "Anyway, I went back over there a couple of nights ago, because someone dropped off another rescue dog, and we're back together."

Libby watched her for a moment. "Did someone really drop off another dog?"

Janelle almost choked on her sandwich. "Libby. Of course they did."

Libby giggled and shrugged, and before Janelle knew it, she was laughing too.

"So who brought the dog over?" Libby asked.

"I don't know."

"And I don't believe that at all." Libby just kept stirring and stirring her soup. "You know everyone in town. Someone shows up on your doorstep with a dog, you know who they are."

"Fine," Janelle said. "It was Will Huff."

"Oh, boy." Libby finally took a bite of her soup.

"He didn't ask me out."

"Uh, honey, I think him stopping by, at night, with a dog, is him asking you out."

"Well, I'm with Russ again." Janelle took another bite of her sandwich.

"Yeah, and I need more details about this reunification." Libby's eyes twinkled, and Janelle really wanted to talk everything out with a trusted friend. So she did, laying out everything that she'd heard on Russ's doorstep to him refusing to kiss her last night to their "date" that night.

"Wow, honey," Libby said. "So he just needs some time."

"Do you think that's what it is?"

"I mean, I don't know Russ Johnson really well," Libby

said. "But from what you've told me, he's very loyal, and well, you broke up with him."

"I know." Janelle stared at the last of her soup. "I just...I shouldn't have freaked out. I know better." She really did. She was old enough not to let her heart rule things and not to let her mind run away with itself. "I'm trying to fix it."

"So you said you need to go slow, and he's respecting that. And he probably needs to go slow too, because he's trying to make sure you're not going to break up with him again."

Janelle nodded. "Okay, I think you're right."

"Oh, honey." Libby laughed again. "I'm *always* right."

"And shockingly, you don't have a boyfriend," Janelle said, plenty of sarcasm in her voice.

"Well, you could help with that," Libby shot back. "I mean, how many brothers does Russ have?"

Chapter 7

Russ fed all the animals on the ranch, that job his favorite. He loved talking to them and calling them by name, giving them their favorite treats, and watching them snack happily in their pens or corrals or fields.

After that, he went out to the dog enclosure and went through the paperwork Seth had for each dog. He didn't have any for the newer dogs, so Russ didn't pick them to take to Janelle's. He sorted out the six tamest dogs, got down leashes, and memorized their names. He texted them to Janelle, but she didn't answer right away.

He knew she was busy at work, and she'd reduced her hours at the beginning of the new school year, so she did the same amount of work in less time. Russ often got messages from her in the middle of the afternoon, while she waited in the school pick-up line for her girls.

So he continued his work, helped Travis begin the order

for the supplies, and listened to his brother give all of the brothers a lecture about Millie's mother, who was coming to lunch the next day.

"Her mom?" Rex asked. "Wow, you guys have gone straight to serious."

"No," Travis said, looking disgruntled. "Her mother is lonely without Millie in the evenings, and I said she could come out here for lunch. Simple. Let's just treat her like Momma."

"Will do," Russ said. "Am I making dinner tonight?"

"Whatever," Travis said. "Don't you—?" He cut off at Russ's glare, and Rex and Griffin looked back and forth between the two of them.

"What?" Rex asked, never one to let things go. He actually thrived on having hard conversations. Sometimes he perpetuated them.

"Nothing," Travis said at the same time Russ sighed.

"They're going to find out anyway."

"Find out what?" Griffin asked.

"The lunch tomorrow is for everyone," Travis said. "Brian, Tomas, and Darren too."

No one even looked at him. Rex and Griffin kept their eyes right on Russ, who rolled his eyes. "I started seeing Janelle again."

"No way," Rex said, but he smiled at the same time. "That's great, Russ. I've always thought you two were good together."

As if what his brother thought counted in the grand scheme of things. "I'll tell her you said that," he said. "I'm sure it'll convince her that we're made for each other." He shook his head, though he did wear a smile.

The brothers laughed, and Russ went with Griffin as they walked into the equipment shed. Griffin was a wizard with a wrench in his hand, as was another of their ranch hands, Darren.

"So what's going on now?" Russ asked.

"Seth bought some new machinery, and it works great," Griffin said. "But we need a couple of new tractors too. Or someone better than me to work on them."

"Better than you?" Russ didn't know such a person existed. He looked at the pair of green tractors sitting in the shed. They looked well-loved, with dirt on the tires. "They won't start?"

"The one does, and it runs for maybe twenty minutes." Griffin moved over to the one of the left. "And no one wants to be in the middle of a field when it quits."

"Yeah, I wouldn't." Russ oversaw the agriculture on the ranch, but he didn't actually do it himself. Griffin did a ton with the planting schedule, the rotation of fields, the fertilization of everything. He was good at keeping records, and he kept a modest office in the corner of the shed here.

"How are things with Rex?" he asked.

Griffin shot him a look. "Okay, I guess."

"Is he as intense in private?"

"He's less." Griffin turned and walked over to a small fridge next to the door. "You want something to drink?"

"Sure. Then I have to get over to the corral and see how the horseshoeing is going. I hired a new farrier."

"I'm going to work on the ATV," Griffin said. "Then I'll get over to the house and clean up for Millie's mom."

"The house isn't that dirty," Russ said. "Me and Travis are fairly clean."

"I know," Griffin said. "But our washing machine is broken, and I need to do laundry anyway. Thought I'd just pick up and maybe vacuum."

"Check out the Christmas tree Millie and Travis put up too," Russ said. "It's really pretty."

"Oh, right." Griffin tipped his hat at Russ and started over to a huge tool chest. He'd tinker with the ATV, and he could probably fix their washing machine too. Maybe he just hadn't had time to do it yet.

Griffin and Rex got along great, but Rex was definitely the most intense of all the brothers, and his personality dominated Griffin's. They lived together in a house in the center of town, and Russ tried to keep in touch with both of them separately to make sure they weren't driving one another crazy.

And for right now, Griffin seemed to be doing okay. Russ left him in the equipment shed in favor of the corral, because he'd much rather work with horses than metal. The new farrier had brought an assistant, and they seemed to have everything under control. All the horses were lined up, carefully tethered to the post where they had access to hay and water.

Only one horse was brought out at a time, and the farrier had a calm, peaceful air about her. "He needs a new shoe here," she said to her assistant, glancing up. She caught sight of Russ, who raised his hand.

"Alex," he said. "He was just shod last month."

"He's throwin' 'em," she said. "And it looks like he's been gnawing at his ankles too." She frowned as she put the horse's hoof down. "Have you had a lot of pests around?"

"Not more than normal." Russ frowned as the woman came closer. She had reddish brown hair that held a tight curl and fell halfway down her back despite the ponytail she'd contained it in.

Her dark brown eyes smiled at him as she approached. "Good to see you, Russ."

"Yeah, I think I was moving cattle when you came last month." He shook her hand, and she sighed as she turned back to the horses. "Overall, they look good. Their shoes are holding strong, and we're working on the regular rotation of horses. But Gallup here doesn't seem to like his shoes. I'm going to try one with a false center. It'll make the shoe lighter, and maybe he won't feel like he wants to kick them off."

"Maybe he needs more support, not less," Russ said.

"Maybe," she said. "I have full support shoes too, but I want to try the lighter center first."

"All right," Russ said. He hired a farrier to come, because he didn't know all the ins and outs of horse foot care. Alex did. "I'm just gonna watch for a while if that's okay."

"Of course," Alex said. "You remember my assistant, Ted?"

"Yeah, of course." Russ shook the man's hand, and they

got back to work. Russ watched for several minutes, and his horses were definitely in good hands. He went to his office, which was in the barn, and looked at the distribution of cattle. Travis had just brought in most of them, so they were much easier to take care of the closer to the center of the ranch they were.

Russ loved the cows, even as stubborn as they were sometimes. He managed all of the sales on the ranch, including cattle and excess crops. He filed a few pieces of paperwork from nearby ranches who'd bought hay from him last week, and he looked up the date of the winter auction, which wasn't until January.

He hoped the price of beef would go up over Christmas, as it sometimes did, and depending on the rate, he might sell a few hundred head. He flipped some pages in a folder, looking at his herd projections for the next year.

He'd need to buy some calves if he sold that many mature cows, and he had good bulls for siring.

An hour later, his stomach reminded him that he needed to eat, and he tidied up his small desk and headed inside. Travis was there, and Russ asked, "How'd everything go with the ordering? Are we on track to get started right away?"

"Yep," Travis said, pouring himself a glass of sweet tea. He left the pitcher on the counter for Russ and moved behind the bar to sit down. "How was last night with Janelle?"

Russ felt his vocal cords dry right up. "Great."

"Okay," Travis said, and that was all. That was the number one reason Russ liked living with Travis over Rex.

First off, Rex wouldn't have asked like a human being. He would've joked about Russ's rekindling with Janelle and how it had gone, said something about how he should kiss her as often as possible, and then laughed if Russ tried to defend her at all.

With Travis, there was nothing to defend. Russ didn't even have to talk if he didn't want to. Out of all the brothers, Travis was the quietest, but Russ didn't fault him for that. "What about you and Millie? The tree looks nice. Sorry I came home and ruined everything."

"You didn't ruin everything," Travis said.

Russ turned to the stove, where Travis had started making a grilled cheese sandwich. Russ flipped it and put together one for himself with the ingredients still laying on the counter beside the stove. "I'm nervous about meeting her kids."

"Understandable," Travis said. "When's that happening?"

"Saturday, apparently," he said. "We'll have all the supplies by then, and she's going to bring them out to the ranch to help with the building."

"The kids will like that," Travis said. "And if they don't, they can play with some of the nicer dogs."

"I'm taking the nicer dogs to Janelle's tonight," Russ said. "Her stables are in great shape, and she can house six of them. I'll teach her how to get them in and out safely, how to feed them, all of it."

"You think she can handle it?"

"Yes," Russ said without hesitation. Janelle Stokes could

handle anything, Russ knew that. She was a powerful woman, with a lot of confidence. At the same time, she'd demonstrated some vulnerability for him, some weaknesses, provided him with a more rounded picture of who she was. She looked no-nonsense and professional on her website, but Russ had seen her with sweat dripping down her face as they hiked, and he'd listened to some of her deepest worries.

"All right," Travis drawled, and Russ finished cooking his sandwich for him.

Later, with the ranch chores done, Russ went back to the homestead at the same time Darren was pulling out in his truck too.

"Cards tonight?" the other cowboy asked him.

"I want to," Russ said. "If I'm done by eight." Really he needed to be on the road, with all the dogs, by seven-forty-five. "Seven-thirty," he amended.

"Brian made sloppy Joes. Come over anytime. We can deal you out at seven-thirty." Darren tipped his hat and continued down the driveway.

Russ decided to get as much loaded up that he could. Then all he'd have to do at seven-thirty is drive out to the enclosure and get the six dogs he'd designated as going to Janelle's.

She'd texted that afternoon that she loved the names of the dogs coming to her stables, and she'd sent six dog emojis. Russ liked her texts; they made him happy. He wasn't sure if that would be considered cute or pathetic.

He decided he didn't care. He liked Janelle Stokes, plain and simple. He wanted to meet her girls to see if they could like him, and he could like them, and they could maybe be a family.

Don't think too far ahead, he told himself. But Russ couldn't help it. He had to think into the future with Janelle. She wasn't the average woman, and she did come with more complications than someone like Millie Hepworth.

After loading up leashes, bowls, and dog food, Russ went home and showered. With a freshly shaven jaw, plenty of cologne, and his best boots on, Russ went down the road to Darren's cabin.

He didn't knock before going inside, where the heater had been running and the food had been simmering. "Smells good in here," he said, and the two cowboys sitting at the dining room table looked up.

"There he is," Darren said. "Food's on the stove, boss."

Russ didn't mind that they called him boss. It wasn't a term of superiority, at least not to him. And it was vastly better than Rex's "bro."

He helped himself to the buns, sloppy Joe mix, and cheese slices before joining his friends at the table. "How'd things go down at the river today?" he asked Brian.

"Good enough," the man said. "The lines all look good. There's something else causing a problem with the pump."

"Travis will have to go look at the wells," Russ said. "I'll talk to him about it." He bit into his sandwich and groaned. "Brian, this is so great."

"Thanks." He grinned at Russ, who had some decent skills in the kitchen.

"Is Tomas coming?" he asked, reaching for the bag of chips in the middle of the table. Russ liked spending time with the cowboys who worked the ranch with him, as he felt it was always better to know the men he employed. That personal connection could keep good help around for a very long time, and Russ liked Brian, Tomas, and Darren.

"He's out with Lucy tonight," Darren said with a chuckle.

"Oh, wow," Russ said. "I can't wait to hear about that."

No one asked him about Janelle, and he was glad for that. Brian started shuffling before Russ had finished eating, and Darren got out the poker chips they used to bet. No real money exchanged hands, and Russ did enjoy an evening or two with his friends, chatting and drinking peach lemonade.

"What are you doin' for Christmas?" he asked Darren. He was from Corpus Christi, but he had a sister only thirty minutes down the road. "Going to Jess's?"

"Probably," Darren said. "I haven't talked to her about it. She's pregnant again." He picked up his cards and looked at them.

"Wow, tell her congrats," Russ said. "Is that number four?"

"Yep." Darren concentrated on his cards, and Russ got the distinct feeling that he didn't want to talk about his sister.

Which was fine with Russ. He studied his cards too, and put down two to trade in. He got nothing, but he put in a couple of red chips to play the hand anyway. Brian was the whiz at cards, and sure enough, he beat Russ and Darren over and over and over.

Completely satiated with potato chips and entirely tired of losing, Russ threw down his last hand about seven-twenty. "Okay, boys. I'm out."

"Me too," Darren said darkly. "I didn't win a single hand."

Brian smiled as he cleaned up the cards and poker chips. "It's not real money," he said.

"Good thing," Darren responded. "I'm going to go sit outside and find something to carve."

"Have you asked Travis to teach you?" Russ asked. "He's great with a knife in his hand."

"Not yet," Darren said, and Russ knew he never would. Maybe he should mention it to Travis instead. But something told him not to, so Russ just picked up his cowboy hat, positioned it on his head, and left the cabin.

"All right, Acorn," he said to the dogs when he entered the enclosure. "We're moving you to Janelle's stable." One by one, he loaded up the six dogs he'd chosen for her, each of them seemingly excited to be in the back of his truck.

"Here we go," he told them before climbing behind the wheel. His nerves accompanied him off the ranch, and he told himself he wouldn't kiss Janelle. Therefore he had nothing to worry about.

Nothing at all.

Chapter 8

Janelle wiped her hand through her hair as she tiptoed out of Kadence's bedroom. Her youngest had demanded a story, then a drink, then a song before she'd settle down to sleep. Janelle had made the girls help in the stables again, as well as cleaning up all of their toys from the backyard. They'd checked the fences to make sure none of the dogs could get out, and Janelle had cleaned up an old pile of firewood she'd never used.

She had good intentions for a lot of things that simply never came to fruition. The firewood had been for a summer hot dog roast that she and the girls had never gotten around to. She didn't want to have to explain such things to Russ, who should be arriving any moment.

He'd texted when he'd left the ranch, and that had been about the time Kadence had started crying because she was so thirsty. Thankfully, water could cure tears, and Janelle knew which songs would get Kadence to settle back down.

The house sat in silence, and that was Janelle's absolute favorite sound. She texted Audrey to come on in, and Janelle went into the kitchen to get down a package of cookies. They hadn't baked anything that afternoon, much to Kelly's disgust.

But Janelle had made them work for more than an hour, and she'd barely had any energy left to cook dinner. She'd put together spaghetti and meatballs in a jiffy, put the girls in the tub, and checked homework before declaring it bedtime.

"It's just me," Audrey said as she entered. She carried her backpack with her, and she sat on the couch and pulled out a math textbook. "The girls are already down?"

"Yep," Janelle said. "And I'll just be in the backyard with Russ. He's bringing all the dogs." As if King knew Janelle was talking about his species, he lifted his head from the floor in front of the TV, where he'd taken up residence.

"Come on, boy," she said to the dog, and he got up and ambled over to her. She scratched him behind his ears, knowing in that moment that she'd be keeping him. Kelly was particularly attached to the dog already, and Janelle didn't have the heart to break her daughter's.

Her thoughts roamed across Henry and how he'd broken so many things in her life, and in their daughter's lives, as she put on a jacket and headed outside with King. "I couldn't get the window open," she told him. "But Russ said he'd bring some tools to do it." She hoped the project wouldn't be too loud so as to not wake the girls.

For some reason, she needed until Saturday to be ready to introduce them to him. She wasn't even sure how that would go. "Kelly, Kadence," she said. "This is my boyfriend, Russ Johnson."

She stepped to the right, as if she were Russ. "Russ, my daughters, Kelly and Kadence." She hated how formal she sounded. And did she need to use the word boyfriend?

He is your boyfriend, she thought. And the girls knew she'd been going out with him for two months. Still, she hadn't introduced anyone as her boyfriend in such a long time. The word felt funny in her mouth.

"Boyfriend," she said again, reaching up to touch her throat. "My boyfriend, Russ."

"Talking about me?" he asked, and Janelle spun toward the sound of his voice, her heartbeat pittering in her chest. She couldn't quite get a proper breath for how handsome he was, standing there haloed in the light from her back porch.

King barked once, but Janelle shushed the dog, who came to sit right beside her. She didn't know what to say, and that literally never happened to Janelle and the lawyer inside her.

He smiled at her and hooked his thumb over his shoulder. "Are you ready for this madness?"

"Totally ready," she said, though her stomach had tied itself into a knot. Six dogs. What had she been thinking?

She followed him around the house to the front driveway, where six wiggling canines waited, almost all of them with their tongues hanging out of their mouths. King did bark then, and he didn't stop.

"Hush," she said, trying to get him to stop pacing at the back of the Russ's truck.

"I'll take him," Russ said, reaching over the tailgate to get a leash. He attached it to King's collar and said, "Stop. Sit."

Miraculously, the dog stopped and sat. Russ handed her the leash, and King whined. He shushed the dog and got back to work, leashing the remaining dogs. They ranged in size, but none were smaller than twenty-five pounds probably. "I picked out the nicest ones," he said. "The ones Seth has been working with the longest. They're relatively calm, and they don't bark, and they should be okay here."

"They'll be okay," Janelle promised. "We'll take real good care of them."

"Seth does adoptions on the last Saturday of every month," Russ said. "But I don't know if he'll do it in December or not. What with him being gone and all."

"Have you heard from him at all?" Janelle asked.

Russ lowered the tailgate and managed to keep all six dogs in the back of the truck at the same time. He turned and handed her two leashes. "You've got Acorn and Snowdrift. They won't pull too much. I'll bring the other four." He added, "All right," and all the dogs jumped out of the truck.

Janelle dang near got her arm ripped out of the socket, but she managed to hold onto Acorn and Snowdrift—and King—while Russ yipped at his dogs and they all sat down like he was their puppet master.

"Haven't heard from Seth," Russ said. "Travis said we can't bother him unless there's a lot of blood or a big fire."

"Probably smart," Janelle said with a smile. "I wouldn't want to be bothered on my honeymoon either."

Russ gave her a look out of the corner of his eye, and Janelle waited for the questions to start. He'd had a lot over the several weeks they'd been seeing each other, and she knew that look.

They'd talked about a lot as they'd been dating, but she had a feeling tonight's conversation would put them on new ground.

"If you got married again," he started. "Would you want another honeymoon?"

"I suppose so," Janelle said. "It's not something you only get once, you know."

"I know," he said, leading the dogs around the side of the house and through the gate. Janelle followed him, securing the gate behind her so she could let go of the dogs.

All of them set about sniffing everything in sight, including each other. King was especially interested in his new friends, and Janelle stood in the backyard with them while Russ went back to his truck to get his tools.

"Where would you go on your second honeymoon?" he asked when he returned.

"Well, Henry and I went to Hawaii on our first, so not there."

"Somewhere else tropical?" Russ unclipped all the leashes and took them with him as he walked toward the stable in the back corner of the yard. He hung the leashes inside the building and went around it to work on the window.

Janelle just tagged along, grateful to be with him, even if it was only for an hour. "Sure," she said. "I like tropical locations. But somewhere like Iceland or Alaska would be fun too."

He paused and looked at her, surprise in his eyes. "It snows in places like that, you know."

"Ha ha," she said, teasing him. "Of course I know that. I've always wanted to see the Northern Lights."

"Ah, I see." He started probing around the edges of the window with a screwdriver, finally driving the tool into the crack and prying it open. "That would be beautiful." He started back toward the gate again. "Let's get the food and bowls."

She once again went with him, asking, "Where would you go?"

"Anywhere," he said, and it sounded a bit evasive to Janelle. She wanted to press him further, but he kneed one huge dog back and said, "Stay here, Benny. You're not coming. No, none of you are coming."

Janelle had the distinct feeling these dogs would not like her as much as they clearly liked Russ. But she helped him carry in food and water bowls, and she listened as he told her how to feed and water them, how much to give them, and when.

"Can they have their food in the stalls with them overnight?"

"If you want," he said. "That's not how we feed them at the ranch, but you can do what you want."

"I'll put them out here," she said, lining up the food

bowls in the small space outside the first couple of stalls. "Do they need constant access to water?"

"Water is good," Russ said. "You can feed out here and put water in there. Don't be alarmed if they share."

Janelle nodded and got to work laying the bowls out where she wanted them. "Have they been fed tonight?"

"Yep." He put the second bag of dog food beside the first. "So in the morning, you give them all a scoop of food. They can come in and out of the stables throughout the day. They'll be fine in the backyard."

Part of Janelle wanted them all to come sleep on her bed with her. Then she remembered how much space King took up, and how stubborn he was about moving if he laid on her blanket the wrong way, and those thoughts dried right up.

With everything done, Janelle faced Russ again. "You have your family dinner tomorrow night, right?"

"Yes." He drew her into his arms, his touch warm and welcome. "You haven't introduced anyone as your boyfriend in a long time, have you?"

"No," she whispered against his neck. His cologne made her pulse accelerate, and the hardness of his muscles in his chest and arms provided her with a sense of safety.

"You have a couple more days to practice," he said, his lips right at her ear. "Good day at the firm?"

Janelle thought about Henry's visit, and she wanted to tell Russ. But the words wouldn't come. He didn't need to know anyway. Henry was *not* coming back into her life, though she'd never truly be rid of him.

"Yes," she said. "You? How's the ranch?"

"Oh, we've got some issues," he said, the same as he always did. He grinned at her. "But we'll get them sorted out."

"When does the excavator come?"

"Tomorrow," he said, a new twinkle entering his eye.

"So you'll call me and tell me about it," she said, laughing.

"Sure thing, sweetheart," he said. "I think we're good here. Are you feeling okay about having seven dogs?"

A keen sense of being overwhelmed hit her, and Janelle exhaled in a low hiss as she glanced around at all the four-legged friends she was now responsible for. "Yes," she said, though she didn't feel it. "We can do this."

She wanted to help Russ if she could. Having the dogs here would definitely keep him in her life, and that was where Janelle wanted him.

"Did you bring hot chocolate tonight?" she asked.

"No, ma'am," he said. "I was playing cards with Darren until right before I came."

"Ah, I see." She smiled at him and stepped over to the stables. "Lucky for us, I put some cookies out here. Want to sit with me for a while?"

Russ reached for her hand and brought it to his lips. "Out here?"

"Yeah," she said. "I have a swing on the back porch. It's not terribly cold."

"And you'll keep me warm anyway," he said, his voice husky.

"I think it's you who's going to keep me warm tonight,"

she said. "Well, and these cookies." She lifted the package and walked down the path that led back to the house. They sat in the swing together, and she offered Russ the box of cookies.

He took several, and they watched the dogs interact in the yard. A couple of them came to sit right at Russ's feet, and Janelle enjoyed the calm presence of them. "Thanks for bringing the dogs here," she said.

"Thanks for taking them," he said. "I think we're going to have to turn away anyone else who stops by with a dog. The Humane Society can take them."

"They only get thirty days at the Humane Society," Janelle said, frowning. She did not like that place, and she didn't want even one dog to go there and risk not getting adopted.

"We'll build the new enclosure as quickly as we can," he said, pushing them gently with the tip of his cowboy boot.

Janelle snuggled into his side, because she could listen to the low, rumbling sound of his voice forever. "Tell me what you're thinking," she said.

"I'm thinking about how much I'd like to kiss you," he said, no hesitation and no embarrassment in his voice.

"Hmm, you better do it then." She tipped her head back and looked up at him. He lowered his head toward her—just as a wail filled the air.

Janelle looked over her shoulder and through the window into the house. Audrey had Kadence in her arms, trying to soothe her.

"I should go," Russ said, standing up. "I'll see you... Saturday morning?"

"Maybe we could go out Friday night," she said. "Out. Away from crying kids."

"I'm free Friday night," he said.

"Great," she said as Kadence's cries continued. "I'll see you then." She stepped into his arms and swept a kiss across his cheek, wanting so much more.

"Come on, guys," he said, walking toward the stables as some sort of Dog Whisperer. All the canines went with him, and he secured them in the stables. King came back with him, and Russ saluted her as he went around the house, and she heard him tell King he wasn't coming with him and to go on back to Janelle.

Then Russ was gone, leaving her with seven dogs and a crying seven-year-old. Janelle heaved a sigh as King came trotting around the corner of the house and together, they went in the back door. "I'll take her, Audrey. You can go on home."

"Sorry, Mrs. Stokes." And Audrey looked sorry too.

"It's fine." She gave her a smile. "Thanks for coming over. You were a great help." She took Kadence and sat in the recliner, already humming to her daughter. She closed her eyes and let her mind wander.

All she could do was think about kissing Russ again, and she dozed with a smile on her face.

Chapter 9

Russ felt like maybe he'd missed his true calling in life—driving heavy machinery. Nothing brought him as much satisfaction as sitting in that seat, the whole world in front of him while he created something where nothing had been before.

And the best part? Travis had marked everything out for him, so all Russ had to do was learn the controls—easy as apple pie—and start digging.

Exhilaration moved through him as he removed scoopful after scoopful of earth, making a neat pile several yards away from the foundation. Not only that, but he'd get to start using power tools that afternoon too, while the cement trucks poured the foundation. Russ liked power tools almost as much as horses—but not quite as much as driving big trucks and tractors.

Since Chestnut Ranch sat several miles out of town, nestled in the hills that made up the Texas Hill Country, he and Travis had been up and working long before dawn. Darren had arrived about six, and he had coffee and the look of sleep still in his eyes. But Russ had asked him to come, because the man had a keen eye for detail and wouldn't let Russ dig somewhere he shouldn't.

By the time he reached the proper depth for the foundation, nirvana had also almost been reached inside his soul. The sun rose steadily through the sky, painting everything in blues, grays, and then gold. Russ hummed to himself inside the small cab of the backhoe, glad to see Darren manning the ATV and loading the clean fill into the back of one of their wagons with a shovel attachment.

Between them all, the hole was dug and ready just after lunchtime, and Travis said he was going back so he'd be there for Millie and her momma. "Oh, right," Russ said, climbing down. "We're right behind you."

Travis bustled off, and Russ looked up into the cloudless sky, a sigh of satisfaction moving through his whole body.

"Let's leave everything," Russ said. "They're bringing lunch for everyone, and we should be there at the beginning."

Darren and Brian, who'd also come to help move the clean fill, didn't argue, and they loaded into Russ's truck and headed back to the homestead. Russ had barely washed his hands in the huge, industrial-sized sink before he heard Travis say, "They're here."

Rex and Griffin were already in the homestead, and the scent of hot chocolate filled the house. So they'd had time to heat up drinks, and Russ entered the kitchen to the wagging of three tails.

Winner barked and scampered off toward the front door, as if Millie and her momma needed herding to the proper place. He'd fed the dogs that morning, but Russ checked on their water and refreshed it as Griffin pulled the pitcher of sweet tea out of the fridge.

"Plates and forks," Rex said, and Russ was quite proud that he and his brothers could put together a meal with all the proper pieces when guests came over.

"Russ," Travis called, and he turned and went through the doorway and into the living, greeting Millie's mother with a warm smile. "Ma'am." He tipped his hat and reached for her arm, as she didn't seem super stable on her feet.

She smiled back at him and shuffled forward. "You can call me Shirley," she said, taking a stronger step now that he had ahold of her. They entered the kitchen, and Griffin beamed at the older woman.

"Ma'am," he said. "Sweet tea?"

Winner barked over her answer, but surely it was yes. She'd lived in Texas her whole life, and Russ wasn't even sure he remembered what regular water tasted like.

"Winner," he chastised the dog. "Leave her be." He pushed the canine back, glad Cloudy and Thunder seemed to know their places.

"Oh, I love dogs," Shirley said, bending down to pat them. "So this is Winner? And you?" She cooed at Thunder, whose tail went *whap whap whap* against the counter—and Rex's legs.

"Tail awareness, Thunder," he said, chuckling.

"Thunder," Russ said. "And Cloud Nine, but we call her Cloudy."

"Sweet tea, ma'am?" Griffin asked.

She accepted the glass of tea from him, and Griffin led her over to the dining room table.

"Pizza's here," Travis said, dropping six boxes on the counter. Six.

Russ's mouth started watering immediately, and chaos ensued as plates got passed out and napkins retrieved from the cabinet. Russ put four slices of pizza on his plate, his stomach thinking he could eat more than that, and took a seat at the table.

"Leave one for Millie," he said, thinking Travis could pull up a barstool. With Darren, Tomas, and Brian here, there was only one seat left at the table. Eight chairs for nine people.

Rex said something to Millie's mother and got up to get her a plate of food.

Russ retrieved her a napkin, and they all sat down before Travis had even picked up a plate. Russ watched his brother, and he was definitely glowing in Millie's presence. At least he didn't fall down, and Russ tuned in to the conversation at the table.

"We need to get out to the south stream," Griffin said. "I think there might be sludge there polluting our water supply."

"It's not the well?" Rex asked.

"I haven't sent Travis out there yet," Russ said.

"I know it's not the river between us and the Wright's," Darren said. "We checked that north to south, didn't we, boys?"

"That we did," Tomas said. "So really, I need to talk about Lucy."

"Oh, boy," Brian said, but Tomas ignored him.

"She's really nice, you guys."

"Lucy McBride?" Shirley asked, and all the conversation stopped.

"Yes, ma'am," Tomas said, his eyes lighting up. "Do you know her?"

"Of course I do," Shirley said. "Her family lives down the block from me. Good folks."

"Everyone thinks she's a bit...odd."

"Oh, she's a bit odd," Shirley confirmed, and Russ wanted to laugh. But Shirley didn't, so he stayed sober too. "But a lovely woman. Bright, and kind, and so talented. I own a few of her paintings."

"She paints?" Tomas asked, and Russ couldn't hold back the laughter then.

"You've been out with her a dozen times," Darren said. "How do you not know she paints?" He shook his head, and Rex practically wheezed he was laughing so hard. It wasn't that funny, but Rex took everything to the extreme. Always had.

Russ caught Travis's eye as he and Millie went outside to the patio, and a slip of guilt moved through him. They should've gotten another chair out of the garage and made sure they could all eat together.

Travis probably wants to be alone with her, he thought. If it were Janelle, he'd want to eat on the patio too, just to get some peace and quiet.

"So I heard a rumor about you," Rex said, zeroing in on Russ.

"Yes?" Russ asked in a monotone.

"You're back together with Janelle?"

"It's not a rumor," Russ said. "I told you yesterday morning I'd started seeing her again." He rolled his eyes, and Shirley said, "Janelle Stokes? Oh, she's a *brilliant* woman."

Russ ignored the smug look on Rex's face and tuned in, because the second-best thing to being with Janelle was listening to someone talk about her.

* * *

RUSS SANG along to the country song on the radio as he drove to town. The cement workers were well into pouring the foundation, and Travis had realized that he hadn't ordered the right kind of nails for the nail gun they owned.

Russ had volunteered to go to town, because he had a hankering for a fresh cinnamon roll, and the bakery did a three p.m. baking every day of the week. If he got in line in time, he could get one with drippy, warm cream cheese frosting before he went to the hardware store.

His mouth watered, and he may have pressed harder on the accelerator. The line for the cinnamon rolls wasn't the usual drive-through line, and only one person waited at the bright blue line in the parking lot. Russ pulled up behind him and increased the volume on the radio. He loved country music, and he had a good twenty minutes to wait before the first cinnamon rolls would hit the line.

Within thirty seconds, three more cars pulled into the reserved line, and Russ smiled to himself that he'd gotten there before them.

His phone chimed, and he glanced at the in-dash screen. *Message from Janelle Stokes* sat there, and he tapped the green button that said *READ* in all capital letters. The words appeared on the screen, and Russ scanned them.

Have fun at your mother's tonight.

Russ smiled, because there was more to the text than just the words. Her text meant she was thinking about him, and he sure did like that.

Thanks, he tapped out on his phone, sending the message. *How's your mother? Your daddy?*

Janelle's parents lived down the highway a bit, in Johnson City. He'd teased her for a solid week that his family had founded Johnson City, though it wasn't true. And boy, had Janelle been annoyed at him when he'd finally come clean. But she'd laughed too, and Russ had kissed her for the first time after that date.

They're doing okay, she said. Her parents were getting older, and Janelle, as the oldest child, bore the weight of taking care of them. Russ was the second oldest, but he saw how much Seth did for their parents that Russ didn't even think of.

And Janelle was a woman, with two younger brothers and a younger sister. She'd liked that he came from a bigger family, and they were both used to a little bit of chaos.

He hadn't asked her if she wanted more kids yet, because he hadn't even met the ones she had. Russ wanted kids, he knew that. What he was less sure about was whether or not he was ready to become a father on the same day he became a husband.

And both were really far down the road anyway.

The music was suddenly too loud for all of his thoughts, so he reached over and turned the volume down. He didn't like the constant up and down with Janelle. Happy she was texting one moment, and then too far inside his mind the next.

So get out of your mind, he told himself.

He wanted to meet her parents, but he didn't want to ask when that would happen. He wondered what her Christmas plans were, as Travis was planning a big party at the homestead, and Russ would like to celebrate the holiday with Janelle and her kids. But he hadn't asked either of them yet, so he'd made no plans.

Let's go to the mall tomorrow night, he messaged her. *Get some Christmas presents. See Santa. Have peppermint hot chocolate.*

Oh, you're trying to get right back into my life. Janelle sent a smiley face with her words. *How'd you know I love the mall at Christmastime?*

Lucky guess, he said, smiling again. *So that's a yes? We can eat there if you'd like. Or stop somewhere first.*

That's a yes, cowboy. And I love that pot pie shop in the

same parking lot as the mall. Have we been?

Oh, they'd been. Russ really liked PotPied, and he'd gone several times since Janelle had introduced him to the fast-casual pot pie shop that had everything from the classic chicken pot pie to a wild mushroom and kale pot pie that made him groan just from the scent of it.

We've been, he sent back. *And I love that place. Seriously love it.*

What's your favorite pie?

Oh, there's too many good ones to choose a favorite.

The minutes passed quickly as he texted his girlfriend, and Russ experienced a new level of happiness in his life.

A girl approached his window, and he tapped quickly. *My cinnamon roll is here. Gotta ride.*

He rolled down his window and paid the girl in exchange for the ooey gooey treat, a smile beaming from his very soul. "Thank you, ma'am," he said, taking the container, which was still warm on the bottom.

His in-dash screen read *Cinnamon roll?* but he dismissed the message. He needed to move out of the way so the rest of the line could get their afternoon pick-me-up, and he still had to go to the hardware store.

He savored the scent of freshly baked dough, butter, and cinnamon on the quick drive down the street to the hardware store. He pulled into a space that was mostly shaded and reached for the treat.

A black plastic fork rested in the container, and he cut off his first delectable bite. The sweet and savory dough made him feel like singing, and he reached over to turn the radio back up. The music filled his soul the same way the cinnamon roll filled his stomach, and he savored every bite until he reached the middle piece.

It was his favorite bite of all, and he held it up a little higher as if offering a sacrifice to the gods of baked goods before putting it in his mouth. He closed his eyes in bliss as he chewed and swallowed, so glad Travis had ordered the wrong nails. Maybe he should come up with a reason to come to town every day at two-twenty so he could wait in the cinnamon roll line and text Janelle.

He reached for his water bottle and drained it. "Back to business," he told himself, taking his trash with him as he exited his truck. No sense in leaving the evidence of his little sugar habit behind. Not that anyone but him drove his truck. And he'd just told Janelle about his cinnamon roll fetish.

The thunder rolled through the sky, and Russ glanced up at the dark clouds that had draped themselves over the Texas Hill Country. He loved rainstorms, and he reached the entrance to the hardware store before the thunder stopped filling the sky.

A man wearing a brand new pair of jeans and a crisp blue polo exited the store as Russ started going in, and they almost collided. "Oh, excuse me," Russ said, stepping out of the way.

The man didn't look like the type to be at the hardware store. In fact, he probably had people who did all of his shopping for him, and Russ was surprised this guy even knew where the hardware store was.

He carried a can of paint by the handle, and he flashed a smile at Russ. "No prob...lem." He did a double-take. "You're Russ Johnson."

The man wasn't asking, and Russ studied him. He decided he didn't know this guy, which wasn't all that surprising. He had grown up in Chestnut Springs, but he'd been living out on the ranch for years now.

"Yes, sir," he said slowly. "Do I know you?"

"I'm Henry Stokes." He extended his hand for Russ to shake. "I think you're dating my ex-wife."

Chapter 10

Janelle looked at herself in the mirror, completely satisfied with the sweater she'd finally settled on. It was pine green—perfect for shopping on the first weekend in December—with white and black stripes around the thicker green ones. It hugged her curves, and she'd paired it with a purposefully ripped-up pair of black jeans.

She wasn't as sure about those, as she was forty-one years old and maybe the jeans said she was trying too hard. Maybe she was trying to relive her twenties.

"Momma," Kadence said, and Janelle turned away from the full-length mirror in her bedroom.

"What, baby?" She ran her hand through her daughter's hair, the silky, fine quality of it so childlike.

"Kelly says I can't watch Mulan with her tonight." Kadence had her pout down pat, and Janelle's irritation rose no matter how she tried to push it down.

"Well, that's just silly," she said. "Of course you can."

"But Momma," Kelly said from the doorway. "She sings *all* the songs, and half the words are wrong. It's annoying."

"Then watch something else."

"I haven't seen Mulan in forever," Kelly whined. "All she wants to watch is Coco."

"That's because I know all the words to those songs," Kadence argued.

"Girls," Janelle said firmly. "All you have is each other. You have to figure out how to get along."

"We just won't watch a movie tonight," Kelly said.

"Not your call," Janelle said, sighing. "Can you two please not spend the night arguing? Audrey doesn't deserve that." She didn't either, but she was their mother, and she couldn't leave at midnight and go back to her regular life.

"Are you going out with Russ again?" Kelly asked, folding her arms. She didn't look happy, but Janelle hadn't gone out while the girls were awake in over two weeks. She was home every morning and every afternoon with her kids, and they'd been doing art lessons, cooking and baking, and going to the swimming hole at the bottom of the springs.

Not recently, of course, but when the weather was warmer. They'd put up their Christmas tree together once the girls had come home from Thanksgiving with Henry, and Janelle had bought each girl the candle she wanted to scent the house with, and they'd made a schedule for who could burn what, when.

"Yes," Janelle said. "And girls." She sat down on the bed and drew Kadence into her arms. She motioned for Kelly to come closer, and the girl did. Janelle stroked her hair too, smiling at her as fondness moved through her. "We're going to go out to Russ's ranch tomorrow morning. He's making breakfast, and he wants to meet you."

Both of her girls just looked steadily back at her, their eyes both a shade of brown that sat somewhere between her light brown ones and Henry's deep, dark ones. They both had brown hair too, with Kelly's being darker than Kadence's.

Kelly pushed Janelle further than Kadence did, but she was smart as a whip and mostly obedient. Kadence was still little and learning, but she seemed to want to please Janelle and her teachers, and Janelle loved both of her daughters with a fierceness that rivaled the power of gravity.

"Do you want to meet him?" she asked. "I really like him. He's my boyfriend."

"Is he going to be my dad?" Kadence asked.

"No, sweetie." Janelle gave her youngest a smile. "You have Daddy. He's still going to take you as much as he always does. Russ and I are dating, getting to know each other."

"Are you going to marry him?" Kelly asked. "Because if you do, then he's going to be our dad."

"I don't know," Janelle said. "You guys know I would never bring someone into your lives that wasn't amazing. And Russ is pretty amazing." She had no idea how to talk to children in a way where they could understand complex, adult situations like this. "He's nice. I think you'll like him."

"What's he making for breakfast?" Kadence asked, and Janelle grinned at her.

"I'm not sure. But he loves cinnamon rolls. Should we get up early and make him some?"

Kelly's face lit up then, and Janelle knew she'd be getting up at five a.m. to make the dough so it had time to rest before going out to the ranch.

"Yes," her daughter said.

"Okay, then," Janelle said. "But if I agree to getting up early to make cinnamon rolls, you have to be kind to your sister tonight." She tapped Kelly's nose, and she saw her daughter's shoulders sag.

"All right," she drawled in her high-pitched Texas twang.

Janelle giggled and echoed her. "We've already made three items this week, but were cinnamon rolls on the list?"

"I'll check," Kadence said, reaching for Janelle's phone. The fact that her seven-year-old knew how to navigate the intricacies of social media wasn't lost on Janelle, but she supposed that was the world she—and they—lived in.

"Yep," Kadence said. "Cinnamon rolls right here."

"Great," Janelle said. "Kel, you need to check the ingredients and make sure we have them all. Text me if we don't, and I'll stop somewhere tonight."

"Okay, Momma."

They went down the hall together, and Janelle took her phone back from Kadence. "Is that what time it is?" Her pulse leapt, and she hurried to step into her ankle boots. "I'm late. Audrey should be here any moment." She stood back as the doorbell rang. "How do I look?"

"Cute," Kelly said at the same time Kadence said, "Sexy."

"Sexy?" She gaped at her seven-year-old. "Where did you hear that?" She moved over to open the front door, where Audrey stood with another girl. Her little sister. "Hello, girls. Come on in."

They did, and Janelle crouched down in front of Kadence. "Where did you hear that?"

Kadence shuffled her feet and looked at the ground.

"Kade," Janelle said, lifting the girl's chin. "It's okay. I'm not mad. I just want to know where you heard that word." And if she knew what it meant. Janelle *had* been going for cute and sexy, but she'd never thought one of her daughters would say it.

"This girl in my class," Kadence said. "She said her sister only wears skirts that make her look sexy."

"Okay." Janelle exhaled. "Well, it's not really a word a little girl like you uses. We'll talk about it tomorrow, okay?"

Kadence flung her arms around Janelle's neck and kissed her cheek. "Okay, Momma. Love you."

"Love you too, baby." She stood up and drew Kelly into a hug too. "Remember our deal."

"Yes, ma'am," Kelly said, and Janelle stepped over to Audrey and Allison to give a few last-minute instructions. Satisfied that Audrey knew Kelly needed to be kind in order to get to make cinnamon rolls, and that she had permission to text Janelle after she went through the cupboards, Janelle grabbed her keys and headed out to the garage.

She texted Russ before she backed out. *Running late. See you in ten*, and then got on the road. He hadn't texted since saying he had to go because his cinnamon roll had arrived, and Janelle couldn't wait to see him.

Her pulse skipped around merrily as she drove, and before she knew it, she'd reached the junction where the road that led out to the ranch met the main highway. Russ waited there in his truck, their common meeting place one they could both reach in a matter of minutes.

Janelle stuffed her phone in her purse, turned off her car, and put her keys in a side pocket before getting out. She couldn't help half-running toward Russ, who'd gotten out and stood near the hood of his truck.

He was the epitome of sexy—and she definitely knew how to use the word. He wore a pair of blue jeans, cowboy boots, a black shirt, and a cowboy hat to match. He seemed to know exactly how to stand to appeal to her, and she practically threw herself into his arms.

Chuckling, he swept his arms around her, and Janelle held onto him as pure joy streamed through her.

"Hey, baby," he practically purred in her ear. "Rough time getting out of the house tonight?"

"Negotiations," she said, stepping back. "But I told the girls about meeting you tomorrow. They seemed excited."

Russ swallowed, the only sign of his nerves. "What time are y'all comin' out?"

"Nine?" she guessed. "Is that too early?"

"Baby, I'll be up by five." He chuckled and laced his fingers through hers for the two steps to the passenger door.

"Do you actually get out of bed at five?" she asked. "Or just wake up?"

"Once I'm up, there's no use of lying in bed."

"Oh, that's where you're wrong." Janelle loved lying in bed almost as much as she loved chocolate and that cowboy hat Russ wore. "But I'll be up early tomorrow too. The girls want to make cinnamon rolls." She cut him a look out of the corner of her eye as she climbed onto the higher truck seat. "I didn't know you loved them so much."

"Trying to hide my flaws for a bit." He chuckled, closed her door, and rounded the hood. He got behind the wheel and turned down the radio. She knew he loved to listen to loud country music, and the first time he'd belted out a song with one of the most popular artists in the world, Janelle had started falling for him.

He had a beautiful singing voice, and Janelle loved it when he hummed as he drove. He didn't even seem to notice that he did it.

"So," he said as he pulled onto the street and pointed the truck in the direction of PotPied. "I met your ex-husband today."

Janelle sucked in a breath at the same time she tried to exhale, and she ended up choking. Then coughing, painfully. "What? Where?"

Russ looked at her for a long moment before focusing on the road in front of them again. "At the hardware store."

"What in the world was he doing there?" she demanded. Her hands shook, and not for a good reason. "Did he know who you were? What did he say?" Janelle was aware her voice had pitched up, both in volume and timbre, and Russ gazed at her again, pure curiosity flowing across his face.

"I don't know what he was doing at the hardware store," Russ said. "But he knew we were dating."

"I didn't tell him about you," she said. "I mean, I did. I told him I was seeing someone, but I didn't give your name…" Her voice trailed off. She lived in a small town, with a rampant rumor mill. Everyone in town knew she and Russ had been seeing each other. They'd been out to almost every restaurant in town and the surrounding area.

"He had a can of paint," Russ said.

"He lives an hour north of here," she said. "Out in a suburb of Austin. And he stopped by my office two days ago, so why—?"

"He stopped by your office two days ago?" Russ asked. "Why?"

Panic flowed through Janelle, and she pressed her palms to her thighs. She took a deep breath in, held it, and pushed the air out. "He stopped by to say he wanted to come home."

Russ said nothing, but the atmosphere in the truck's cab changed. An electric charge filled the air, and Janelle struggled to breathe against it.

"He's not coming home," Janelle said. "I moved after the divorce, and I don't want him back."

"That so?"

"Russ," she said, realizing that she didn't say his name very often. "That's very so. I told him that in no uncertain terms."

"And yet, he's still in town." Russ made a turn, and he could've looked at her, but he chose not to.

"I'll call him and tell him to go home."

"Is he hanging around for the girls?" Russ asked. "He is their father."

"No," Janelle said. "He took them for Thanksgiving. He's not supposed to see them again until January." Janelle rolled her shoulders, which were suddenly so tight. "I mean, there's no 'supposed to.' We have an open custody agreement. He can ask to see them more often, and if it works, it's fine with me."

"Did he ask to see them?"

"No." Janelle swallowed, her mouth sticky. She couldn't wait for a tall soda from PotPied, as they had some of the best diet cola in the county. "We talked for maybe five minutes. He interrupted my meeting, and I was annoyed. He left without a fight."

"Okay," Russ said, but his voice seemed a bit too high.

Janelle didn't want Henry to ruin their magical, holiday evening together. The streetlamps on Main Street now bore Christmas wreaths, and Janelle loved the holidays in Chestnut Springs.

"The City Center has the lights up," she said as the bright, colorful lights came into view.

"How they do that all the way to the top of the trees is impressive," Russ said, and his voice seemed normal now.

"Isn't it?" Janelle tucked her hair behind her ear, wishing the conversation they'd just had didn't still seethe under her skin. "I had a client once who worked for the city, and he said it takes a crew of ten men to get all the lights up. Only takes them two days."

"Is that so?" Russ gave her a smile, and Janelle returned it. Hers felt a little shaky on her face, but Russ didn't seem to notice.

The mall loomed ahead, and Russ made a left turn into the parking lot. Plenty of Christmas lights had been put up on the mall too, and some of Janelle's tension leaked out of her muscles.

"I love Christmas," Janelle said. "Tell me what you're thinking." She forced herself to look at Russ, though she was afraid of what he'd say.

He remained silent until he pulled into a space near the restaurant. Then he put the truck in park and faced her too. "I'm thinking that I like Christmas too," he said. "But what I'm really thinking is that I need to know more about you and Henry."

"What?" Janelle asked. "Why?"

Russ cleared his throat. "Because what ex-husband thinks he can show up and interrupt his wife's meeting, only to ask her if he can come home?" He looked away, pure frustration pouring off of him. "So just be honest with me. What's really going on with you and Henry?"

Chapter 11

"There is nothing going on with me and Henry," Janelle said, and Russ really wanted to believe her. He told himself for the tenth time that she wasn't the best lawyer in five counties for no reason. She could put together a killer argument, and he couldn't forget that. He hated that he didn't fully trust her, but he couldn't ignore the facts.

And the first fact was that she had been married to Henry. They had two children together. She'd always be connected to him, and Russ needed to know what he'd be dealing with for the rest of his life—if he stayed together with Janelle.

"Janelle," Russ said, and she held up both hands.

"Okay, listen. This doesn't mean anything, okay?"

"What doesn't?"

She inhaled slowly and looked him squarely in the eye. He sure did like that, and he wished his crush on this woman wasn't quite so large. "Henry and I were married for twelve years," she said. "We've been divorced for three, and…and… I've taken him back three times. I guess he thought it was time for a fourth."

"And is it?"

"No," she said emphatically. "Absolutely not. I told him that. My personal assistant was there. I am *not* taking him back. I don't want him back. That's why I told him I was seeing you, so he could see that I'd moved on—and that he should too."

Russ looked away from her, his mind spinning through everything. He sometimes needed to get out of his own head, but he didn't know how. Not for something like this.

"I've been cheated on before," he whispered, almost to himself. "I don't want to go through that again."

"Russ." Janelle's voice held only agony, and that was the reason he looked at her.

"Henry cheated on me for five years before I left him. Both times I took him back, he said he'd changed. That he wouldn't ever do that to me again." She wrapped her arms around herself, and Russ's heart started to bleed for her.

He wished it wouldn't. He needed to think clearly when it came to this relationship, not let his heart lead.

"The last time, he was only faithful for six days before I found him with another woman." Her chin shook, but she didn't cry. Russ wondered what would make a woman as strong and confident as Janelle Stokes cry. "I would never —*never*—do that to someone else. I know exactly what that feels like, and I would *never* do that to you."

Russ nodded, because he believed her. "All right," he said. "Are we still feeling festive?" He was starving, but he could drive Janelle back to her car if she didn't want to go out with him.

"I am," she said. "You?"

"I could at least eat," he said.

She smiled and swiped at her eyes, though he still saw no evidence of tears. "You can always eat, Russ."

He reached for her hand, glad when she let him hold it. "I'm sorry, baby. I just...had to ask."

"I know." She nodded and put his palm against her cheek. "I'm glad you did."

"Promise me you'll tell me if you want to move on," he said. "Get back with Henry. Whatever it is." He couldn't promise that he wouldn't crack and break, but at least he wouldn't have to guess about what she wanted. He hated the guessing, the speculating, the obsessing, most of all.

If Janelle would just tell him when she wanted to move on, he could at least turn up the music and keep the damaging thoughts from keeping him on the ranch for another five years.

"I'll tell you," Janelle said. "I had no problem telling you I was uncertain about you meeting the girls, right?"

"Right." Russ got out of the truck and went around to Janelle's side. He leaned into the space between the door and the seat so she couldn't get out. "And so we're clear, I want you to know I sure do like you, Janelle Stokes. I don't want to break up. I want to meet the girls. I want to celebrate Christmas with you."

Janelle's eyes searched his, and they softened by the moment. "I like you too, Russ. I don't want to break up either, and I'm a little nervous about tomorrow morning, but it feels right. And I can't think of anything better than spending Christmas with you." She gave a little nod at the end of her speech, and Russ really wanted to kiss her.

But the foot traffic going in and out of PotPied made him uncomfortable. He wasn't a fifteen-year-old with his first girlfriend, unable to control his hormones. There was an appropriate time for kissing a beautiful woman, and in the parking lot of a busy restaurant wasn't it.

"Let's go eat," he said. "And then you can educate me on the finer points of holiday shopping."

Janelle's face lit up from within, and Russ grinned too. He'd spoken true, and he was glad Janelle hadn't gotten scared by it. The last time he'd tried talking to her about something serious, she'd said she needed a break.

"Oh, the special is green chile pork," she said. "I'm getting that. It's fantastic."

"Is it spicy?" Russ asked, his eyes scanning the menu for his favorites.

"Not at all," she said. "It's a green chile verde sauce. Really great. It comes with potatoes and carrots and a creamy gravy. It's so good."

"Mm." Russ kept examining the menu until it was their turn to order, and then he said, "I'll take a large braised short rib, and we need a large special, too."

"Braised short ribs," Janelle said, linking her arm through his. "I should've known."

"I like red meat," Russ practically growled, and he got rewarded with Janelle's feminine giggle. He could listen to that sound all day, every day, and he tucked her closer to his side.

They ate, the conversation light and easy now that they'd gotten the harder topics out of the way.

"All right, cowboy," she finally said, standing up. "Let's hit the mall."

Normally, those words would strike fear in the heart of any man. But tonight, they held great promise for Russ.

Christmas music played in earnest inside the mall, and Friday night was apparently the time when couples descended on the stores in great force. Russ held Janelle's hand and let her lead him from store to store as she exclaimed over the "perfect wrapping paper" or the "most adorable Christmas ornaments."

"I buy one of these every year," she said, placing two globes in her basket. "One for each girl. Kelly has a teddy bear theme, and I started a collection of ornaments with a rabbit theme for Kadence."

"Wow," Russ said. "What do they do with them?"

"We decorate a couple of trees," she said. "Our main tree is already up. That's where all of my ornaments go. The girls put up and decorate their own trees on Christmas Eve. Well, if I have them. Henry's only taken them for Christmas once."

"When do you do if he takes them?"

"The morning before they leave," she said. "Their trees are small, only four feet tall."

"Three Christmas trees," he said, glad Travis was upping the ranch's holiday game. Russ couldn't even remember the last time he'd put up a Christmas tree.

"Oh, come on," Janelle said. "Don't tell me you don't have stockings for every horse and every goat on the ranch." She laughed, and Russ joined in.

"No stockings for the livestock," he said. "Sorry to disappoint. But I do go out and give them treats on Christmas morning."

"Of course you do." She looked at an assortment of snow globes, picking one up and putting it back on the shelf. "What kind of treats do goats like?"

"Oh, all the animals like butterscotch," Russ said. "We buy them in bulk in December."

"You must really need to budget for that," she said.

Russ said nothing about that, because he'd stopped budgeting much of anything a couple of months ago when his mother had gathered all the boys around and told them she owned half of a multi-billion-dollar cosmetics company.

Consequently, Russ had become a billionaire along with the rest of his brothers. He'd bought himself a truck and not much else. Besides all the meals out, that was. Russ sure did love to eat good food, and he sometimes made it and sometimes bought it.

"What do you want for Christmas?" he asked. He caught her looking at him, but he kept his eyes forward, on the crowds of people in the mall. He didn't particularly like crowds or noise, but the scent of pine needles and the jolly holiday music did have a certain appeal.

"What do I want for Christmas," she mused. "I don't know. I usually buy myself a new pair of shoes or another sweater. I love sweaters."

Russ loved the one she was wearing. It said Christmas without all the gaudy colors and reindeer antlers. He glanced down at her shoes, which added a couple of inches to her height.

"What would a boyfriend buy you for Christmas?" he asked.

"Oh, a *boyfriend*," she said playfully. "Now, that's a different story, isn't it?"

Russ grinned as she steered him toward the check-out register. She just bought the ornaments, which the clerk took great pain to wrap in copious amounts of paper. She handed Janelle a red bag with gold handles, and smiled them out of the store.

"Jewelry?" Russ guessed. Janelle always had something glinting from her ears, but her fingers were gem-free.

She automatically moved her hand to the necklace he'd seen her wear.

"You always wear that," he said.

"Yeah, it's a mother's necklace," she said. "It has the birthstones of my girls on it."

"Ah." Russ couldn't top that, and he wondered who'd bought it for her.

"My sister gave it to me last year, for my birthday," she said, and Russ got that question answered.

"I know," he said, "A year's supply of coffee from Brew Time."

"Do you know how much a year's supply of coffee from Brew Time would cost?" Janelle scoffed and shook her head. "That's something my brother would get for me."

"Definitely not interested in being your brother," Russ said, dipping his mouth closer to her ear. It could've been his imagination, but he thought he detected a shiver as it moved down her arms and into her hand, which held his.

"Candy?" he suggested as they walked by a store full of caramel apples and chocolate covered truffles. "No, that's lame." He honestly didn't know what to buy for a woman. "I usually get my mother a pair of slippers or something she likes to read."

"If you buy me a pair of slippers, ever, it's over," she said. "That's the death knell for a relationship, isn't it?"

"Is it?" Russ looked at Janelle. "I think slippers can be sweet. Like, sometimes I'm annoyed when I have to run the garbage can out to the end of the driveway and it's been raining and I have to put on my shoes and socks. Slippers are so much easier."

"Do you need me to buy you a pair of slippers?" she teased.

"Actually," he said. "I *was* hoping to find some tonight."

Janelle laughed, quieting when he just smiled at her. "Oh, you're not kidding."

"No, I am not." He steered her toward a department store. "So let's go in here. See what they have." The music changed once they'd stepped through the wide entrance, and he said, "Look. Tons of sweaters."

"A sweater would be romantic," she said, dropping her hand to finger the fabric on the one closest to her.

"You'd let an old cowboy buy your clothes?"

"First off, you're not old," she said. "And second, yes, I think clothing gifts are sweet."

"Slippers could be counted as clothing."

"You're never going to let that go, are you?"

"Nope." He took her hand again and led her toward the shoe section. He wasn't fussy, and he knew what he liked, sometimes just by looking, and he picked out a pair of slippers fairly quickly.

He wasn't planning on buying her a Christmas gift that night, but he sure would like to know what would constitute a boyfriend gift so he could start thinking about it. He still liked the idea of jewelry, but his mind also moved in the direction of a pet.

"What about a kitten?" he asked.

"For a Christmas present?" Janelle looked and sounded horrified, and Russ crossed a pet off his list.

"Never mind," he said, setting his slippers on the counter for the clerk to scan. The guy rang him up, and Russ pulled out his card to pay. "You're a man," he said to the man. "What do you give your girlfriend for Christmas?"

Janelle giggled quietly beside him, and they both watched the guy, who was easily ten years younger than them. Maybe fifteen.

"Perfume?" he guessed. "I got that once for my girlfriend."

"Are you still with her?" Janelle asked.

"No." He ran Russ's card while Janelle cocked her head and looked at Russ meaningfully. So no perfume.

Russ took back his card and his bag with his new slippers in it, and he and Janelle headed back out into the mall.

"You know," Janelle said. "It's not about the cumulative gift once a year."

"Oh?"

"It's about all the little things," Janelle said. "Flowers for no reason. Doing the dishes for me before I get home from work. Sacrificing something you want to do to spend time with me, doing what I want to do."

Russ nodded, because he believed that too. "So I'm really getting some points for being at this mall tonight, aren't I?"

"*You* suggested the mall," she said, looking at him with surprise in her eyes.

"Yeah," he said, putting his arm around her waist and bringing her close to him. "Because I knew *you* liked it."

Janelle's eyes softened, and she melted into his side. "That's so sweet, Russ."

"All right, baby," he said. "Let's go find Santa Claus. I have a few questions for him, and I want to make sure he knows what I want for Christmas."

Chapter 12

Janelle turned in a full circle, looking for something in her house. What, she didn't know. She just knew she was nervous about putting the girls in the car and driving out to Chestnut Ranch.

"Keys," she muttered. "Phone. Purse. Cinnamon rolls." She'd gotten up early with Kelly to get the dough made, and then she'd spent the hour while it proofed getting their hair braided and curled. They wanted to "look cute" when they met Russ for the first time, and Janelle hadn't even suggested it.

When Kelly had wanted to wear her blue and yellow flowered dress, Janelle had told them about the construction on the new dog enclosure. "So sneakers and jeans, girls," she said. "We can still look cute in clothes like that, trust me."

Russ had told her last night how much he liked her sweater, and Janelle had caught him looking at her several times. He still didn't kiss her when they pulled up to the patch of dirt off the side of the road where she'd parked her car.

As she'd driven home last night, she realized why. He didn't want to kiss her on the side of the road at an intersection he passed every time he came to town. He wanted to kiss her somewhere romantic—and Janelle wanted that too.

Though she'd kissed him before, this time would be important too—almost like the first time all over again.

Janelle had been thinking about it nonstop that morning. She needed to plan the perfect date, with the perfect ending spot, so she and Russ could have their special, romantic moment. She wanted to kiss him so badly, and she turned around again, still searching for something.

"What am I missing?" she asked the girls.

"Nothing," Kelly said in her cute Texas drawl. "Let's go, Momma. We're going to be late."

"Are we?" Janelle looked around. They'd fed and watered the dogs. They'd been let out of their new stable-pens. The oven was off. She had everything she needed. Now, if she could just find the steel nerves required to drive the twenty minutes to the ranch, getting out of the car, meeting Russ on the front porch...

"Come on," she said, exhaling. "I'm ready."

The girls went first, and Janelle turned back, something still on her mind. She wasn't sure what it was, so she followed them into the garage and handed Kelly the roll of cinnamon rolls they'd carefully frosted only twenty minutes ago.

The miles disappeared under her tires as Kelly sang every

lyric to nearly every pop song that came on the radio. Janelle didn't even have the wherewithal to be annoyed, though she certainly would've been in any other circumstance.

Before she knew it, she drove past the elaborate fence that marked Chestnut Ranch, and then under the arch that had a giant J carved into the wood.

"This place is nice, Momma," Kadence said from the back seat.

"Real nice," Janelle agreed. "Russ is nice too, and I'll bet we'll get to meet some of his brothers too. Y'all remember your manners, now. Make me proud."

"Yes, ma'am," the two girls chorused back to her.

Janelle drew in a deep breath and continued past the cabins on the left-hand side of the road. The driveway held two trucks and a sedan, and she parked beside Russ's truck.

"That is a huge house," Kelly said. "Momma, he must be really rich."

"He must be," Janelle agreed. She'd never really thought about it before, and Russ had never said anything about money. A huge pine wreath decorated the front door, with a brilliant, bright red bow on the lower right side.

She stretched as she got out of her car, and she took the pan of cinnamon rolls from her oldest. The girls joined her at her door, and she said, "You two go first. There's nothing to be afraid of. It's like going to visit Pops."

"Is he old like Pops, Momma?" Kadence asked.

"No, silly." Janelle laughed. "That wasn't a good comparison. I just meant sometimes you two are afraid of Pops, but he's always nice, and he always has candy, and you always love seeing him as soon as you get past your fear."

Janelle wondered how she was going to get past her fear, because the ball of nerves in her throat wouldn't go away no matter how many times she swallowed.

The wreath moved as the front door opened, and Russ himself stepped out. He was a cowboy god, and Janelle's pulse rioted in her chest. "There he is," she whispered.

Kelly and Kadence kept walking, and they were the only thing that kept Janelle's feet moving too. She smiled at him as he leaned against the post at the top of the steps, a huge smile on his face too.

"Well, look what we have here," he said, his Texas drawl bright and unrushed. "Three pretty ladies. Who are you guys here to see?"

Kadence giggled, and Kelly said, "We came to see you."

"You came to see me?" Russ came down the steps then, his boots making plenty of noise against the wood. "Wow." He crouched in front of Kadence, his eyes never wavering from hers. "You must be Kadence. Your momma talks about you all the time. You like to draw and paint." He looked at Kelly. "And you're Kelly. Did you make the cinnamon rolls?"

"Yes, sir," she said, and Janelle was proud of her manners.

"Do you draw?" Kadence asked.

"Only if I want to make people guess about what they see." Russ chuckled. "But my younger brother, Travis, is a real good artist. He draws whole buildings."

"Wow," Kadence said.

"Girls," Janelle said. "This is momma's boyfriend, Russ Johnson."

"Nice to meet you, sir," the girls rehearsed, and Russ chuckled as he straightened.

"Nice to meet you ladies too." He touched the brim of that sexy cowboy hat and finally, finally, looked at Janelle. "You look great, baby." He smiled at her and reached for her hand. "I have coffee, milk, and juice inside. Everyone else is out on the ranch. Let's go eat before we get to work."

"Momma helped with the cinnamon rolls," Kelly said as she climbed the stairs. "But I did a lot of it."

"Did she braid your hair so pretty?" Russ asked as they brought up the rear.

"Yes, sir," Kelly drawled.

She stepped into the house, and Russ said, "Straight ahead, girls. Go on into the kitchen."

They did, and Russ had more than a few beverages on the counter. Yes, he had the coffee, the juice, and the milk, but he also had bacon, scrambled eggs, and a huge platter of fruit.

Janelle squeezed his hand, and he looked at her. His eyes danced with a spark of life she hadn't seen in him before, and his smile was brighter than any she'd seen previously too.

"I told you he liked to cook," she said to Kelly as she slid the pan of cinnamon rolls onto the counter with the rest of the food. "Which is a very good thing, because I'm starving." She released his hand and moved around the counter to pick up a plate.

She handed it to Kelly and said, "Go on, girls. You can eat."

The mood relaxed from there, as everyone loaded up something to eat. Russ helped scoop fruit, and he carried Kadence's plate to the table for her before returning to get his own food. Janelle couldn't help watching him, and she sure did like his gentle touch with her kids, the kindness in his actions and eyes, and the way he kept flitting his gaze toward her.

He was still nervous, but doing such a great job of acting like he wasn't. Truth be told, Janelle was a little nervous too. Kids were unpredictable; they could say anything at anytime.

Kadence asked Russ if he likes Taryn Sawyers, and he glanced at Janelle with a blank look on his face.

"She's a pop star," Janelle said with a smile.

"You don't know Taryn Sawyers?" Kelly demanded. "Momma, let me see your phone."

Janelle passed it over, and Kelly started looking up her favorite music video. "It's not country," she warned Russ, who looked from her to Kelly and back again. "He only likes country music, girls."

"She has some country songs," Kadence said.

"Not since her first album," Kelly said, rolling her eyes.

Janelle wished her eyes were equipped with lasers as she glared at her oldest daughter. *Be kind*, she thought. Kelly seemed to get the message, because she put her head down and found the video.

She put the phone on the table in front of Russ and watched him. He exchanged a glance with Janelle and peered down at the phone as the music started to blare from the small speaker.

"Oh, wow," he said. "This is rock-country. I think I've heard this before."

"See?" Kelly asked. "Everyone's heard of Taryn Sawyers." She put another bite of bacon in her mouth while Kadence belted out the lyrics to the song still playing from Janelle's phone.

"You're a great singer," Russ said to Kadence, who had eaten very little for breakfast. She rarely consumed more than a few bites in the morning, and Janelle would have to watch her out on the ranch. It wasn't terribly hot, and it had been raining off and on for the past couple of days, but Kadence could be delicate.

Janelle finished her cinnamon roll and looked at Russ. "Not as good as the bakery, but not bad, right?"

"It's delicious," he said. "Just as good as the bakery, actually. Just not as big."

"No one can eat those huge cinnamon rolls," Janelle said.

"Uh..." Russ gave her a sheepish grin, and Janelle burst out laughing. Russ chuckled too, his hand landing on her knee and sliding up a few inches.

Sparks and showers of shivers moved through her whole body, and she enjoyed this man so much she couldn't imagine her life without him. She wondered how she'd survived before they'd met, and she was so glad he'd given her a second chance.

"All right," Russ said with a sigh. "The new dog enclosure isn't going to build itself. Who's ready to swing a hammer?"

"I am," Kadence chirped, and Janelle wondered if she could even lift the tool. A powerful dose of love moved through her as she watched her daughter slide off the chair, most of her food still on her plate.

"I can, too," Kelly said, getting up and picking up her plate. Pride filled Janelle now as her daughter carried her dishes into the kitchen with Russ. The two of them standing side-by-side at the sink made everything inside her melt, and she told herself not to get too far ahead of the situation. This wasn't her house. He wasn't her husband. And she was just here for the day—or for as long as the girls behaved—to help Russ build a new dog enclosure.

She stood up too and took her plate and Kadence's into the kitchen.

"She didn't eat much," Russ murmured, and Janelle handed him the plate.

"She's not a big breakfast eater," Janelle said. "What can I help clean up?" All the eggs were gone, and only one slice of bacon remained.

"I'll bag the fruit." Russ opened a drawer in the island, pulled out a plastic zipper bag, and started putting the grapes and strawberries into it. Janelle put the beverages into the fridge, and a few minutes later, they were ready to go outside.

"We let our dogs out here, just like you guys do at your place," he said as they went through the back door. "We'll drive over in my truck. Do you girls want to ride in the back?"

"Yes," Kadence cheered, and Russ lifted both girls into the back of his truck before helping Janelle into the cab.

"They're great," he said the moment he climbed behind the wheel. "How am I doing?"

"Russ, you're doing amazing," Janelle said. "Better than amazing."

"Do you think they like me?" He started the truck and looked at her, pure concern in every line of his face.

"Yes," Janelle said with confidence. "I think they like you. The extra food was a definite good move. Kelly loves having a hot breakfast." Janelle herself didn't cook much, and she put a few boxes of cereal on the table for the girls to eat before school.

Russ drove around the back of the house and on a dirt road out to the dog enclosure. Plenty of pups ran around inside a fenced area, and Janelle easily made out the construction site. "Is it ready?" she asked.

"Not quite," he said. "The foundation has to cure, but we're putting together the frames anyway. I spent yesterday morning cutting wood, and Travis and I worked on building the walls in the afternoon. But his girlfriend came over, and well, he didn't help a whole lot."

"And now you have two little girls and your girlfriend here," Janelle said, watching him. "I don't think you're going to get very far today either."

"We'll see," he said. "Travis will be over to help in a little bit."

Janelle put her hand in his, wishing this truck had a bench seat instead two bucket seats with a console between them. "Thank you for inviting us," she said. "The girls are going to love 'helping' you." She grinned at him, and Russ returned the smile.

"Happy to have you," he said. "Really happy, Janelle. Thank you for letting me meet them."

Janelle settled back into the seat though Russ was already slowing down. She closed her eyes in a long blink, happier than she'd ever been.

Now she just needed to get that second first kiss.

Chapter 13

New energy existed on the ranch, and Russ knew it had everything to do with Janelle and her girls being there. He couldn't adequately describe what it felt like to see them walking up the sidewalk to the homestead, and his heartbeat still jiggled a little in his chest.

Kids were a tough nut to crack, he knew that. But Kelly and Kadence seemed warm enough to meeting him, though Janelle had said she'd never introduced them to any of her boyfriends before.

To be fair, she'd only had one before him, and she'd said it didn't last longer than a few weeks.

Russ practically floated as he got out of the pickup and turned back to open the tailgate. Two brown-haired girls waited there, both of them dressed for a day of work on the ranch. His dreams of working Chestnut Ranch alongside his wife and kids had materialized right before his eyes.

He smiled at the girls. "All right, ladies. Are you ready to put together some wall frames?"

"I am," Kadence said, gripping the side of the truck as she scooted to the edge of the tailgate. Russ stayed close by in case she toppled out of the truck, but she managed to get down easily. Henry Stokes didn't seem like the type of man to own a pickup truck, but Russ reminded himself that Janelle and her kids did live in Texas. A lot of people drove trucks.

Kelly got down just fine too, and Russ met everyone at the front of the vehicle. "Okay," he said. "I have a lot of wood cut. We need to build sections like these." He walked down past the huge hole he'd dug, which now had the cement foundation curing inside it.

"Two tall ones," Kelly said. "With these in between."

"Yep," he said, picking up one small section of what they'd use to frame in the walls. "I have all of these smaller ones cut, and my brother and I marked where they go." He moved over to the trailer they'd first used to haul away the dirt. It now rested out near the fields, where it would be plowed into the ground before they planted their crops for next year.

"So you take a smaller one," he said, lifting one out of the trailer. "And you have to be real steady. We don't go trying to hammer something in our hands." He took the two boards a little farther down, where several sawhorses waited. "This here is called the stud," he said, laying the long piece of wood across three sawhorses.

"The sawhorses support it at a height where we can sand

it, cut it, or nail into it." He turned and looked at the girls, Janelle included. "You with me?"

"Yes, sir," the two little girls said.

"Your mom or I will put the studs here," he said. "And you get to attach what we call the blocking." He smiled at them and bent to pick up two child-sized hammers he'd purchased last night. He handed one to each girl. "Nails are in the bin on this here sawhorse."

He wasn't as carpentry inclined as Travis, but Russ did love seeing a building come together. He could measure, cut, nail, and make things line up. And he and Travis had spent a couple of hours that morning already, marking a couple dozen studs with blue marks for where the horizontal support blocks should go.

He'd be making the doorframes and attaching them to sections of prepared frames, and he'd teach Janelle how to take the studs with their blocking and put the ceiling plates and sole plates on them to make them sturdy, square, and strong.

"I think it's easiest to nail down," he said. "So what you do is you take your blocking and you line it up with the blue mark we put on the stud. See?" He held the block in place. He was well-aware that he'd done this a thousand times before. For him, it was like pouring milk on cereal. For the girls, they probably hadn't seen anything like this in their lives. He waited to make sure they'd all nodded, and then he looked at Janelle.

"Can you hold that block there, sweetheart?"

Their eyes met, and the heat from her gaze made every

cell in his body light up. He thanked his momma for calling him honey, sweetheart, baby, and darling for his whole life. Saying such things was simply second-nature to him, and he sure did like the way Janelle looked at him when he did.

"Right here?" she asked, putting her hands on the block and keeping it in place.

"Yep." Russ inched to the side. "You guys can work together, and you can stand on opposite sides of the stud. Okay?"

"Okay," Kelly said, her fingers gripping her hammer a little too tightly.

"Hands out of the way," Russ said. "Then you line up the nail." He did so. "And drive it in." Five taps of the hammer, and he was done. "Easy."

For him, he knew.

Kadence stared at the wood and then Russ, her mouth slightly open. "Kel, I want to hammer."

"I was going to say that," the other girl said.

"You can take turns," Janelle said.

"And we're not done," Russ said, glancing around at all of them. Janelle looked the teensiest bit frustrated, but Russ didn't know why. A powerful feeling of...love came over him, and he had no idea what to do with it.

He looked around, his train of thought derailed. "Uh..." He caught sight of a longer section of wall. "Right. Then you can lay the stud and blocking on the ground." He did so, making sure he didn't hit anyone as he moved the long stud. "And you attach another stud to the other side of the blocking. They go straight in, ladies." He pointed straight horizontally through the stud to the blocking. "Okay?"

"Okay," they all chorused, and Russ grinned as he looked around at them.

"So we've got things for y'all to work on, and we'll help you get a good rhythm going." He looked at Janelle. "I'm going to have you cap the frames as they make them."

"Oh, boy," she said. "Sounds hard."

"It's super easy," he said, shaking his head.

"Mornin' y'all."

Russ turned at the sound of Travis's voice, a bit of relief pulling through him that he had more help. "Hey, Travis." He wanted to rush over to his brother and hug him for a reason he couldn't name. He didn't, but grinned at him and adjusted his cowboy hat. "This is my brother, Travis. Travis, you remember Janelle Stokes."

"Of course," Travis said, a perfectly placed smile on his face. He stepped forward and shook Janelle's hand.

She likewise smiled at him and said, "Nice to see you again, Travis." She immediately retreated back to Russ's side, and he sure did like that.

"And her daughters," Russ said, looking at the girls who had also come to stand on his other side, as if they belonged to him. Emotion crowded into his throat, making everything tight for a moment. "Kelly's the oldest." He nodded at her. "And Kadence is the youngest."

"Are you guys going to help us build this new place for the dogs?" As if on cue, Winner barked, and Russ glanced over at her.

"And the dogs," he said. "Winner, Thunder, and Cloudy."

Kadence squealed and ran toward the mutts, lavishing them all with hugs and scratches behind the ears. Winner barked at her and licked her face, which caused Russ to laugh. He sure did like having these small people on the ranch, and he thought he was doing a decent job of interacting with them.

"Millie all set up with the chickens?" he asked Travis.

His brother looked back toward the barns and pens where they kept goats, chickens, and horses. "Yeah. I hope she doesn't get pecked or anything. She seemed a little freaked out about going into the coop."

Russ chuckled and shook his head. "She'll be fine."

"Millie Hepworth?" Janelle asked.

"That's right," Travis said, looking at her. "She's working out here today." He looked back at Russ, who was surprised Travis didn't claim Millie as his girlfriend. "I'll go out to the well once she's done. Take her with me in case I need help clearing the debris."

"Sounds good," Russ said. Travis had never taken anyone out to the well to help before, and he knew by the time Millie finished with the feeding, Travis would be ready to be alone with her.

Russ turned back to the girls, his thoughts suddenly on being alone with their mother. "All right," he said. "Who's starting with the hammer?"

"Me," both girls said in unison, and Russ sent laughter into the sky.

"Kelly can start," Janelle said. Kadence immediately started to protest, and Russ had no idea what to do about the whining. Janelle simply waited for her to stop and then she said, "Kade, you got to do all the dogs this morning. You went first for that. Kelly gets to go first for this."

Kadence pouted, but she said, "Fine," and turned to go get a block.

Russ slipped his hand into Janelle's, impressed by how she'd handled the situation. He would've had no idea what to do, and flipping a coin to see who got to nail first had sounded like a good idea to him.

Janelle squeezed his hand and leaned her head against his shoulder. "Thanks for having us, Russ."

"It's so great you're here," he whispered, dropping her hand and moving to reposition the stud so Kelly could put in the second horizontal support.

* * *

Russ served taco soup for lunch, and Millie pulled out her party planning folder. The conversation didn't go super well until Janelle jumped in with a comment about apple fizzers. Russ appreciated her then, and he knew Travis did too.

Rex had made some smart comments about the food until Millie glared him into silence, and the ranch hands just watched everything. Russ felt somewhat exposed, having his girlfriend and her family there, and he knew he'd have to talk about it next time he got together with Darren and Brian to play cards.

And he'd have to talk to Travis too, see how the conversation at the well with Millie had gone.

For some reason, he wanted everyone out of the homestead, and he asked, "Back to work?" to get everyone to clear out. Darren, Brian, and Tomas thanked him for lunch and left through the back door.

Rex and Griffin went to catch a siesta on the couch, their usual midday activity. Russ took Janelle's hand in his and leaned right into her. "I want be alone with you," he whispered.

She tensed next to him, but her face lit up. "Girls," she said. "Why don't you go play in the backyard for a few minutes before we get back to work?"

Travis started cleaning up the kitchen while the girls ran into the backyard. Russ didn't know where to take Janelle to be alone with her. But he desperately wanted to kiss her, and he could not let her leave that day without doing it.

With the kitchen clean, Millie and Travis went into the formal living room, already talking about the party again.

He had no idea where to take her. He had brothers everywhere. Kids in the yard. They didn't have time for a walk, and he sure didn't want to kiss her in a shed or a smelly stable.

Then Janelle was tugging on his hand and leading him into the small half-bath off the kitchen. "Really?" he whispered.

"You wanted to be alone," she said, ducking inside with a smile.

Russ closed the door, the space not terribly big. His heart pounded in his chest, and he mentally commanded himself to calm down. He'd kissed this woman before.

But this felt new, and exciting. He felt like he was fourteen and sneaking off for his first kiss with the hottest girl in school.

Janelle wrapped her arms around his neck and leaned into his body. "Why'd you want to get me alone, cowboy?"

Russ gazed down at her, easily accepting her into his arms. "How do you think things are going?" he asked.

"Great," she said. "You?"

"Amazing." He whispered the word as he lowered his head. His cowboy hat got in the way, and he swiped it off his head and tried again. His lips touched hers hesitantly at first, and then he pulled in a breath and kissed her.

He felt fused to her after that, wanting her to know that everything about her amazed him. That he sure did like her, and he didn't want her to welcome anyone else into her life. Just him. Only him.

"Janelle," he breathed, breaking the kiss.

But she formed her mouth to his again, and Russ sure wasn't complaining.

Chapter 14

Janelle loved kissing Russ Johnson. Simple as that. The man made her feel like the only woman in the world worth having, and she hadn't felt like that for a long, long time.

Discovering Henry's infidelity had been terribly hard for her. She'd learned a lot through the experience, and she thought she made a more sympathetic lawyer now for her female—and male—clients who came in looking for a divorce because their spouse had been unfaithful to them.

She'd felt thrown away. Used. Like she'd never be good enough for anyone again.

Her husband had chosen someone else over her, his wife, because he didn't care about her. Didn't love her.

But when Janelle kissed Russ, all of that disappeared. He cared about her, and he wanted her to know it.

His hands moved through her hair, down her shoulders,

and back up to cradle her face. She couldn't stop kissing him, and he wasn't slowing down either.

She felt twenty years younger, making out with a man in the most unlikely of places. But it didn't matter. All that mattered was Russ. The smell of his skin, his cologne. The touch of his hands. The taste of his lips.

She couldn't get close enough to him, though he'd backed her into the wall and pressed himself right against her.

"Janelle," he said again, and she didn't reunite their mouths.

"Hmm?"

He didn't speak, instead sliding his lips along her throat. She leaned her head back and clung to his shoulders, fire exploding down into her chest as he kissed his way up to her ear. She wasn't sure, but she might have moaned. Everything felt liquid, like it wasn't quite solid or real.

"Baby?" he asked, finally removing his mouth from her skin.

"Yeah?"

He pressed his cheek right against hers, positioning his mouth close to her ear. "Do you want more kids?"

She pulled in a long breath, imagining what a child with Russ's DNA mingled with hers might look like. "Yeah," she whispered. "You want your own kids, right?"

He backed up enough so they could look at one another. "I'd love your girls as my own," he said. "But I do want a child or two that comes from me."

Janelle pressed her lips to his again, relinquishing control of the kiss to him immediately. He moved slowly now, though the kiss was still full of passion and desire and hunger. She loved that the most—the fact that Russ acted like he couldn't get enough of her.

Everything in the world felt far away, muted, as she focused on kissing Russ. She'd been in love before, and she sure felt like she was sliding in that direction with him. And fast.

She became aware of someone whistling at the same time someone opened the door. Russ pulled away from her and looked over his shoulder as Rex swore. He stomped away, leaving the door open so his footsteps echoed right into the bathroom.

Janelle couldn't help the giggles that erupted from her throat. Forty-one and caught making out in the bathroom, of all places.

Russ didn't laugh with her, but stepped back and picked up his cowboy hat from the floor. "We better go check on the girls," he said. He didn't leave her standing in the bathroom alone, but waited for her to make sure her T-shirt was covering her properly. She also ran her hands through her hair to straighten where he'd mussed it with his big, cowboy hands.

She shivered as she thought about those hands touching her in other places, and then she left the bathroom with him. Thankfully, they didn't see anyone else in the homestead as they made a quick escape through the back door.

A wail filled the air, and Janelle's excitement waned.

"That's Kadence. Sorry, she and Kelly have been going through a stage where they fight all the time."

"You don't have to apologize to me," Russ said. "I grew up with four brothers, remember? And one of them just walked in on us and didn't seem too happy about it."

"He didn't, did he?" Janelle gave another light laugh and headed for the swing set where Kadence had her arms folded as Kelly benignly swung in one of the swings. Probably the one Kadence wanted—or had already claimed. Kelly seemed innocent a lot of the time, but she was just quieter about her defiance.

All three of the dogs Russ had introduced them to earlier loitered nearby the girls, and Janelle thought the canines made pretty good babysitters.

"Yeah, I'll have to talk to Rex about it," Russ said with a sigh. "And that won't be fun."

Kelly shook her head, and Kadence wailed again. "Yeah, this isn't fun either, so I understand." She dropped Russ's hand as they approached the girls. "Kade, what's going on?"

"She said I can't swing because I'm a baby." Kadence glared at her sister for an extra moment and then ran toward Janelle.

She received her youngest daughter into her arms while glaring at her oldest. Kelly didn't even look up from the ground as she continued to sway back and forth in the swing. She hugged Kadence while she tried to figure out what to do.

"I'll take her," Russ said, easily taking Kadence right out

of Janelle's arms. "We'll go visit the horses. You want to, Kadence?"

"Mm hm," the little girl said, still sniffling. She clung to Russ as if he were her father, and the strong, sexy cowboy walked away with the little girl wrapped around him. But he was the one wrapped around her little finger, Janelle knew that.

She sighed as she took the last few steps to the other swing and sat down. "Kelly, what's goin' on?"

"Nothing."

Janelle toed the ground, which set her to swaying too. "Why can't you just let Kadence swing too? There's two swings."

Kelly looked up at her. "I want to go see Daddy this weekend."

Confusion pulled through Janelle, making her eyebrows pinch downward. "What?"

"He called and said he's in town and wants to see us. He said he went to the house, and we weren't there."

Janelle held her breath, because she hated with the heat of a volcano that Henry called Kelly without her knowledge. But he'd bought her a phone that only did texts and calls, and he was her father. He and Janelle had exchanged words about it a dozen times, but the fact was, Henry did what Henry wanted.

Always.

Janelle wished she could tell Kelly that, but she never had and she wouldn't.

"He hasn't called me," Janelle said, taking out her

phone. "Look." She handed the phone to Kelly, who did look at it.

"Can you call him?" She handed the phone back. "When I told Kadence, she whined—she's *always* whining—and said she didn't want to go with Daddy. But I do."

Janelle gazed out over the peaceful land at Chestnut Ranch. She didn't want to drive her daughter back into town for Henry, but she sure didn't want him coming out here. It angered her that he'd gone to the house too, because that was just another ploy to try to get back into Janelle's life.

"You just spent last weekend with him," she said. "More than that. Wednesday to Sunday."

"He said that movie I want to see is playing tonight," Kelly said. "And he can take me."

Janelle resisted the urge to exhale loudly. Classic Henry, trying to swoop in with a gift or something that made him look like the good guy. Janelle couldn't blame Kelly for falling for it though. She herself had too—many times. More times than she cared to admit.

Foolishness raced through her at the memories of how she'd swept his behavior under the rug. How she'd made excuses for him for years. How she'd let his flowers, gemstones, and boxes of chocolates make things "right" between them when they'd been shattered for so long.

And she didn't want Kelly's heart to be in tatters the way hers was. But she couldn't keep her husband from her daughter, or vice versa.

"Just you?" she finally asked.

"I guess Kadence can come," Kelly said, her voice sullen.

"I'll talk to Daddy," Janelle said, getting out of the swing. "Maybe it would be good for Kadence and I to spend some time together alone." With that, she walked away from Kelly, who said something under her breath.

Janelle wanted to march right back over to her and tell her to stop acting like such a brat. She didn't, because she didn't need to get into a full-blown fight with her ten-year-old on her boyfriend's ranch.

With level-ten annoyance filling her, she dialed her ex.

"Janelle," he said pleasantly, as if they were getting together for a dinner-movie date later that night.

"Henry," she bit out. "You called Kelly about a movie tonight?"

"Oh, right," he said, as if he'd forgotten. Janelle rolled her eyes heavenward and sent a prayer up too that maybe the Good Lord could help her out for just a moment. "Are the girls available?"

"They haven't been getting along," Janelle said, her tone angry even to her own ears. "So I think it would be best if you just took Kelly tonight."

"Well, the movie's at three-thirty…" He let the words hang there.

Janelle sighed. "I'll meet you at the intersection of highway thirty-seven and Longmire in thirty minutes."

"Really? We have to meet on the side of the road?"

"You already went to my house," she snapped. "We're not home. You're putting me out as it is."

"I can just come get her. Where are you?"

"Not happening," Janelle said. "See you in thirty

minutes." She hung up, not caring that Henry was in the middle of a sentence. She stared straight ahead for several long moments until her vision faded from bright red and back to normal. Then she sighed, turned around, and walked back over to where Kelly still sat in the swing.

"Let's go," she said.

"Right now?" Kelly looked up at her, surprise in her face. "It's my turn to nail first."

Janelle glared down at her daughter. "Do you want to go to the movies with Daddy or not?"

"Yes, ma'am." Kelly stood up, her eyes bright and zero guilt on her face. She was already turning into a teenager, where everything was about her. Janelle wasn't ready for it, and she was ill-equipped to deal with her attitude and manipulations.

"Then we're going now. Come on." Janelle started across the lawn toward the driveway, already lifting her phone to her ear to make another call, this one to Russ.

He'd be fine with Kadence while she drove Kelly in to meet Henry. She knew that. She just didn't want to explain to him why she was leaving.

"Hey, baby," he said easily, nothing like the false tone she'd heard in Henry's voice. Everything that was tight inside Janelle loosened, and she sighed. "You okay?"

"Yes," she said, deciding this little hiccup in the plans was not going to ruin her day. "I'm taking Kelly into town to meet Henry. Can you keep Kadence while I'm gone?"

"No problem." Curiosity rode in his tone now, but Russ didn't ask any other questions.

"Thank you," she said. "I'll be back in a little bit."

"Can't wait," he said, and the call ended. Janelle didn't say anything to Kelly, the tension between them as thick as mud.

The drive happened in silence, and Henry's sports car waited on the patch of dirt where she usually left her sedan when she met Russ here. "Go on," she said to Kelly after she'd stopped.

Kelly got out of the car and said, "Thanks, Momma," before closing the door.

Janelle's fingers gripped and re-gripped the steering wheel as she glared at the shiny, black car. Henry had apparently just washed it, as it gleamed in the weak winter sunlight.

Kelly got in the car, and a moment later, Henry got out.

Janelle wanted to peel out, spitting gravel in his face as she left. But she took the high road and rolled down her window as he approached. "Thank you," he said, and he seemed genuine.

Janelle reminded herself that he'd seemed that way a lot in the past, and it was never once true. "Yep."

"I'll bring her home tonight? Say around nine? Is that too late?"

"Nine is fine." Janelle kept her eyes out the windshield, refusing to look at him.

"I didn't mean to interrupt you at the ranch," he said.

Janelle swung her gaze toward him, and he was oh-so-handsome and perfectly perched as he'd balanced one arm against the top of her car and leaned down to see her through the open window.

"Yes, you did," she said. "Don't lie to me. That might work on the girls, but I know better."

Henry looked like she'd splashed ice water in his face, and he straightened. He tapped the top of her car a couple of times and said, "All right. See you later, Janelle," before he walked away.

A mixture of guilt and powerful satisfaction dove through her. Her heart pounded with the extra doses of adrenaline, and she clutched the steering wheel again. Why couldn't she be a little mean? The tiniest bit unkind?

He'd cheated on her with eight other women while they'd been married. Eight. He'd thrown her to curb time and time again, and she was supposed to just turn the other cheek? Forgive him over and over? Welcome him back into her life—and her daughter's lives?

No.

But maybe yes.

She sighed, some of her fury going with the air as it left her lungs. She could forgive him. She could turn the other cheek.

But that didn't mean she needed to forget what he'd done. It didn't mean she condoned it, or that she had to open herself up to getting hurt again. She didn't have to be his doormat—she wouldn't.

Her phone rang, and Russ's name sat on the screen. Sweet, thoughtful, kind Russ. He was white if Henry was black. Day while Henry was night.

She swiped on the call, tears gathering in her eyes. "Hey."

"Sweetheart," he said. "You okay? Kadence and I can come get you, and we'll go get ice cream."

She nodded, because she didn't want him to hear the tears in her voice. She never let them fall, and she blinked them back now too. Henry fired up his fancy car and left, turning to go south instead of north where he lived.

"Kadence says ice cream sounds awesome," Russ said. "So we're already heading to the truck, okay? Where are you?"

Janelle drew in a deep breath and cleared her throat. Cleared all the emotion from her chest. Cleared all the painful memories and hurt feelings and inadequacies from her memory. "Our usual place," she said.

"Be there in ten," Russ promised, and Janelle knew that when the cowboy promised something, he would follow through, unlike her ex-husband.

"Okay." The call ended, and Janelle slumped in her seat. She had ten minutes to rid herself of the anxiety, the worry, the fear, and the tears. Russ deserved the best version of herself. Kadence did too.

And she would give it to them.

Chapter 15

Russ pulled up to Janelle's house, a new kind of freedom beating its wings through his bloodstream. Because today, he was going to go in through the front door. In fact, Janelle appeared on the front stoop while Russ still sat in his truck, and he reached quickly to unbuckle his seatbelt.

When he and Kadence had arrived to pick her up for ice cream yesterday afternoon, Russ had sensed her turmoil. But she'd covered over it with a smile and her cute Texas twang. She'd held her daughter's hand as they scoped out the ice cream flavors, and she'd kept the conversation going even when Russ ran out of things to say.

She hadn't come back to the ranch after that, and he'd said goodbye to her on the side of the road again. Needless to say, there was no kissing involved, and Russ's heart had hurt for the rest of the day.

He didn't know how to deal with an ex-spouse, and he

didn't know how to ask Janelle what she was thinking about Henry. He didn't want to anger her again, or upset her, and while he'd previously believed ice cream could fix everything, after yesterday afternoon, he wasn't so sure anymore.

"Hey," he said as he closed the truck door. "How's your day?"

She wore a long, black dress that flowed in waves around her body. She was sleek and sophisticated, and Russ wondered what in the world she was doing with him. This woman, with her beautiful brown hair that fell in curls over her shoulders and those perfectly painted pink lips, belonged with the posh, casual man Russ had run into at the hardware store.

No matter what, Janelle definitely didn't look like a rancher's wife.

"Good," she said, her fingertips touching the brim of his cowboy hat. He tensed as she removed the hat completely and gazed at him silently.

Russ didn't move and he didn't speak. So much was said between them anyway, and Russ hoped he was conveying the right things.

"Kelly's already set up in the kitchen," she said, her voice pleasant. She seemed normal today, and Russ wondered how she compartmentalized everything so easily. Maybe she didn't. Maybe she was pretending.

"What are you thinking?" he asked as she started to move.

She froze again, her eyes coming back to his. "I'm thinking I'm sure glad you're here." She dropped her gaze to his hand, which she took in both of hers. "Henry was here all morning, and it's a relief that he's gone."

Surprise darted through Russ, and his pulse picked up speed. "Henry was here all morning?"

"He kept Kelly overnight and brought her back this morning. And then." She exhaled heavily. "He wouldn't leave. Kept asking me questions about the dogs, and you, and your ranch." She wouldn't look at him, and Russ didn't know what to make of that.

Russ really didn't like that her ex had hung out all morning at his girlfriend's place. But what was he supposed to do? He'd worked all morning, first with the animals, then on the dog enclosure, and then held a staff meeting for that week's task list. They had their final mowing of the year to do, as well as the last of the winterizing. The cattle needed to be checked more regularly when the weather turned wet, and Russ had scheduled himself and Darren for that, hoping to get some insight from the older cowboy about his relationship with Janelle.

He hadn't spoken to Rex about what he'd seen in the bathroom, and Travis had disappeared into his woodshop, leaving the homestead to Russ and the dogs last night. In all honesty, Russ had been fine with that. He didn't want to talk about his relationship with his brothers anyway. Maybe Travis.

He missed Seth, and he couldn't wait until his even-keeled, good-natured brother returned from his honeymoon.

"What did you tell him about me, my ranch, and the dogs?" Russ asked.

"Normal stuff." Janelle shrugged. "He asked if we were serious."

"And?" Russ really wanted to know how she'd answered that question.

She finally looked at him, and she was as serious as a nun in church on Sunday. "I told him we were."

A smile played with Russ's lips.

"Is that what you would've said?" she asked.

"Yes." His whispered word barely met his own ears, but he knew Janelle had heard him by the way her eyes crinkled as she gave him half a smile.

She enveloped herself into his arms then, and Russ held her right there on her driveway. She didn't shake or shiver, and she didn't cry, but Russ felt strong as she relaxed into him. She needed him, and he hadn't been needed by a woman in a very long time.

After a few minutes, he said, "Maybe we shouldn't keep Kelly waiting."

"She's fine," Janelle said, but she stepped back. "She's turning into a teenager already." She sighed in that frustrated way Russ had heard before. "I miss my little girl already." She threaded her fingers through Russ's and they walked toward the front steps.

Russ had never been inside the house, and it was obvious Janelle had spent at least part of today cleaning up. The air held the scent of pine needles and the sterile crispness of air freshener. All the pillows on the couch matched and were perfectly placed. There were no shoes, no backpacks, and no jackets in sight.

"This is a beautiful house," he said, glancing around the open concept. A hallway led out of the living room to his left, back to bedrooms and bathrooms, he assumed. The dining room sat in the back right corner, with the kitchen beside it. Kelly sat at the bar, and she looked up from the book in front of her.

She didn't smile, but she did slide off the barstool and come toward them. "Good afternoon, Russ," she said, almost formally. Almost like she'd been coached.

Russ cleared his throat and glanced at the girl's mother. "Afternoon, Kelly."

"Russ!"

He turned toward the little girl barreling down the hallway toward him, barely catching her as she launched herself at him. He chuckled as he swept Kadence up and into his arms.

"Hey, baby," he said, touching one finger to her nose. "Were you good for your momma last night?"

"We watched *My Little Pony* and made caramel popcorn by ourselves." She sounded so proud, and Russ set her on the ground, glancing at Kelly as he did. She was clearly too mature to be swept into a hug and far too advanced in the kitchen for mere caramel popcorn. She almost held her nose in the air, and Russ found himself wanting to connect to her anyway.

"Sounds amazing," he said. "Did you eat all the caramel popcorn?"

"Nope." Kadence skipped into the kitchen and opened a bottom drawer in the island. "Hey, where's the bag of popcorn?"

"Kade," Janelle said, her voice already taking on a diplomatic tone. "Kelly ate it this morning, remember?"

"It's fine," Russ said, but he saw the daggered look form on Kadence's face.

"Mom said I could," Kelly said.

"I was savin' that for Russ," Kadence said.

"It's sav*ing*," Kelly said. "There's a G on the end of the word." She stalked away from Russ and Janelle, who wore a weary look on her face. "And we're making peanut butter bars today, so there will be plenty of treats." She closed her book and looked at Russ. "Can we start?"

He didn't need to give his permission, but Kelly wasn't looking at her mom. Janelle turned and got out a giant jar of peanut butter. "Kadence gets to measure everything today."

"Momma," Kelly whined.

"Or we can skip it entirely." Janelle gave Kelly a pointed look. "And you haven't washed your hands. You can't mix if you don't wash up first."

"I did wash."

"Let me smell your hands."

Kelly's fists balled up, and she marched around the island to the sink. "Fine, I'll wash up."

Russ could've cut the tension with a knife, and he didn't know where his place was in all of it. Janelle motioned for him to come into the kitchen, but it almost felt like he'd be entering a war zone. He did it, though, and he glanced at the book Kelly had been reading.

"I have this one," he said, a blip of happiness filling his heart. "It's got some amazing recipes in it. What have you tried?"

"Nothing yet," Kelly said from the sink. "Daddy just bought it for me last night."

"Oh." Russ picked up the book and leafed through it. "The peach tarts are awesome. The triple chocolate chip cookies. We've had those. I tried the baked potato chowder, but my momma's corn chowder recipe is better, and it has potatoes in it too, so…"

Kelly returned to his side. "Will you mark the ones you've tried?"

"Sure." He smiled down at her. "I didn't know you cooked too. I thought y'all were into baking."

"She's branching out," Janelle said at the same time Kelly said, "I'm trying new things." They looked at each other, and Russ could practically feel the awkwardness in the kitchen dissipate.

"All right," Kelly said. "Kade, you better climb up and get ready. I'll start getting everything out."

Russ caught the ghost of a smile on Janelle's face, and he sat down at the bar to watch the women work. No one invited him to help, and he rather liked simply basking in their presence. He couldn't help thinking about Henry, and where he'd sat. What conversations they'd had. Had Kelly run to him when he'd arrived?

He banished the thoughts as far as he could, but they

kept creeping back. Steadily, until they'd infiltrated his mind again. By the time Kelly melted the chocolate glaze to pour over the cooled peanut butter bars, Russ could no longer ignore the questions in his mind.

"How was the movie with your daddy?" he asked her.

Kelly barely glanced up. "Uh, it was okay."

"Just okay?" He looked at Janelle and back to her daughter. "Your mom said you were excited to see it."

Kelly looked at Janelle too, and Russ would have to learn how to communicate with children the way she did. Maybe it was a mother-daughter thing he'd never know how to do.

"We got there late," she finally said. "So we missed the first little bit." She shrugged. "I don't know. It was okay."

"You got there late?" Janelle asked. "Daddy said it didn't start until three-thirty, and he picked you up at just after one." She wore alarm on her face when she looked at Russ. But what was he supposed to say?

Kelly kept her eyes on the glaze as it poured over the peanut butter bars. "The movie was all the way down in San Antonio."

Janelle sucked in a breath. "What? You drove almost two hours to go to a movie?"

"Don't be mad, Momma."

"I'm not mad," she said, though Russ probably would've classified her that way too. He couldn't imagine driving that far for a movie when there were probably fifty theaters between Chestnut Springs and San Antonio. "I'm just surprised. Why did you go all the way down there?"

"We met someone at the theater," she said, finally looking up. Pure fear lived in her expression. "A lady."

Horror washed across Janelle's face, and Russ got up to go stand next to her. "You met one of your father's girlfriends." She wasn't asking, and Russ really didn't like how she'd phrased it as "one of" his girlfriends. If Kelly or Kadence noticed, they didn't say anything.

"She wasn't his girlfriend," Kelly said. "I think he said she was a therapist."

Even Russ didn't believe that, and he swept his arm around Janelle as she sagged into him. Apparently, she and Henry had different views about nearly everything, including when it was appropriate to introduce their children to their new significant others.

"What else happened last night?" Janelle asked, her voice the slightest bit hysterical. She backed away from Russ and Kelly. "Never mind. I don't want to know."

Kelly ignored the question just fine and turned to open the fridge. "These just need to set up." She'd already cleared a spot in the fridge, and she slid the tray of treats inside. With that done, she looked at Russ. "Do you want to go see the dogs? We've been taking really good care of them."

"Absolutely." Russ shot a look at Janelle, but she just shook her head. So he went out into the garage with Kelly, and then into the backyard behind her. All of the dogs bounded toward him, a couple of them barking as they came.

"Hey, guys," he said, chuckling. "Hey. How are you?" He scratched and patted all of them, letting them sniff his jeans, where they could probably smell Winner, Thunder, and Cloudy.

"So Kelly," he said. "What do you guys do for Christmas?"

"Do?"

"Yeah, do you go see your grandparents? Stay here? Decorate?"

"We'll go see Granny and Gramps in Johnson City." Kelly bent and picked up a ball, tossing it as far as she could. Three dogs took off after it, and she picked up a bucket and a scooper. "It's pretty fun. They have two treehouses in their backyard."

"Wow," Russ said. "Did your grandpa build them?"

"His grandpa," Kelly said. "So they're old."

"Sounds like it."

She set about cleaning up the backyard with the pooper scooper, and Russ followed along beside her. "What do you want for Christmas?" he asked next.

"I was just going to ask you that." She smiled at the ground. "I want a stand mixer, but Momma says they're really expensive."

Russ did a little bit of cooking, but he didn't pay attention to prices. "Does your momma pay you for chores?"

"Yeah," she said. "That's why I'm out here cleaning up."

"Maybe you can get one then."

"Even Daddy says it's too big of a gift for Christmas." Kelly sighed. "But he'll probably pay a ton of money to take us to Florida or something."

"Does he travel a lot?"

"Sometimes," she said. "He took us to Disney World last year."

"I bet that was fun." It sure didn't sound fun to Russ. Crowds. Noise. Lines. Heat.

"It was. I got a light saber, and Kade got like, a hundred water bottles. She loves water bottles." Kelly smiled and kept cleaning up.

Russ liked talking to her, and he wondered if he could figure out a Christmas present for her beautiful mother during this conversation.

"What do you get your mom for Christmas?"

"Kadence usually paints her something at the Girls Club we go to after school sometimes. I make her breakfast in bed, and then my aunt or someone helps me buy her something."

"Like what?" he pressed.

Kelly looked up at him, but he couldn't read her expression fast enough to know if she was onto him or not. "Nail polish one year. She loves notebooks and planners. I got her that last year. A picture frame with a picture of me and Kadence. Stuff like that."

Nothing Russ could get her, unless he wanted to take a picture of himself and stick it in a frame for her desk at work. He almost snorted out loud at the very idea of doing that.

No, he needed something meaningful and romantic. Something that showed he cared about her, knew her, and wanted her, all at the same time.

He couldn't go with clothes. Slippers were out, obviously. He wasn't going to buy her nail polish or something for the house or kitchen. So what could he get?

"If you have any ideas about what *I* could get for her for Christmas," Russ said. "Let me know, okay? She's hard to shop for."

Kelly giggled and nodded. "That's what Daddy always says too."

Russ suddenly found it very hard to swallow, and thankfully, Kadence came skipping outside with a request to play jump rope, which both Kelly and Russ readily agreed to do.

* * *

The next morning, Russ had just gotten out of the shower when his phone rang. He couldn't get to it fast enough without falling on the tiles in wet feet, so he let it go to voicemail. Not two seconds later, it rang again.

"Momma," he answered. "What's goin' on?"

"The house flooded," she said. "We've tried Griffin and Rex, and neither of them are answering their phones."

Russ's pulse shrieked through his body. "Are you guys okay? Are you inside?"

"We're inside," she said. "As near as we can tell, a pipe burst in the night and has been gushing ever since."

"I'll come right now," he said. "Hang tight, Momma." He hung up and dressed quickly, hurrying downstairs, where he heard Travis doing something in the kitchen. "Trav?"

"Right here," he said, stepping around the corner still

wearing a pair of gym shorts and yesterday's T-shirt. "What's wrong?"

Russ finished tucking his shirt in and entered the kitchen to get his keys. "Momma called. She said the kitchen is flooded, and she can't get ahold of Rex or Griffin."

"They're probably still asleep."

"Yeah." Russ swiped his keys from the drawer and looked at Travis. "Want me to go alone?"

"No," Travis said. "Give me two minutes. I'll meet you in the truck."

Russ nodded and headed outside, ready to be going already. He had a ton of work to do that day, and no time for house floods. Not only that but getting his father to leave the house would be tricky. And getting him and his momma to stay in the homestead while they cleaned everything up?

Russ wasn't even sure that was possible. But he would try, just like he'd decided to keep trying with Janelle.

Chapter 16

Janelle put herself together on Monday morning the same way she did every other weekday. Makeup in muted tones. Lip gloss in the perfect shade of pink for her complexion. Professional hoops for earrings. Her mother's necklace. Conservative, dark clothes, with her bunion-approved flats.

She got her kids ready for school and dropped them off exactly on time. She drove through Perky For Another Day and ordered her favorite coffee blend with cream and caramel. She walked through the door at the firm at precisely nine o'clock, her briefcase bag swinging at her side.

No one would've thought anything in her life was wrong, or even slightly off.

But Janelle knew. She knew that so many things had been blown wide open that weekend, starting with Henry.

He'd called as she was getting out of the shower, and she'd put him off with, "You can't call me in the morning.

We're busy getting everything ready for the day. I'll call you when I get to work."

She'd hung up before he could say another word, and he hadn't called back. So the message had been delivered and received.

"Morning, Libby," she said, pausing at her friend's desk. "I need you to hold all my calls for the next twenty minutes. Then interrupt me no matter what and say I have an important client waiting for me."

Janelle never scheduled important clients on Monday morning, because she needed to ease into her week.

"You're due in court at eleven," Libby said, handing her a file.

"Yes, I reviewed this last night," she said.

Libby stood up. "Henry?"

"Unfortunately." Janelle gave Libby her best smile, but it must not have come off very well, because Libby didn't return it.

"Good luck," she said instead. "And we still need to talk about how things went on Saturday with Russ and the girls."

"Yes, we do."

"I'll block out time after your hearing."

Janelle felt like she never had enough time in the day, but now wasn't the time for that lamentation. She entered her office and closed the door behind her. She didn't need to lock it, as she'd just given Libby instructions.

She'd barely set down her bag and her coffee before she called Henry. He answered on the first ring with, "Morning,

Janelle." He sounded like he was relaxing in his back garden as he watched the sun rise over the Hill Country.

She really disliked that picturesque vision of him, not when she'd been up since before dawn to make sure the three of them got up, brushed, bathed, fed, and had everything they needed for the day in just a couple of hours.

"You called?" she asked, keeping the phone on speaker. Then, when Libby came in, Henry would be able to hear her.

"Yes." He cleared his throat. "I didn't get a chance to thank you for letting me keep Kelly overnight on Saturday."

Janelle pressed her lips together, trying to decide if she wanted to bring up San Antonio with him or not. "She's your daughter, Henry."

"And I wanted to let you know that I'm in town until the New Year."

Surprise filled her, rendering her mute for a moment. "All month?"

"Yes."

"You're living here, in Chestnut Springs?"

"Yes."

The town that smothers you? She bit back those words, as she really didn't need to fight with him. But he'd told her this small town "smothered" him and that was why he constantly needed to drive to the city.

Turned out, that was only one reason, and Henry had left the moment Janelle had told him she was going to file for divorce. Her firm had handled all the legal proceedings, and she still relied on Regina Hessler if there were any legal considerations when it came to the girls and Henry.

"Why?" she asked instead.

"I'm on a leave of absence from my firm, and I thought it would be good to spend time with the girls. Take them Christmas shopping, help them decorate their trees, all of that."

"A leave of absence?" Janelle was a very good lawyer, because she could pick up on the little things people said. Henry had said something big though. Janelle ran a law firm, and she didn't just grant leaves of absences for no reason.

Usually people only requested one if they had a loved one going through a terrible health crisis, in the case of a birth or death, or if they were in some sort of legal trouble themselves.

A lightbulb went off in Janelle's head, and she said, "What's going on, Henry? For real. Tell me the truth."

For once.

She didn't say that last part, because she wanted Henry to keep talking.

He sighed, but Janelle wasn't going to let him off the hook. She could out-wait him, and they both knew it. She sat down behind her desk and reached for her coffee. Taking a sip, she could practically hear the wheels in his head start turning.

He was going to lie to her.

"I've been accused of something I didn't do," he said. "I have a friend at my firm representing me, and until it blows over, I'm on administrative leave."

"What's the accusation?" she asked, already reaching for her laptop. If there was a formal charge, she'd be able to find it in the state's system.

"It's nothing, honey," he said smoothly. "The allegations are completely false, and I just have to get through the hearing, which isn't until December twenty-seventh."

She opened the Internet and started logging into the lawyer side of the court document system.

"So anyway," he said. "I got an apartment here, and I'd love to pick the girls up from school. Take them to a gingerbread-making class I found at the community center. Take them ice skating up at Marble Falls. All that stuff we used to do as a family."

Janelle leaned away from her computer, needing every brain cell to focus on the man's words. "You want to pick them up from school?" He wasn't even on the emergency contact paper, as he lived over an hour away and had literally never picked up one of his children from school. Ever.

"Sure," he said. "I'm just sitting here right now. In fact… I also found a stocking sewing class at Buttons and Bobs, and I know Kelly would love that."

"She would," Janelle said, somewhat numbly. She didn't have time to take the girls to very many after-school or weekend activities and classes. Certainly nothing where she'd need to go sit with them or supervise the use of a sewing machine or the oven. Just baking their three items each week had been a huge challenge for her. One they'd knocked out of the park, sure. But still a challenge.

"So what do you think?" Henry asked. "They go to River Springs Elementary, right?"

Her blood boiled, but Janelle couldn't say no to him when he wanted to be a father. She could say no to him when he wanted to come back into her life. But for Kelly and Kadence…

"All right," she said. "They get done at three-fifteen. The pick-up line is a bear, so I usually get there about fifteen minutes early. You'll need to go into the school and ask about getting an emergency contact paper. I don't think you're on either of the girls' forms."

If Henry found that odd, he didn't say so. "Sounds good," he said, perfectly at ease. "I'll get it all taken care of. Thanks, honey."

With that, the call ended, and Janelle watched as her ex-husband's face faded into blackness on her phone's screen.

"What is going on?" she asked herself. Then, shaking off the numbness, she leaned forward and finished logging in. She quickly typed in Henry Stokes to the search box, and sure enough, one case popped up.

It was a protective order case, filed almost two weeks ago by a woman named Marissa Gillmore from Austin. She claimed he'd been stalking her after their break-up and had shown up at her work, demanding she go outside with him so they could talk in private.

Janelle read the order quickly, and if she'd been hired to represent Henry, she'd bet good money she could get the order dismissed. Number one, he'd never touched Marissa in a negative way. At least, she hadn't claimed any of that in the order.

She had filed a police report when he'd shown up on her doorstep one night, "clearly drunk" and wanting to spend the night with her. She admitted to having sex with him previously, but they'd broken up, and she'd turned him away that night.

She alleged he banged on her door for fifteen minutes and only left when the police showed up.

Janelle quickly navigated to the associated police report, and sure enough, he had been escorted off her property.

But Henry wasn't dangerous. Was he?

Janelle reasoned he'd probably just been stressed. The next week, she'd dropped the girls off at his house northwest of Austin, and he'd seemed fine. She knew how emotionally tumultuous it was to break-up with a boyfriend. He'd just been upset about the ending of his relationship with Marissa.

Her throat felt unusually dry, and Libby poked her head into the office. "Miss Stokes. You have—oh. You're off the phone." She ducked into the office and strode toward Janelle's desk. "And you're white as a ghost. What's going on?"

Instead of answering, she turned the computer toward Libby, whose mouth dropped open as she read the report. "Oh, my." She looked at Janelle. "What are you going to do?"

"He's here through the New Year," she said. "As in, he

rented an apartment here and wants to do all kinds of Christmas things with the girls."

Libby wore concern in her eyes, but all Janelle felt was misery. She didn't want to share the girls with Henry on a day-to-day basis. Having him live farther away and not really be interested in their lives was so much easier—for everyone.

"Maybe you'll have more time with Russ," Libby suggested. "No babysitters at night. Henry can take them while you go out with your boyfriend."

"That feels weird," Janelle said.

"Yeah, I know." Libby leaned back in her chair. "I don't know, Janelle. What did you tell him?"

"I told him the pick-up line at the elementary school was a bear and to get there fifteen minutes early." Her mind felt like one giant blank space, and Libby stood up as her phone rang.

"I'll be right back." She left the room, and Janelle picked up her cell as it vibrated against her desk.

My parents had a flood at their place this morning, Russ had sent.

That's terrible. Janelle didn't know how to tell him about Henry. Maybe she didn't need to.

Of course you do, she thought, and she tapped out another message. *Can I call you real quick?*

Give me a few minutes, he said. She set her phone facedown and closed the lid on her laptop. The black words on white paper still ran behind her closed eyes, and she focused by drawing in a deep breath and opening the folder for her court hearing that morning. She had already gone over it, and she knew what arguments she was going to make to the commissioner.

Sometime later—definitely more than a few minutes—her phone vibrated again, and she picked it up to see Russ's name and face on the screen. Her heart pounced, and she answered the call with, "Hi," and a sigh.

"Mornin', sweetheart," he drawled. He sounded tired too. "This week is going to be a killer."

"Yeah?"

"Yeah, my parents will stay out at the ranch while their house gets restored. It was a broken pipe that went to the dishwasher."

"Oh, wow," Janelle said. "That stinks."

"Yeah, the entire main level is full of water. And we have our last harvest this week, and Travis and I are going whole-hog on the dog enclosure, because Seth gets home next Sunday." He exhaled. "But this wasn't about me. What did you need?"

Janelle opened her mouth to tell him, but the words flew. "Uh, nothing."

Russ didn't say anything for a moment, and Janelle hated that she hadn't just told him. "You wanted to call me for nothing?" he asked.

"It's Henry," she said, feeling the weight of the world settle right on the back of her neck. "He's actually rented an apartment in town and wants to spend the next couple of weeks doing holiday things with the girls."

"Oh."

"Yeah, that sums it up," Janelle said. "I just got off the phone with him."

"He doesn't have a job in Austin?"

"He's on leave," she said, going on to explain briefly what she'd seen in the reports and cases he was dealing with. "And I don't know. I feel like maybe I need to supervise the visits or something."

"I'll be honest, I'm not going to be much help this week," he said. "It's fine. My family party is next Friday, though, and I really want you and the girls there."

Janelle had started to shake off some of the paralyzing thoughts, and she clicked over to her calendar. "Next Friday…I can do that. It's at the ranch?"

"Yes," he said. "Dinner at six."

"Gifts?"

"Nope," he said. "But it'll be my parents and my brothers, and all of their significant others. So just Jenna and Millie. I think Jenna's brother might be coming too. I'm not sure."

She started adding a calendar event. "I'm putting it on right now. We'll be there." In the past, she wouldn't have had to clear it with Henry, but now she did. She also wanted him to know she knew what the allegations against him were, and that she didn't trust him to be alone with the girls. Not if he was drinking.

So she had another hard phone call to make.

She didn't want to let Russ go quite yet, but she didn't know what to say to him. They just breathed on the line together, and Janelle stole some of his powerful, quiet energy before she managed to say, "Thanks, Russ. I'll talk to you soon."

"Anytime, baby," he said, his voice husky and contemplative too.

Janelle took a few minutes to let her emotions wash through her. Over her. They threatened to pull her right into a black pit, but she fought against them. She squared her shoulders and picked up her phone again.

She'd make this call. She'd go to court. She'd get through the day. She'd done it all before, and she could do it again.

She just wished she didn't have to do it alone.

Chapter 17

Russ called a meeting for everyone at Chestnut Ranch, and they met in his tiny office on Monday afternoon. He filled everyone in concerning the flood, ending with, "And Momma and Daddy will be living in the homestead for this week. Travis has been working with the restoration company the most, and he's going to keep doing that."

His brother nodded, and so did Rex and Griffin.

"Sorry we didn't get their calls," Griffin said.

"You wouldn't have done anything different anyway," Russ said. "It's fine. We got them out, and we've hired someone to clean it all up." He looked down at his clipboard. "This week, Travis and I are going to focus on the dog enclosure. Griffin and Rex will take over all the chores except for the dogs. That leaves Darren and his crew to do all the crops. It's our last week of that for a couple of months, and we need all the fields cleaned up, mowed, and set for the winter."

As if Mother Nature wanted to make his life a little harder, a clap of thunder filled the sky.

"And it's supposed to rain a bit here at the beginning of the week," he said.

"We have ponchos," Darren said. "We'll get it done, boss."

And Russ knew they would. Darren was an excellent cowboy who'd landed at Chestnut Ranch several years ago after an ugly divorce and a bankruptcy at his own ranch just outside of Fredericksburg.

"And Seth is coming back on Sunday," Russ said, his emotions sneaking up on him. He had no idea where they'd come from, but he missed his older brother powerfully in that moment. He cleared his throat and continued. "We'll have dinner at the homestead that night to celebrate with him. Everyone is invited."

"Everyone's invited to Thursday night dinner too," Travis said. "And our ranch party next Friday night." He nodded at Darren, Tomas, and Brian, and they all nodded back.

"Okay, that's it," Russ said. "Oh, wait. We need to have one more check of the cattle this week sometime..." He flipped a page. "I don't like it when it rains and we don't know if they're standing in water all the time."

"The farthest field is soggy," Griffin said. "I was out there on Saturday, and it was bad then."

"Let's move them somewhere else then." Russ thought

about the winter pastures they had ready. "Maybe section eleven?"

"We put the bulls there," Rex said, moving to stand next to Russ. "What about over here?" He pointed to the southern sections on the map.

"That's close to the river," Russ said. "I don't normally put cattle there in the winter. We lose ground every year to the floods when it rains."

"It's just today and tomorrow," Rex said. "I'll move them in the morning, and we'll see how it goes." He looked at Russ for his approval, and he simply gave it. He didn't have another pasture at the moment, and if Rex was willing to take lead on a chore none of the brothers liked that much, Russ wasn't going to argue.

"Great." Rex clapped Russ on the shoulder, and the cowboys started to disperse. Before he could even set his clipboard down on the desk, his phone buzzed. That was his mother—again—and Russ tried not to be frustrated by her constant messages. It was like she'd just gotten a phone and learned how to text for the first time.

Daddy needs his weighted blanket to sleep. Do you think you could run to town and get it?

Russ sighed, because no, he couldn't just "run to town" and get the blanket. A drive there and back took a half an hour, minimum, and he'd skipped lunch as he'd already driven back and forth from the ranch to their house twice that day alone.

I miss you, he sent to Janelle, because it was past the time where she normally texted him from the pick-up line at the elementary school. He hadn't gotten a single text, and Russ felt like he had a mountain of chores to finish all by himself.

He reminded himself that he loved this ranch. He loved horses, and cattle, and even mowing down winter wheat.

He loved his parents, and he'd do anything for them. Since his father's injury, Seth's responsibilities had picked up, but Russ and the others hadn't really had to do much.

He did now. He could do it.

Miss you too, Janelle said.

Russ stared at the words as warmth moved through him. Life got busy sometimes, he knew that. He went back to his mother's message and answered it with, *Sure. I'll go now. Anything else you need?*

No, dear. Thanks.

He messaged Travis and asked him if he needed anything in town, but he also said no.

Russ was an hour late for the cinnamon rolls, and he didn't have time to wait in line anyway. They'd probably be gone already, besides. But he grabbed his keys from the homestead and checked on his parents, who were both seated on the couch in the living room. "I'm goin' now, Momma."

"Thank you, baby," she said, not bothering to look up from her crochet. She did look over to Daddy, who snored softly. "This is too much excitement for him."

Russ wondered how in the world he was going to go on the service mission to the Dominican Republic if a couple of inches of water tuckered him out, but he didn't say anything. His parents were grown adults, and they'd never done anything all too exciting. His daddy had worked the ranch, with Momma right beside him. Russ hadn't even known she was part of a huge cosmetics company until a few months ago.

"Be back in a few," he said, and he left the homestead.

In his truck, he called Janelle, who picked up on the first ring. "Hey," she said, and she sounded a bit better this afternoon than she had that morning. Music came through her speaker, and he feared he'd interrupted something.

"Hey," he said. "Where are you?"

"Oh, uh, just my house."

"Are you baking this afternoon? I can hear music."

"Yep," she said, and the music quieted. "You know how Kelly is with her pop songs."

Russ had the distinct feeling that Janelle wasn't telling him the truth. He'd felt it this morning too. "I do," he said. "Are you really at your house baking?" He didn't want to question Janelle, but if she was lying to him now, what could he expect her to do in the future?

"Yes," she said. "It's just that...Henry is here too."

"Ah." Russ didn't like that one little bit, and the small storm cloud that had been hovering over him since he and Travis had run from the homestead that morning to see what was going on their parents' house morphed into a full-blown tornado.

"It's nothing," Janelle said. "I just don't trust him to be alone with the girls. So I'm hanging out on my laptop while they make cake pops." She lowered her voice and added, "Ugly ones, too."

For some reason, that got Russ to laugh, and everything seemed brighter after that. "All right, sweetheart. I'm driving to town for the third time today, and I need a good story. What have you got?"

"You want me to tell you a story?"

"Anything," he said. "I just like hearing your voice." He didn't even care if he was revealing too much about how he felt about Janelle Stokes. Surely she already knew. He couldn't hide anything when he kissed her, and he had the sudden thought of asking her to sneak away for a moment so he could do just that.

She started talking about her friend, Libby, at work, and Russ just drove, her sweet voice painting pictures for him and making the drive go by so much faster.

* * *

On Tuesday, Russ stood in the kitchen, trying not to listen to Travis and Millie argue in the formal living room. But it was really hard, as only he and Rex were in the kitchen, and neither Travis nor Millie seemed to care about how loud they were talking.

"I'll go get Daddy off the back porch," Rex whispered.

"Hurry," Russ said back, practically slamming a cupboard after he took out plates. Maybe Travis and Millie would then be reminded that sound travels.

He heard the front door open, but he didn't hear it close, and Russ continued getting everything ready for lunch. The back door opened, and voices filled the house.

Darren laughed at something one of the other cowboys said, and relief rushed through Russ.

Travis appeared in the doorway between the kitchen and the living room, his face a perfect mask of anger. Russ stared at him in shock. Had he and Millie really just broken up?

He seemed to be able to ask the question without words, because Travis nodded and turned to go up the steps. He disappeared at the same time the boys came into the kitchen, and Brian said, "Russ, can you cook for us every day?"

"No, sir, I cannot," he said. He'd barely had energy to do it today. The only reason he'd put together the baked chicken and potatoes was because Momma had made a comment about everything in the homestead being frozen or from a box. She wasn't entirely wrong, but the brothers had managed to survive without her for several years now.

They laughed, and Rex came in with Daddy on his arm and Griffin right behind them. Momma brought up the rear, and Russ waited for her to ask about Travis. But there was a lot of noise, and it only increased as the cowboys went through the line to get their food. Once everyone was seated at the table, Russ asked, "How did the cattle move go?"

Rex had already reported to him, but he looked up and made eye contact. "Good," he said. "The south fields along the river don't seem to be compromised right now. I'll check on them this afternoon and every morning to make sure."

"Thanks, Rex," Russ said, grateful for more than just the ranch report. Rex could be very loud, sure. He made a lot of things into a joke that usually annoyed Russ. But he was incredibly loyal too, and he worked hard, and he never complained about anything.

He'd left town for a while several years ago, and Russ had wondered then if they'd ever see him again. But he'd come back about five years ago, and while Russ wished he hadn't walked in on him and Janelle kissing, Rex was a good brother.

"Is Travis in his shop?" Momma asked. "Doesn't he know lunch is ready?"

"I texted him," Russ said. "But he doesn't get great service out there."

"He's not out there," Griffin said, glancing at Russ and back to Momma. "I stopped by when I came in. Shop was empty."

"Where is he then?" Momma peered out the glass doors that led to the patio, and Russ wished he could kick Griffin under the table without it being too obvious. But he sat too far away.

"Winner and Cloudy aren't here either," Rex said. "He's probably out with the dogs." He didn't seem to care, but Russ met his eye again, and definite anxiety lived there.

"I'm sure he's fine," Russ said. "We don't all eat at the same time every day, Momma." Thank goodness. Russ loved his men and his family, but he felt near the end of his rope, and it was only midday on Tuesday.

The conversation moved on to something else, and eventually the cowboys got up to get back to work. Rex helped Daddy to the couch, and Momma cleaned up the kitchen.

Russ started for the stairs, because he needed to check on

Travis—and make sure he knew Momma had already been asking about him.

He knocked on his brother's door and said, "Trav? It's Russ."

"Come in," he said from behind the closed door, and when Russ entered the bedroom, he found Travis standing at the window, which overlooked the front of the house and out onto the ranch.

"Hey," Russ said, moving to stand beside him. His brother wasn't the neatest person on the planet, but he made his bed every day. He put his dirty clothes in the hamper. And he kept his desk relatively clean. The scent of cologne and leather hung in the air, and Russ didn't know what else to say.

Several minutes went by, and he finally said, "Momma was asking why you weren't at lunch."

"She's still downstairs, isn't she?"

"She sure doesn't have anywhere else to go," Russ said, and maybe it came out a bit darkly. He wasn't sure. But she'd criticized him for how late he'd come in last night, and for making too much noise that morning. It was almost like she'd forgotten how early ranchers rose and how much work they had to do before the day was truly done.

Travis chuckled, surprisingly. "She sure doesn't." He sighed. "I'm not talking this to death. Millie thought I was cheating on her, and I broke up with her."

"Because of Caroline?" There had been some incident at the bell choir concert where Caroline Landy had kissed him and Millie had seen it. Some sort of scavenger hunt that Russ—and Travis—didn't understand.

"No," he said. "I had to go meet with the restoration company this morning. She thought I was with another woman, which I mean, I was. But Gabby works for Oakwood Restoration, and she literally just walked me through the cleanup and how much it's going to cost."

"Wow," Russ said. "I'm sorry, Travis. You really liked her."

"Yeah." He nodded, and Russ wondered what he was looking out at.

"Did you leave the dogs outside?"

"Oh, shoot," he said. "Yes, I put them in the enclosure because you were busy and I didn't want them to bother Daddy."

"I'll go get them," Russ said. "They like taking an afternoon nap with him."

"How is he going to go to the Dominican Republic?" Travis asked. "Do you think they'll let him sleep every day?"

"I have no idea," Russ said. "But we should find out more about it so we can talk to them about the likelihood of them going. For real."

"I agree."

"We'll talk to Seth about it when he gets home," Russ said, adding it to the list of things he needed to discuss with his brother.

He wanted to call Janelle as he left Travis standing in his bedroom and went to get the homestead dogs from the enclosure. He wondered what she was doing that afternoon, and he decided to text her to find out.

Gingerbread houses, she texted back. *Community center at four. You could come...*

Russ actually snorted at the idea of him taking time from his day to go watch her girls make gingerbread houses—with her ex-husband.

He wanted to see Janelle and the girls, but he felt choked off by Henry's presence. Intellectually, he knew that if he and Janelle continued their relationship and it became even more serious, he'd have to figure out his place among the four of them.

But right now, he couldn't see it, and he didn't know how to do it. So he just said, *I wish I could,* and left it at that.

Chapter 18

Janelle stepped out of her front door and sighed. Audrey had just arrived, and she'd brought a cake decorating kit to keep the girls occupied that night.

She stopped at the top of the steps, though she was in plain sight of Henry. She couldn't believe she was doing this. Going out with him.

"You're *not* going *out* with him," she muttered to herself. They were simply going Christmas shopping for their kids. That was it.

She'd spoken to Russ every day that week, both on the phone and through texting. He'd just finished telling her that his parents were moving back to their house tomorrow morning. She was happy for him, because he'd been stressed dealing with his momma and daddy in the homestead, and she didn't blame him.

She didn't live in Johnson City for a reason, though she loved her parents and wanted to go visit them often. She and the girls were going next Saturday, as a matter of fact, and she needed a couple of gifts for her parents too.

That was all this evening was. Shopping. She'd told Henry that in no uncertain terms. He'd said he was fine with that. He just wanted to provide a "nice Christmas" for their kids, and Janelle couldn't argue with that. She wanted the same thing.

So she went down the steps, the sidewalk, and around his sports car to the passenger side. She sank into the seat, feeling like she'd just folded her body in half the car was so low. She didn't complain about it, though.

"Ready?" he asked.

"Yes," she said. "Audrey can stay until nine." The mall closed then anyway, and she and Henry didn't need to stop off for coffee or ice cream.

"We better get going then."

"It's six-fifteen."

"And I haven't bought them a single thing," he said.

Janelle worked not to roll her eyes. At the same time, she wondered what her life would be like if Henry was capable of being true to her and their family. The past week with him hadn't been terrible, though there were still little clues that he hadn't changed. He checked his phone almost constantly, and every time he texted, Janelle wanted to rip the device from his hand and see what he was saying, and to whom.

She'd had to tell herself over and over that it was none of her business. He wasn't her husband. She had a boyfriend. Henry couldn't hurt her anymore.

But somehow, having him here this week had also

endeared him to her, reminded her of what it was like to have a family with a mom and a dad and kids. And the fact was, Henry Stokes was Kelly's and Kadence's father.

Russ Johnson was not.

Everything inside Janelle felt knotted and confused, and she didn't know what to do about any of it.

Henry did not turn up the radio like Russ did. He didn't sing along, and he didn't say anything. Janelle stared straight out the front windshield too, only looking at him when he asked, "Did you eat?"

"Yes."

"I didn't, so do you mind if we stop somewhere?"

"Yes," she said. "You just said we might not have enough time to get everything you want by nine. We don't have time to eat out on a Friday night. Everywhere will be packed." She glared at him. "And this is not a date. I'm not going to dinner with you."

Henry blinked at her, his dark eyes so mesmerizing.

No, she told herself. He was *not* mesmerizing. He was *not* handsome. He'd cheated on her dozens of times. She was not taking him back.

"Do you ever think about us being a family again?" he asked, swinging his car into a drive-through line at a fast food joint.

Janelle sighed heavily, the only answer she was going to give him. Besides, he already knew the answer to the question.

"Because this past week has been really nice," Henry said, his voice quiet, almost like he didn't want to scare her away.

"I love seeing the girls every day. I like spending our evenings together, like we used to. It feels...good, don't you think?"

The past few evenings had held a new kind of charm that Janelle had previously been missing in her life. But she didn't want the life she'd had with Henry before. And he didn't seem capable of a different kind of life.

"Henry," she said. "It has been nice. But that's because you're on your best behavior. It's been four days."

"Five," he said.

"And you never discipline the girls, and you're not there in the morning when it's completely chaotic and we're all trying to get ready to leave. This morning, Kadence purposefully left her gum on Kelly's chair, and there was a screaming match, crying, and then a wardrobe change."

She cocked her eyebrows at her ex. "So you get to see them after school, when they're so excited to tell you about their day. You take them for food and sweets, and spoil them rotten. So yeah, it's great. But it's not *real*."

"I'm willing to get more real," he said, and he seemed so genuine. "I'm different now, Janelle. Honestly."

"Really? A month ago you showed up at your ex-girlfriend's house, drunk, and wanted to sleep with her." Janelle lifted her eyebrows and stared him down. "Do not tell me you'd be faithful to me, or that you even have feelings for me."

Henry reached over and took her hand in his. "I do, Janelle. You're my first love. My wife."

She snorted and delicately removed her hand from his. "The only reason I've allowed you to even stay in this town is because of Kelly and Kadence. I can pretend for them. They're not here. I don't have to pretend right now. And you know what, Henry? Neither do you."

He didn't deny that he'd been pretending, and he inched forward to the speaker to place his order. With that done, he said, "I want to try again."

"Henry."

"I think we can make it. I've always thought that."

"I have a boyfriend."

"That's easy to fix," he said, taking her hand again. "Come on, Janelle. Just tell me you'll think about it."

Janelle looked at him, and so many thoughts entered her mind. So many emotions flooded her. She had no words, and she couldn't speak.

"Just think about it," Henry said again, and this time, Janelle nodded.

* * *

THE NEXT MORNING, she rose early despite it being Saturday. Shopping with Henry had been…nice after their talk in the drive-through. They'd walked around the mall, with the festive music playing, and the scent of marshmallows and hot chocolate on the air.

They had shared coffee after the mall closed, and Audrey had stayed until ten after Janelle had asked her to. The teenager didn't care why Janelle had needed to stay out later, and she didn't ask any questions. She didn't judge.

But Janelle felt all kinds of uneasy. She shouldn't have

agreed to go shopping with Henry, simple as that. He'd promised to give her the weekend to think, and the next time he'd see her would be Monday evening, after he picked up the girls from school.

Janelle really needed to figure out what she was doing. Russ had a family party in less than a week, and she'd told him she'd be there. She gazed up at the ceiling, helplessness filling her. "Why did Henry have to come back into town now?" she whispered. "What am I supposed to do?"

She hadn't spent a lot of time in church, but there were dozens of chapels around the Texas Hill Country. Maybe she should go tomorrow. See if she could find some answers to the mess her life had become.

After she'd finally decided to end her marriage, she'd gone to church with her parents. She remembered the peace and comfort she felt there, and she reached over to her nightstand to pick up her phone.

Her mother never slept past seven, so Janelle didn't feel bad dialing her despite the early hour. "Momma," she said when her mother had answered. "How are you?"

"Janelle," her mother said. "It's great to hear from you. We were just talking about you and what you might be doing for Christmas."

Janelle did not want to tell her mom that she'd been spending any time with Henry. She could practically feel the disappointment coming through the line already. "We're coming on Christmas Eve," she said. "Is that still okay?"

"Oh, yes. Daddy just bought the ham and the turkey."

She gave a light laugh. "He couldn't decide what to have this year."

"Should I make my sweet potato casserole then?" Janelle asked. "It goes well with ham or turkey, and Kelly's been dying to learn the recipe."

"Sure," her mom said. "I love seeing her creations online. What did y'all make this week?"

Janelle went on to tell her about the gingerbread cookies that Kelly had insisted they make after the class at the community center. "And cake pops," she said, though she hadn't posted those on any social media, nor had she taken any to her co-workers. "And upside-down caramel apple cake. That was a big hit." And her suggestion.

"Sounds lovely," her mother said. "And how are the dogs?"

"Doing really well," she said. "Russ's brother comes home tomorrow, so we'll see what happens with them after that. If they're ready for adoption, I might not have them much longer."

"But you're going to keep King, right?"

"Yes," Janelle said with a sigh. "I don't see how I can give him up. It would break Kadence's heart." And Janelle had grown quite fond of the mutt sleeping on her feet too. He was warm and comforting, and she never had to be alone.

"What else is going on?" her mom asked. "Are you still seeing Russ?"

"Yes," Janelle said. She'd never told her parents that she'd freaked out about him meeting the girls. And she hadn't told them about last weekend either. "He met Kelly and Kadence last week. We went out to his ranch and helped him with a project."

"Oh, my," her mother said. "So it's serious."

"I mean, yes," Janelle said. She had plans to go to his family party. They were planning a Christmas celebration for next Saturday too. Him, her, and the girls. Privately.

If that wasn't serious, what was?

Plus, she'd told Henry she was serious with Russ. She couldn't bring up Henry, and she never wanted to mention her doubts to her mom. But she did say, "Momma, if I wanted to go to church up here, where would you recommend?" and that probably told her mom how uncertain she was anyway.

"Let me call Pastor Belluise. He'll know, as he has a sister who lives up by you."

"In Chestnut Springs?"

"Oh, I think she's in Llano, but closer than we are."

"Mom, Llano is pretty far from here."

"Closer than here. I'll call him and call you back."

"Okay," Janelle said, barely getting the word out before her mom hung up. She shook her head, wondering if she'd just made the biggest mistake of her life. Her mom had always been a little disappointed in Janelle for her lack of faith, despite her other accomplishments in life.

Since she was up, she dialed Russ, almost desperate to see him. She needed to be reminded that she liked him more than Henry, desperately.

"Hey, sugar," he said, and Janelle smiled at the simple sound of his voice.

"It's so good to hear you," she said. "I've missed you this week."

"I know," he said. "I've missed you too. What are you doing this morning? I'm moving my folks back to their place, and then maybe we could go to breakfast."

"That sounds amazing."

"All of us?"

"Yes," she said, though she could call Henry to take the girls if she had to. But then she'd be going back on their deal for her to have the weekend to think.

"And we're having a big meal tomorrow afternoon to celebrate Seth and Jenna's return. Do you want to come to that? Girls and all."

"Yes," she said again, though a tingle of nerves ran through her at such a big family gathering. Then she reminded herself that she knew the Johnsons, and she knew Jenna Wright. She worked at the elementary school where Kelly and Kadence attended, and the atmosphere at the ranch was calm and peaceful.

Only her business dinners were made of stress. And Henry's friends, who wore stuffy suits and constantly carried tumblers of scotch. Janelle had not missed those outings, and she wouldn't even be able to dress the part anymore. Not with her bunions.

"Great," Russ said. "So I'll stop by after I finish with my parents, maybe around nine or nine-thirty."

"Sure," she said. "I can't wait." She hung up, knowing she'd spoken true. She couldn't wait to see Russ again. She needed the reassurance that the feelings she had for him were real and shouldn't be ignored simply because her ex had come back into town and asked her to think about getting back together with him.

She knew what heartache that brought her, and she couldn't endure it again. She wouldn't put her girls through having Henry back for a week, only to wake up and find him gone again.

"Momma?"

She rolled over at the sound of Kelly's voice. "Yeah, baby?"

"Where's Daddy?"

All at once, Janelle realized with horror that she'd already done that. She'd already allowed Henry back into their lives for a week, and then he'd left for the weekend.

Probably has to go check on a girlfriend somewhere, she thought, *and San Antonio came to her mind.*

"Daddy will be back on Monday," she said, smoothing back Kelly's hair. "It's just us this weekend, and we're going to go to breakfast with Russ in a couple of hours."

"Russ?" Kelly didn't smile. "I don't want to go to breakfast with Russ."

"Why not?"

"I thought you and Daddy were going to get back together," Kelly said, her fists curling into balls. "Why did he leave?"

Janelle wanted to tell her the truth about her beloved father. But she couldn't bring herself to do it. "I don't know, baby. He said he'd be back on Monday. That's all I know."

Kelly sat down on the bed, and Janelle wished she knew

what to say. Kadence pushed open the door a few inches, and she said, "Come on in, sweetheart."

Her youngest climbed right into bed with her, and Janelle liked the two of them with her, as well as King. "The dogs are barkin', Momma."

"Well," Janelle said with a sigh. "We better go get them fed and out for the day. We need to clean their pens too. Then we're going to breakfast with Russ."

Kadence cheered as if Janelle had just told her they were going to Disneyland, and Janelle smiled at her. At least one daughter was excited about seeing Russ that day. But Janelle couldn't help wondering if what she was doing was okay. Would Kadence be confused about things if Janelle spent all week with Henry, and then dated Russ on the weekends?

Janelle sure was confused, and she hoped her breakfast in a couple of hours would help shed some light on her situation so she'd know what to do. She didn't want to hurt her girls, and she didn't want to lose her heart. But would one always be at the mercy of the other?

Chapter 19

"All set, Momma?" Russ looked around the living room, the new flooring looking amazing. "I think this looks so good." He toed the rug Griffin had chosen. Griffin had taken care of all of the remodeling, and Russ was grateful for that.

"Yes, baby," his mom said. "Thanks so much, Russ."

His daddy already lounged in a new recliner, the TV remote in his hand. "Yes, thanks, Russ."

"No problem," Russ said, though having his parents at the homestead hadn't been his favorite thing ever. But it had only been six days, and they'd all survived. His parent's house was now water and mold-free, with new flooring and furniture if what they'd had couldn't be salvaged. "See you guys on Thursday."

"Love you, sugar."

Russ loved his mother too, and he gave her a kiss on the cheek before he left. He had twenty minutes to get to

Janelle's, but he was already in town. He never could quite figure out how to waste time, so he simply pulled up to her house ten minutes early.

He could sit on her couch as easily as behind the wheel, and he climbed the front steps and knocked on the door.

A scream came from inside the house, and it sounded like Kadence. Russ wasn't sure if he should open the door and go help, or give Janelle her privacy to calm down her kids before she let him in.

He decided to hold his ground, and the door opened a few seconds later. Kelly stood there, and she looked down at Russ's cowboy boots and back to his face. "Hey," he said, feeling completely out of place. "Did your mom tell you we were goin' to breakfast this morning?"

Kelly didn't say anything. She simply left the front door open and walked away.

"O-kay," Russ said, not quite sure what he'd done wrong. He hadn't seen Kelly since last weekend, but she'd seemed happy enough to be on the ranch. She'd laughed, and she and Kadence hadn't fought hardly at all. She had left early, but there hadn't been a reason other than a movie with her father.

Ah, her father, Russ thought. He'd spent all week wrestling with his inadequacies to be Janelle's boyfriend, let alone an instant father to two little girls. And Henry was back in town for a few weeks, and Russ knew Henry had been spending a lot of time with the girls.

"Hey," Janelle said, out of breath. "Come in. It's not super warm out there."

"Right." Russ stepped into the house and closed the door. "I know I'm early. Anything I can do to help?"

"No, Kadence just stepped on something." Janelle gathered her hair into a ponytail, revealing her slender neck, and Russ's hormones fired. She exhaled and gave him a fast smile before dropping her arms. "That was a lie. Kelly took her painting and ripped it in half, because she doesn't want to go to breakfast."

Janelle's bottom lip trembled, and she looked away. "I just need a few minutes to get everyone together."

"We don't have to go to breakfast," Russ said.

"Yes, we do." Janelle turned around and went into the kitchen, where she helped Kadence tape together her painting. She said something to the little girl, dried her tears, and Kadence faced Russ and skipped over to him, the painting held in her tiny fingers.

"Look," she said. "It's your dogs."

Russ took the painting, which definitely had three figures on it. "Would you look at that?" Thunder was black and white. Winner was brown and white. Cloudy Nine was white. He could easily distinguish them, and he beamed down at Kadence, a sense of love overcoming him that he didn't entirely understand.

"Momma said for us to go wait in the truck," Kadence said. "You can keep the painting."

Russ surveyed the kitchen again, but Janelle was gone. "All right." He reached for Kadence's hand, another sense of satisfaction and love moving through him as they went outside and walked down the sidewalk to his truck together.

In the truck, he fired up the engine and turned on the heat. It wasn't freezing, but the thunderstorms had returned to the Hill Country. He wanted to ask Kadence about her dad, but he didn't dare. He didn't want to use a seven-year-old to get information, and he'd have to figure out how to deal with Henry in his life if a relationship with Janelle made it very far.

So he swallowed the questions, and asked Kadence instead about what she'd done last week.

"We made gingerbread houses," she said. "And cookies. And Daddy took us to this stocking class. Kelly called me a baby because I couldn't use the sewing machine, and Momma finished mine for me. Daddy told Kelly not to call me a baby, and she didn't for a whole day." The little girl continued to talk, and Russ listened to her high-pitched voice with happiness streaming through his soul.

He knew Henry had cheated on Janelle, and while he couldn't fathom that, he also didn't understand how the man had risked his family. These little girls were precious, and Russ wanted to be a good father.

The front door opened twenty minutes later, and Kelly walked out with Janelle right behind her. Neither of them looked happy, but Russ got out of the truck and opened the back door for Kelly.

"Kelly," Janelle said, her voice full of warning.

"I'm sorry, sir," she said, looking up at him. She'd obviously been crying, and her chin wobbled now too. "I'm glad we get to go to breakfast together today. It was fun at your ranch last weekend." She looked at Janelle, who nodded exactly once. "Can we come back out there tomorrow night? I hear your brother is coming back from a vacation."

Russ chuckled and crouched down in front of the ten-year-old. "He sure is. And you can come to the ranch anytime you want. You, or Kadence, or your momma." He looked up at Janelle, who looked like she wanted to crawl back into bed, not go to breakfast.

"Thank you for the apology." Russ drew the little girl into a hug, and surprisingly, Kelly gripped his shoulders as she hugged him back. "And you should maybe apologize to Kadence," he whispered as that same powerful emotion he'd felt earlier raced through him again.

He released her, and Kelly stepped back. She climbed in the truck, and Russ heard her say, "I'm sorry for ripping your painting, Kade," in her most sincere voice.

Russ looked at Janelle, who lifted one shoulder in a shrug. "We're kind of a mess," she said. "I'm surprised you haven't run screaming yet."

Russ drew her into a hug too, not sure what to say. Maybe there was nothing to say. Maybe she just needed to know he wasn't going to run screaming, but that he actually liked her and her kids, no matter what.

"I'm not sure what time Seth and Jenna will be back," he said. "But why don't you guys plan on coming out about six? I'll make sure there's something to eat then."

"I won't be intruding on your brotherly Sunday afternoon?"

"Nope," he said. "Six o'clock isn't afternoon, baby." He stepped back and walked her around the truck to the passenger door. On his way around the hood, he made a mental note to get a text out to the brothers about having Janelle and her kids out to the homestead at six tomorrow night.

* * *

Change of plans, Russ sent to Janelle. *Dinner and games at Jenna's house at six.* He almost expected Janelle to cancel, but she sent a thumbs-up emoji and the words, *We'll be there.*

He'd welcomed Seth back to the ranch. Travis and Russ had shown Seth the dog enclosure, and he'd been thrilled. They'd eaten lunch with just the brothers, as Russ had asked to bring Janelle and her kids to the game night at Jenna's.

Travis had said he wanted to pull back from the ranch, and that he wanted to build a house near the ranch's entrance. Russ wasn't sure how he felt about it. He'd lived with Seth and Travis for a few years now, and he didn't want to be in the homestead alone.

Don't get too far ahead of yourself, he told himself again. Travis wasn't even talking to Millie right now, and it took a few months—at least—to build a house.

Russ hadn't even talked to Janelle about marriage yet. Things between them felt like they moved really fast sometimes and then slowed way down at other times. They were in a slow period at the moment, and Russ was okay with that.

He went upstairs and surveyed the bags on the coffee

table in the upstairs family room. He'd bought three different patterns of wrapping paper, and he started by pulling out the painting kit he'd bought for Kadence and wrapping it in the red and white checkered paper. He wasn't in the habit of wrapping gifts, and he struggled to get the package wrapped so it looked like a grown man had done it.

He continued wrapping her gifts—a new scooter, a jump rope, a ten-DVD set of Disney movies, an easy-bake oven, and several dog bandanas. Kadence liked taking care of the dogs, but she couldn't do as much as her mom or Kelly. The bandanas would allow her to dress them up and feel accomplished.

Kelly was much harder to shop for, and Russ probably should've consulted with Janelle before buying anything. But he'd asked the department store clerk for the single best piece of kitchen equipment for a child who loved to cook, and she'd said a stand mixer—the same thing Kelly had already mentioned to him.

And it was *heavy*, and Russ thought the wrapping job looked like Winner had done it with her four paws. Since the mixer had cost so much, he'd gotten Kelly a few smaller things—rubber spatulas and a set of stainless steel measuring cups, along with a cookbook of desserts made specifically with pie dough.

He needed something more for her that wasn't associated with the kitchen, but he hadn't found it yet. And he had nothing for Janelle. They'd planned a holiday celebration for Saturday, and five days didn't feel like long enough for him to get the just-right gift for her.

But he would.

"Russ," Travis called, a measure of excitement in his voice that made Russ lift his head quickly.

"I'm upstairs," he said.

Travis came thundering up the steps, and he paused to take in the gift wrapping center. "Oh." His chest heaved. "What is all this?"

"Christmas for Janelle and the girls." Russ stood up and wiped his hands together. "What's goin' on?"

"Millie just texted to say she got a job."

"Wow, did you call her?" Russ wanted to grab his phone and look at it.

"No, she texted me out of the blue."

"Okay, so this is perfect," he said. "Did you respond?"

"Not yet."

Russ smiled at the pure terror on his brother's face. "Okay, you need to respond." He started thumbing something out on his phone, and Russ said, "Read it out loud to me."

"That's so great, baby. Congrats." He looked up at Russ with questions in his eyes.

"Yes, send that."

He did and then met Russ's eye again. "And?"

"And what, Travis? Do you want to get back together with her or not?"

"Yes," he said quickly. "Yes, I *so* want to get back together with her."

"Okay," Russ said. "Where did she get a job?"

"Furniture Row. She starts tomorrow."

"What time does the store open?"

"I have no idea."

"Probably ten." Russ's mind fired at a million miles a minute. "So here's what you do. You've got that desk you built for her for Christmas, right?"

"Right."

"So you call Chantelle down there, and you tell her you need just ten minutes before they open."

"Ten minutes for what?"

"To give Millie her Christmas present," Russ said. "And tell her what you want for Christmas." He nudged Travis out of the way and started for the stairs.

"Wait," his brother said behind him. "What do I want for Christmas?" His footsteps sounded panicked behind Russ's.

"Her," he called over his shoulder. When he reached the bottom of the steps, he turned back to his brother. "Travis, you want her."

Travis looked like he might throw up, but he nodded. "Okay, so I call Chantelle." His phone buzzed, and he glanced at it. "Millie wants to meet about the party. We do need to do that."

"You only have room for one thing in your life right now," Russ said. "And that's getting Millie back. You can talk about the party tomorrow."

"Right." Travis tucked his phone in his back pocket. "Okay. I show up at Furniture Row with the desk. Say it's her Christmas gift and I only want one thing for Christmas."

"Yes." Russ went into the kitchen to pour himself a cup of coffee.

"So I need something that says 'you' on it." He opened a drawer and pulled out a piece of paper. He wrote the three letters on it and held it up, his eyebrows lifted.

Russ almost spewed his coffee out of his mouth. "You can't even read that." He chuckled, the laughter filling the room soon afterward. "Try again."

Travis did, a few more times, getting more and more frustrated with each attempt.

"Wait, wait," Russ said. "I've got this. Just a sec." He pulled out his phone and called Janelle. "Hey, baby."

Travis looked like he might deck Russ, so he held up his hand in a universal sign of *just wait*.

"Hey, what's up?"

"Can you have Kadence bring out some art supplies tonight? My brother needs help with a project, and she's just the person to do it."

"Art supplies?" Travis looked so confused.

"Sure," Janelle said. "She'll love that."

"Thanks, baby." He hung up and grinned at his brother. "There. Done. Kadence will make you a pretty paper that says *you* on it. Done."

"Thank goodness." Travis sagged onto the nearest barstool. "Thanks, Russ."

"Sure thing, brother." Russ patted Travis on the shoulder. "Plus, you're helping me by keeping the girls busy."

"Rough time with them?"

"Kind of," Russ said with a sigh. He sat down at the

counter too and sipped his coffee. "But it's still great. I really like Janelle."

"Yeah, I saw all those presents upstairs."

"None of them are for her." Russ cut a look at Travis out of the corner of his eye. "I could use some help with that."

"Gift ideas for your girlfriend?" Travis rolled his shoulders as if he were gearing up for the battle of his life. "All right. Let's brainstorm."

Chapter 20

Janelle walked between her two girls as they walked up to the front door of a beautiful home that stood proudly on some of the most beautiful land Janelle had ever seen. Her nerves rattled around her ribcage, but she managed to climb the steps and ring the doorbell.

This was more of an estate than anything, and Janelle absolutely loved it. She could just see herself living in a place like this, with a lot of rooms, big windows, and merry Christmas lights twinkling into the twilight.

The double doors opened, and a tall man stood there. "Janelle Stokes," he said, sending a huge belly laugh into the air in the next moment. Seth Johnson engulfed her in a hug and just as quickly let her go. "And these must be your girls. Let's see…Russ told me your names."

Kadence giggled, and Janelle herself couldn't help grinning like a fool. Seth's enthusiasm was simply infectious.

"Kelly," he said to the right girl. "And Kadence. Ah, yes,

you have the art kit. Travis is going to be so happy to see you." He stepped back. "Come in, come in."

Janelle didn't have to nudge the girls to get them to enter, and she willingly stepped inside too. Noise came from the back of the house, and Seth led them in that direction. The table had a stack of paper on it, and Kadence went skipping over to the cowboy there.

Travis looked relieved as he caught sight of her, and he jumped to his feet and gave her his chair. Janelle looked around for Russ, but she couldn't see him. Jenna stood in the kitchen with Rex, and they were talking about something she couldn't hear over the music playing throughout the house.

"He's coming," Seth said. "He stopped to pick up the boys."

"The boys?"

"Yeah, Darren, Tomas, and Brian?"

"Oh, right." Janelle took a cup of steaming hot chocolate from Griffin, who joined them in a three-way huddle.

"So I have a question for you," Griffin said, lifting his hot chocolate to his lips.

Janelle braced herself. She often got legal questions, and she'd just be sure to give him a disclaimer about how he needed to hire a real lawyer. She shot a glance at Seth, whose smile felt a little fake now.

"All right," she said.

"There's a woman who works at your law office," Griffin said. He cleared his throat, a definite flush crawling into his face. "A Libby Harward?"

Janelle didn't want to give too much away, so she simply nodded. "Yes, I know Libby."

"Do you happen to know if she's seein' anyone?" Griffin coughed, but he held his ground.

"I happen to know she is *not* seeing anyone right now," Janelle said. "And I happen to have her phone number." She held up her phone and waggled it back and forth. "Do you want it?"

"You'd give it to me?" Griffin asked, looking at the phone like it was a juicy steak and he hadn't eaten for a month.

"Let me text her and find out if it's okay first," Janelle said, firing off a text to Libby in a matter of seconds.

"What did you say to her?" Griffin asked, swallowing.

Janelle turned her phone to Griffin, who read aloud, "Hey, I'm with the Johnson brothers. Do you care if I give your number to one of them?"

"Good?" Janelle asked. Griffin Johnson was so cute, and Libby would look darling on his arm. Excitement flowed through Janelle as Griffin nodded.

"Yeah, great."

Her phone chimed, and she turned it back to her. "Oh, it's Libby," she singsonged.

"What did she say?" Griffin asked.

"Settle down," Seth said, almost under his breath.

Janelle read the text and pressed her device to her collarbone, her own pulse firing. "Oh."

"What did she say?" Griffin asked again.

"I don't want to read it out loud," Janelle said.

"She said no, didn't she?" Griffin turned away, clearly disappointed.

Janelle looked at Seth. "What's his number? I'll text him Libby's number."

"She said yes?"

She handed Seth her phone, and he quickly read the messages. "Oh, okay. I'll delete these and you can text him the number." He tapped a couple of times and handed the phone back, a smile on his face. "I mean, I happen to agree with her. Rex is a special kind of man." He chuckled, and Janelle was glad Seth hadn't taken offense to what Libby had said.

Only if it's Griffin. That Rex is too loud for me.

Seth gave her Griffin's number, and she sent him Libby's contact info. She watched him pull his phone out and check the text, only to spin back to her, a huge grin spreading across his face. "Thanks, Janelle." He hurried away, his thumbs already moving over the screen.

Janelle giggled at the same time laughter filled the room as Travis and the girls had obviously just done something funny. She stepped away from Seth to see what they were doing, and Travis held up a pathetic looking paper that appeared to have the word "you" on it. At least Janelle thought that's what it was supposed to say.

The front door opened, and Russ said, "We're here."

Janelle's heartbeat went wild, and she quivered in anticipation for him to walk across the room and join the party in the kitchen.

"Y'all didn't eat without us, did you?" He set a huge slow cooker on the kitchen counter.

"We couldn't eat without you," Rex said. "You have the main dish."

"Finally," Seth said. "Let's eat."

Janelle loved the energy and vibrancy of this family and their ranch hands. She fit here, and she felt it keenly. Everyone spoke to her girls, and Travis helped Kadence through the line while Kelly went through in front of Seth.

Janelle hung back with Russ, curling her arm around his back and leaning into his side.

Russ pressed his lips to her temple and said, "Hey, baby. How's your day?"

"Better now," she said, smiling up at him.

"I'd kiss you," he whispered, his lips getting dangerously close to hers. "But Rex is already glaring my face off, and I'm starving."

She laughed along with Russ, and they joined the line for pulled pork. This party and time with Russ was exactly what she needed after a tumultuous week of doubt and worry. She knew as soon as Henry came back into the picture, her thoughts would scramble, and she concentrated extra-hard to be able to hold onto these specific memories.

She enjoyed herself immensely during dinner. During game night. While Travis explained his plan to get Millie back. And when Russ took her hand and leaned down to say something to Seth, Janelle felt like she'd lost twenty years of her life as she snuck out the back door and into the chilly night.

"Ah," Russ sighed as the door closed behind them, sealing most of the noise in the house. Janelle admitted the quiet night sure was refreshing, and she drew in a long, deep breath of the winter air.

"So, family party on Friday night," she said. "Our Christmas celebration on Saturday."

"Right," Russ said. "Six for dinner on Friday. At least that's the plan right now. Travis will know more when he talks to her tomorrow."

"Do you think they'll get back together?"

"Yep." Russ leaned against the railing on the deck. "You want to walk over to one of the bridges?" He took her hand again, and Janelle had a feeling she'd go wherever he wanted her to.

"Sure." They went down the steps to the lawn and crossed it, moving east toward Chestnut Ranch.

"What do you want to do for our Christmas thing?" she asked. "Kelly and I can just make dinner or something."

"I have gifts for you all," he said.

Surprise moved through Janelle. "You do?"

"Yep."

"When did you have time to shop this week?"

"I may have made up a reason to leave the homestead once or twice," he said. "My Momma has a way of treating us boys like we're not quite grown yet." He chuckled, and Janelle joined him.

"Honey, that's all Texan mothers." She bumped him with her hip.

"Are you gonna be like that?"

"Probably," she said.

"You did get Kelly right in line before breakfast yesterday." Russ glanced at her, but it was much too dark to read his expression before he looked away.

Janelle's stomach clenched. "Yes, well, sometimes I have to get really firm with her. She usually comes around for a while, and then she slips again." Janelle sighed. "Kelly is going through a hard time right now." Truth be told, Janelle was too. "Having her dad back is hard on her."

"And meeting me probably didn't help."

"I don't know," Janelle said honestly. "She seemed happy to meet you, but then Henry came back…" She let the words hang there, because she didn't know how to explain her own confusion. It was easy to pass it off as Kelly's, but also a bit untruthful too.

"She loves her dad."

"They both do."

"So, I just gotta ask. Do you see us…I mean…are you looking to get married again?"

Janelle had once sworn never to walk down that particular aisle again. But she found herself saying, "Yes, Russ. I'm only forty-one. I don't want to live alone forever."

"Technically, you're not alone. You have the girls."

"And what happens in just eleven years when Kadence is eighteen? They'll go off and live lives of their own, and I'll be chained right back to that law office."

Russ's hand squeezed hers, and that was enough of a comfort for her. It said that he was in this for the long-term, and that he'd been thinking about marrying *her*.

"You don't like the law office?" he asked, leading her down a gentle slope. A bridge sat ahead of them, and Janelle loved the beauty and majesty of this place.

"I like the law office," she said. "I like it a lot, but it has a way of consuming me."

"Oh, you just described the ranch." Russ chuckled. He sighed as they reached the top of the curved bridge and stopped walking. "I love the ranch, but it's the exact same thing."

"So we just have to make sure our jobs don't become our lives." She gazed up at him. "Easy enough, right?"

He smiled and shook his head. "So easy." He leaned down and touched his lips to hers, and Janelle hadn't kissed him in far too long. She pulled in a breath as her pulse started to pound, and she ran her hands up his arms to his face.

"My hat," he said, breaking the kiss as he turned his head away from her. "Oh, there it goes."

"Did it fall into the river?"

"Yep." He chuckled. "It's gone."

"Sorry," she said, grinning as she tucked herself into his arms.

"Oh, you're worth it," he said, lifting her chin to kiss her again. She loved the feel of his hands on her face, the strength in his stature as he kissed her, and kissed her, and kissed her.

Chapter 21

"Russ, baby, you're throwin' Daddy around up there."

Russ eased up on the accelerator at his momma's words. He couldn't help his excitement to get back to the ranch, where the family Christmas party was set to start very soon. He'd volunteered to drive to town and get his parents, as Travis had to go get Millie's momma. Millie was already at the homestead—had been for hours—getting set up.

"Sorry, Daddy," he said, glancing over at his father, who did look a little tense. "You sure you two can go on your service mission? It's a long flight."

"Yes," his father said. "I'm starting some new physical therapy in January."

"Oh?" That was news to Russ, and he hadn't heard it from anyone else either. "Well, that's great."

"We still need to ask Rex or Griffin to drive you,"

Momma said from the back seat. "Oh, I hope we have a lot of steak at this party."

Russ chuckled softly to himself. "Momma, it's going to be an upscale party," he said. "You've got to trust Millie."

"Trust her?" Momma scoffed. "I barely know her."

Russ looked in the rear-view mirror and met his momma's eye. "Momma," he said. "She's a real nice woman, and Travis is in love with her. So be nice. Please."

"I'm always nice," she said.

"Yes, but in a Momma-kind of way."

"What does that mean?"

"It means that you'll go around and examine every plate and fork. And she doesn't need that." He cocked his eyebrows at her. "You just go in, and you start gushing. You're good at that."

"Am I?"

"Sure," Russ said, slowing as they approached another curve in the road. "You go, 'oh, Millie, this is beautiful. Wow, look at that candle. Where did you get these dishes? They're *lovely.*'"

Momma laughed, and Russ did too. "I do not sound like that," she said, patting her hair, which she'd just had set.

"Mm hm," Russ said, looking at his daddy. "She sounds like that, doesn't she?"

"A little," Daddy said, and that got Russ to laugh even louder.

"My voice isn't that high-pitched," Momma said.

"All right, I may have gone a little high," Russ drawled. "But that was the only difference."

"Mm hm," Momma said. "And we finally get to meet your Janelle too."

His stomach twisted and turned. But he said, "That's right, Momma. And please, I really need you on your best behavior. Both of you." He shot his dad a look too. "No asking her about hunting or guns, Daddy. She's a single mom."

"So that means she doesn't hunt?" Daddy asked.

"Yes," Russ said immediately. "That's what it means. She runs a law office." He took a deep breath and braked to make the turn onto the lane that led to Chestnut Ranch. "And I really like her. Like, a whole lot. Please, Momma?"

"Okay," she said. "I already agreed to be nice."

"Like, normal-person-nice," Russ said. "Right? Not Momma-nice."

"Yes," she huffed. "Normal-person-nice."

Russ grinned and passed the Wright's house as Seth and Jenna came out onto the front porch. Russ had driven fast, and he suspected they'd be the first back to the homestead. Sure enough, Travis's truck wasn't there, and neither was Rex's or Griffin's. He wasn't sure which one of them would be driving tonight, but they hadn't arrived yet.

"All right," he said, opening the garage and pulling inside. "Everyone's on their best behavior starting…now." He parked and went around to help Daddy. Momma could get out on her own, but she didn't, and Russ helped her down next.

They entered the house to the scent of steak, and Russ's soul sang. His momma would be happy with that.

"Oh, my," Momma said, pausing in the doorway of the mudroom.

"Go on, Momma," Russ said. "We're trying to get in too." He nudged her gently out of the way, but one step into the kitchen and he knew why she'd stalled. The homestead had been transformed since he'd left forty-five minutes ago.

The scent of pine needles mingled with the trays of food waiting on the counter. Millie had set the table with fine china, lit candles, and covered all the pillows in festive wrappings. The fireplace crackled, and it seemed like every detail was exactly right.

"Millie, this place is magical," Momma said, stepping over to Millie and hugging her. "I do like this new tradition."

Russ kept one eye and ear on Momma while he helped Daddy over to the couch. "Seth has the dogs, Daddy. They'll be here soon."

His dad groaned as he sat on the couch, and Russ smiled at the garland on the mantel and turned back to tell Millie how amazing this was. No wonder Travis liked her. He thought of Janelle, and this was definitely the upscale party Millie had mentioned weeks ago.

"We're here," Rex called as he and Griffin walked in the back door. A moment later, Seth and Jenna followed them, the dogs' claws clicked on the tile floor as they came inside too.

Winner barked, scampering around the homestead to sniff everyone already there, getting a good scrub from Millie as she laughed. Rex whistled and said, "Millie, this is amazing."

"It doesn't even look like the same house," Griffin said.

"Hey," Millie said, swatting his hand away from one of the trays of food on the counter.

"Sorry." He grinned at her. "But I'm *starving*."

"Travis isn't even here," Russ said. "So calm down." The doorbell rang, and his heart gave one loud boom in his chest. Janelle. The girls. It was a lot to meet so many people at once, but he told himself that they'd met most of them already. Maybe not all at the same time, and never his parents, but Janelle was a champion.

"That'll be Isaac and Luisa," Jenna said, moving toward the living room and the front door. Russ heard more than two voices in that direction, and he kept his eyes on the doorway, glad when Jenna returned with her brother and his girlfriend—and Janelle, Kelly, and Kadence too.

Joy filled his whole soul, and he knew then that his Christmas crush had bloomed into a lot more than that. He was falling in love with this woman and her children, and he hoped he wouldn't do anything to scare Janelle away again.

"Hey, baby." Russ gave her a quick kiss and bent down to give the girls each a hug. "Thanks so much for coming, guys. You wanna meet my momma?"

"Sure," Kadence said, but Kelly seemed a bit on the sullen side tonight. Russ had probably pulled her from something with her father, though Janelle hadn't said anything. He hadn't seen any of them since Sunday night, but he and Janelle had texted a lot more this week than they had last week. He liked it better, because he didn't feel like Janelle was trying to hide from him. Run from him.

She told him what she was feeling, and he'd been toying with the idea of suggesting that he go with her for Christmas Eve with her parents. But he didn't want to bring it up. He wanted Janelle to take some of the steps to advance their relationship.

"Who are we missing?" Momma asked, her spot at the kitchen counter unwavering. So she was going to be nice, but she was still in charge. Russ wished he'd given her that lecture on the way here, but he couldn't rewind time now.

"Travis," Seth said.

"I'll call him," Millie said. "He went to pick up my momma." Before she could even dial the number, Travis came through the back door.

"We're here." He escorted Millie's mom, who Russ had met several times. Travis gave Seth a big hug, then Griffin and Momma. He held her for an extra moment as she said something to him, and then Russ gave Travis a hug.

For some reason, he wanted to make sure Travis knew that this party was *awesome*, and that he approved. Travis needed that right now. Millie did too, and Russ made a mental note to thank her profusely and tell her how great of a job she'd done.

Travis went to help Daddy over to the table, and Momma said, "Okay, everyone. Let's do introductions, as there are some of us that might not know everyone." She smiled at everyone as if she'd pulled together the amazing holiday décor and catered the food herself.

Momma looked right at Janelle, and Russ tensed beside her. "You're turn, baby," he whispered.

"My turn for what? Oh." She looked at Momma, who was watching her expectantly. "I'm Janelle Stokes," she said as the ranch hands came in the back door. At least they were semi-quiet about it, though cowboy boots did seem to echo on everything they touched. "And these are my daughters, Kelly and Kadence. We're here with Russ."

Russ raised his hand as if anyone there didn't know him. Millie went next, and everyone else was someone who'd been on the ranch for a while. He'd warned Janelle about the compliments they usually did, and she'd obviously prepared her girls, as they both had something to say.

Rex tried to cover up his anxiety with snide comments until Momma put him in his place, and Griffin complained when Travis kissed Millie at the table. Russ thought they were cute, and he couldn't help threading his fingers through Janelle's as they finally got food.

He wanted to tell her he loved her. He felt it so powerfully in that moment, but he couldn't say it in front of so many witnesses. And the verbal beating he'd take from Rex…

Russ tucked the words away for later, hoping he could tell Janelle tomorrow at their private Christmas celebration.

"Russ," Kadence said on his other side, and Russ swung his attention toward her.

"What, baby?"

"Can you help me with my meat?" She handed him her knife, and Russ got to work on cutting it. It felt like such a parental thing to do, and he was quite proud of himself as he completed the job.

* * *

THE FOLLOWING DAY, Russ made four trips up and down the steps to load all the Christmas presents into his truck. The majority of them were for the girls, and he only had a single, legal-sized envelope for Janelle.

He almost turned around five times in the twenty minutes it took for him to drive into town and to Janelle's house. The sun was going down, and her porch light kicked on as he pulled into the driveway.

The front door burst open before he'd even put the truck in park, and both girls came running down the steps and then the sidewalk. He laughed as he got out of the truck and stepped to open the back door. "Help me with all of these, would you?"

He snagged the envelope, as he wanted to give that to Janelle. He'd written her name on the outside of it, and he suddenly had more empathy for Travis as he'd tried to write the word "you" on a piece of paper for Millie. Russ had cowboy handwriting, which meant it wasn't great. But the envelope wasn't the gift, and he collected the stand mixer and hauled it inside.

"Russ," Janelle said as the girls went to get another load of presents. "This is ridiculous." She gazed at the gifts and back to him. "What—?"

He glanced over his shoulder. "Janelle, there's something I haven't told you."

She folded her arms and leaned all of her weight on one foot. "Oh?"

"Yeah." He set the mixer down on the dining room table, where the girls had put the other gifts. "I have a lot of money."

"Obviously."

"No," he said. "This is nothing." He swallowed. "My mother was a cosmetics heiress." Her eyebrows went up, but Russ had committed to telling the secret now. "And she cashed out a few months ago, and well, we all got billions."

"Billions." Her face paled slightly, and her eyes searched his. She was a very good lawyer, and he figured she could spot a liar from a mile away. But he wasn't lying. "So you're a cowboy billionaire."

"That's right," he said, grinning. "So please don't make a big deal about this." He put the envelope on the table as the girls came back into the house.

Janelle glanced at the envelope as more presents got piled on the table. "About what, exactly?"

"Momma, look at all these presents!" Kadence spread her arms wide as if Janelle couldn't see the presents. Russ watched only her.

"Yeah, baby," Janelle said, making her voice falsely bright. "I see 'em." She looked at Kadence and stroked her hand through her hair. She smiled at her youngest and then her oldest, and Russ took a look at Kelly.

She looked excited too, and he thought he might have finally done something to win over the ten-year-old. But he didn't want to buy her love. He knew that wouldn't last—and that he'd never be the girl's father.

With each day that passed, Russ came to terms a bit

more about that, and it hadn't bothered him as much that week that Henry was picking the girls up from school and spending all afternoon and evening with them—and Janelle.

He trusted Janelle. He knew she liked him.

"Merry Christmas," he finally said, and Janelle relaxed.

"Momma," Kelly said. "Can we open presents before we eat?"

"That wasn't the plan," she said, stepping into the kitchen, where she had a pot bubbling on the stove.

"Please," Kadence asked.

"Yeah, please," Kelly whined.

Russ stepped in between them and put one arm around each of them. "Please," he added, and he grinned as Janelle spun toward the three of them, shock on her face.

Chapter 22

Janelle could not believe Russ had joined forces with Kelly and Kadence. Could not believe it. She stood there with a wooden spoon in her hand, staring at the three of them.

"Fine," she said, almost slamming the spoon into the sink. "Let's open presents first. Kel, will you get Russ's for him, please?"

Kelly and Kadence cheered, and Kelly went to do what Janelle had asked. She didn't look away from Russ, who chuckled, his face so handsome it hurt.

"Come on, sweetheart," he said, taking her into his arms. She resisted him for only a moment before melting into his embrace. "It's Christmas."

"I said we could open presents," she said.

"No," he whispered, his lips dangerously close to her ear. "You said fine, and that's never good." He chuckled in her ear, and she liked this easy-going side of Russ.

"Open mine first," Kadence said, skipping back over to Janelle and Russ. She carried a bright green bag with elf legs on it, and she was so proud of it.

"She made that in school," Janelle whispered, as if Russ needed coaching to be beautifully kind to Kadence. But she'd had to sometimes remind Henry that their girls were little and needed to be told the art projects they did were wonderful even when they were somewhat hideous.

"Oh, wow," Russ said, stepping away from Janelle and taking the gift bag. "You made this?"

"Yep." Kadence swayed on her feet, her face filled with only the joy a seven-year-old could muster. She was about to burst with the secret, and Janelle hoped Russ would open the gift quickly.

He pulled out the white tissue paper, his face full of a smile too. Janelle's heart softened as she watched him, because he was just so…good. He was calm, and gentle, and wonderful.

"Wow," he said, pulling out the snow globe. "You made this?"

"Yes," Kadence said, bursting now. "And look, Russ! It's the ranch. There's the horses, and the dogs, and that's your truck." She kept pointing but the globe was small, and every poke was in the same spot.

"I see that." Russ grinned at her and held up the globe, studying it. "This is so awesome, Kade. I love it." He set it down on the table and picked up Kadence, hugging her tight and cradling her in his lap. Janelle could only watch, everything inside her turning soft.

This was right. This was good. This was perfect.

"My turn," Kelly said, and she held a square package that Janelle had helped her wrap in blue paper with snowflakes on it. She handed it to Russ, who held her eye for several moments before he turned his attention to the gift.

"Feels heavy," he said before peeling back the paper. "Oh, yes." He started laughing. "I love this stuff. Love it. Thanks, Kelly." He held up the two-pound box of fudge Kelly had wanted to get him. Janelle knew Russ had a real sweet tooth, and he opened the box and pinched off a chunk of fudge right then. "Mm. I love this stuff."

"Merry Christmas," Kelly said, stepping forward awkwardly and rocking back. Russ grabbed onto her and drew her into a hug too.

"Merry Christmas," he said.

She stepped back, and Janelle could tell she was pleased.

"All right," Russ said. "Who wants to go next? Should we go round and round?" He reached for one of the smaller presents wrapped in red and white checkered paper. "I only have one for your mom. That one should go last."

"And I have one for you," she said. "So let's let the girls go back and forth."

Russ handed the present to Kadence. "Yours are all red, Missy. Kelly, yours are green."

"My favorite color," she said, beaming at him, and if it was, that was news to Janelle. The girls opened their presents one by one, and Janelle was shocked at how thoughtful and perfect they were for each girl.

Jump ropes, art supplies, and movies for Kadence.

Kitchen gear—including a very expensive mixer—and a couple of books for Kelly.

Finally, there was just the two of them left. "Open yours, Momma," Kelly said. "I want to make something with this mixer."

She smiled at her daughter, because this had been an amazing Christmas so far. "I want Russ to open his first." She picked up the slim package, a tremor materializing in her chest. She almost wanted to hurry and get rid of it. Instead, she handed it to him. "Don't be too disappointed."

"Janelle." He rarely said her name, and Janelle really liked hearing it. He took the present and started unwrapping it. Janelle's heart beat faster and faster with every second it took him to peel back the paper. "Are these the McGavin gloves?" He looked at her, pure excitement in his eyes.

"You're hard to shop for," she said. "Especially now that I know how much money you have."

"I've wanted these forever," he said, unboxing the gloves. He put them on, flexing his fingers as joy emanated from him. "I love them. Thank you so much." He leaned forward and kissed her, and Janelle didn't even care that her girls were watching.

Russ put his gloved hands in her hair and kept her close. "I love you, Janelle." Their eyes met, and pure love lived in his, plus a hint of nerves.

Nerves seemed to be all Janelle was made of, and she swallowed as Kadence said, "Momma, open yours."

Russ leaned away from her and said, "I'll take that, little

lady." He took the envelope from Kadence and held it toward Janelle. "Remember what I said about the money."

She took the envelope, her heartbeat jumping and hammering and doing all kinds of other things to her body. She unclasped the envelope and took out a couple of pieces of paper. Behind them was a color photograph of a hot tub.

"Russ," she said, sucking in a breath. "You didn't."

"Now you can relax after one of your hard days at work," he said. "That's the work order, but if you don't like the style I picked out, the guys said you could choose any one you want."

"I can't...Russ." She wrapped her arms around him and held on tight. "This is too much." She pulled away just as quickly. "I mean, I can't. This is too much." She felt frantic and out of control.

"You can," he said. "Merry Christmas, sweetheart."

Janelle kissed him while Kelly said, "We're getting a hot tub?" and then started cheering. Janelle felt like cheering too, and she wondered what on earth she'd done to deserve a man as good as Russ Johnson.

✷ ✷ ✷

"Take the salad bowl, Kelly," Janelle said as her daughter got out of the car. Janelle glanced up to the front stoop, where her daddy stood. He looked much older than Janelle remembered, and her heart squeezed.

She only lived an hour away. She really should get down to Johnson City more often.

"Kade, you grab the rolls. I'll get the basket of gifts." She got out of the car too and called up to the porch, "Hey, Daddy."

"Need help?" he asked, but he didn't look like he could traverse the steps, and he leaned against the pillar.

"No, stay there," she said. "We've got it." And they did. Her mother never let her bring very much to Christmas Eve dinner, and Janelle had put all the gifts into a single laundry basket for easy carrying.

She set the presents down on the porch when she arrived and hugged her dad. "Oh, it's good to see you, baby," he said.

Janelle pressed her eyes closed and smiled, the embrace of her father always welcome. "Thanks. Good to see you too. Is Jess here yet?"

"He just called," Daddy said. "He's going to be late."

"As usual," Janelle said dryly. It had been several years since all of her siblings had come for Christmas Eve dinner at their childhood home. Everyone was married, and they had in-laws to visit and their own family traditions to cement. Janelle had been coming for the past three years, and she'd seen all of her siblings over the years. They just hadn't been all in one place at the same time in a while.

This year, only Janelle and her oldest brother, Jess, were coming. Jess had two kids too, boys instead of girls. Michael and Hudson got along great with Kadence and Kelly, and Janelle really liked Jess's wife, Shelly.

So today should be fun.

Janelle entered the house to the scent of candied ham

and butter. "Wow," she said, glancing around the living room. "Something smells good."

She found her mother in the kitchen, and Kelly and Kadence put their contributions to dinner on the counter before hurrying back into the living room with calls for their Grandpa to show them the rabbits out back.

"Can Daddy navigate the steps to get to the backyard?" Janelle asked.

"Oh, sure," her mom said. "He's just a bit slower than usual." She kept her attention on the pot in front of her, stirring as the gravy thickened. "So tell me before Jess shows up…how are things going with Russ?"

Janelle drew in a long, deep breath. "I really like him, Mom."

She looked away from the gravy, interest in her eyes. "I can see you do." She glanced around the kitchen too. "And?"

"And I don't know."

"Why not?" Her mother wouldn't look away from her.

Janelle wrestled with what to tell her mom. Maybe she needed someone to talk everything out with. She'd been holding it all in, dealing with one piece of her life at a time.

"Henry's been in Chestnut Springs," Janelle said, and her mother's eyes widened. "For the past few weeks. He picks the girls up after school and spends time with them in the evenings. We're spending Christmas together tomorrow."

Momma just blinked at her, and Janelle had literally never seen her speechless.

"Say something."

"Janelle, I don't know what to say."

"That's because you've always disliked Henry."

"Now, that is not true," Momma said.

Janelle looked out the window and saw her girls each holding one of Daddy's hands, leading him to the rabbit pen. "The girls love Henry." Which only made everything so confusing.

"Are you saying…What are you saying?"

"I don't know," Janelle said again, pure helplessness filling her. "I just need someone to tell me what to do."

"I can't tell you that, honey," Momma said. "God maybe could."

Janelle suppressed a sigh, though she'd already considered taking her problems to church and asking for an answer.

"Family is important," Momma said. "But you know that, baby. You'll do what's right for you and the girls."

"We're here," Jess called, and Janelle glanced toward the kitchen doorway.

"Don't say anything, Mom, okay? He'll do his psychotherapy on me, and I just want to eat a lot of mashed potatoes for my therapy."

Momma laughed, and Janelle's brother came into the kitchen. "What's so funny?"

"You and that beard," Janelle said, giggling as she stepped over to give her brother a hug. His boys came in behind him, chattering as they went up to Momma.

She laughed and hugged her grandsons as Shelly brought in a pumpkin pie and an apple cobbler.

"Hey, Shelly." Janelle hugged her too, while Momma told her the girls were out back with Grandpa and the rabbits. Michael and Hudson went in that direction, and Janelle looked at her brother and his wife.

She remembered what it was like to be part of a couple. A happy couple. A married couple, who co-parented their children and spent holidays and weekends together.

Her doubts swelled, and Janelle had no idea what to do with her girls, with Russ, or with Henry. He'd asked for another chance, and the last couple of weeks with him at her house or taking care of the girls had been…nice. The girls definitely loved him, especially Kelly.

Janelle had struggled to file for divorce the first time, and maybe… *No*, she told herself. Henry would not be faithful to her. He had a temporary protective order that would get dismissed. He'd either go back to the woman who'd filed it, or he'd find another piece of arm candy to spend his nights with. She didn't need to open herself up for that hurt again, just because she felt a little bit guilty right now.

So she'd enjoy dinner and singing Christmas carols with her family. And she'd endure Christmas Day with Henry tomorrow. And then she'd get back to Russ.

* * *

"Morning, Daddy," Kelly said after Henry had walked through the front door without knocking. Janelle looked over to him from where she stood in the kitchen. She'd decided to go simple and non-traditional for their family

Christmas dinner, and she was making the girls' favorite food: spaghetti and meatballs.

The scent of garlic bread filled the air as Kelly and Kadence giggled in their daddy's arms. Janelle stalled in her browning of the meatballs at the sight of Henry with both little girls. It was a picture-perfect scene, with stockings hung along the mantel and the Christmas tree lights glinting in his smiling eyes.

He laughed with them and wished them a Merry Christmas before he looked at Janelle. She quickly looked away and turned the meatballs that were starting to get a little too brown on one side. She felt like crying, and she didn't even know why.

She'd managed to keep her new hot tub a secret from her parents, and the girls had enjoyed their origami cash that her father did for them every year. They'd gotten books and puzzles and water park passes for when they went to stay with Gramma and Grandpa in the summer.

"Let me go get the presents," Henry said, and Kelly went with him.

"Momma, can I let in King?" Kadence asked.

"Yes, baby. Did you feed him like I asked?"

"Yes, Momma." Kadence went out the garage and returned a few minutes later with the dog. He went straight to his food bowl and started eating, and Janelle felt a bit bad for him.

"We should've let him in earlier," she said. She'd just gotten so busy with the food.

"I put out food and water for the other dogs," Kadence

said. "Did Russ say when the new dog enclosure would be done?"

"No," Janelle said. "I haven't heard about that for a while." She'd texted Russ last night after she'd gotten home from her parents, but their conversation hadn't deviated to dogs or the enclosure. She did like talking to him, but guilt ran through her as Henry walked through the door, a huge smile on his face, Kelly right behind him.

She was laughing, and Janelle wondered if she was doing the right thing by pushing Henry away.

"Meatballs," he said, and she glanced up at him.

"Yeah," she said. "Hope you weren't expecting a turkey with all the trimmings."

A brilliant smile filled his whole face. "Whatever is fine with me, sweetheart." He beamed down at her. "The house looks great. Very Christmasy."

"That's all the girls," Janelle said, focusing back on her last batch of meatballs.

"Have you thought about what we talked about a couple of weeks ago?"

Janelle didn't dare look at him again. "I haven't stopped thinking about it."

"And?" Henry asked, his hand sliding down her arm to hers.

And Janelle still didn't know what to do. But she knew she couldn't have Christmas with two men and expect things to feel good. She didn't feel good. The problem was, she didn't know who to cut out of her life and who to keep.

Chapter 23

Russ woke the day after Christmas to a string of texts, and he reached for his phone, his heart pounding in a bad way. The day his momma's house had flooded had started out this same way, and he had visions of inches of water soaking the brand new floors and his parents moving back into the homestead.

But all of the texts were from Janelle.

Russ smiled and sat up as he tapped to get the string open. She'd texted a lot, in a very short amount of time, which meant she'd had these all planned out and ready to go.

And he didn't like them. Not one little bit.

Her first text started with *I've been thinking*, and things quickly devolved from there. She'd sent five or six texts, and the gist was that she didn't want to see him anymore.

"This can't be happening," he muttered to himself. He tapped the phone icon and lifted his phone to his ear. The line rang a couple of times, and his heartbeat accelerated with every passing moment.

"Hey," Janelle said.

Russ didn't know what to say, because the emotion in his throat made everything too tight. He finally asked, "You're breaking up with me through a text? The day after Christmas?" He thought of all the gifts he'd bought for her and her girls. Foolishness filled him from top to bottom, and the wallpaper across the room started to blur.

"I just need some time to think," she said. "With Henry back in town, he wants another chance, and I have the girls to think about..." Her voice trailed off, and Russ didn't want to hear it anyway.

"Okay," he said, because what was he supposed to say? "Talk to you later."

"Russ," she said, but he hung up anyway. He left his phone on the nightstand and went to get in the shower. He got dressed and went downstairs. He set coffee to brew, and he made breakfast. He didn't know where Travis was, but he'd been spending more and more time out in the woodshop, so Russ went out to take care of the dogs alone.

He breathed as he cleaned out bowls and pens, refilled food and let the dogs into the yard. The work wasn't hard, and Russ's mind was free to roam. The only topic revolving through his brain was Janelle.

He was in love with her, and he knew it. He'd told her three blasted days ago. She hadn't said it back, but Russ had felt confident in his feelings. He'd thought she was falling for him too.

Henry.

He'd known her ex was back in town, but he'd thought it was temporary. He'd thought Janelle had been telling him everything. He worked through his chores, finally returning to the homestead for lunch. Rex and Griffin were already there, eating leftovers from Christmas dinner at their parents'.

Russ kept his back to them as he poured himself more coffee. Thankfully, they were engaged in a conversation about the New Year's First Night in town, and Russ didn't have to talk. He'd already said he wouldn't be going to that, and now he had a very good reason never to leave the ranch again.

He felt utterly confined to the ranch now, and while he loved the land and the work, he'd had some hope of having a wife he loved and a family filling the homestead with laughter.

Rex left first, and Griffin looked at Russ. "You okay?"

"Fine," Russ said, as he didn't feel like talking about anything right now. In fact, he just wanted to heat up the steak bites and go back to bed.

"Okay, well, I have to go check on the goats. They've been breaking their hay cradle every morning, and I've been giving them a stern talking-to."

"Keep that up," Russ said, as if the goats really cared what Griffin said to them.

He was alone in the homestead now, and he hated it. The silence pressed in around him, but he couldn't get himself to get up and leave. Or even get something to eat. He pulled out his phone and looked at it again, almost expecting to see a text from Janelle. He didn't.

He was vaguely aware of the back door opening and people coming in, but he didn't look up. It was as if her words had branded themselves on the back of her eyelids.

"Hey, Russ, we have—" Travis cut off and then added, "What?"

Henry wants another chance.

"Russ?" Travis asked, and Russ finally looked up.

"Yeah?"

"Uh…what's goin' on?" Travis asked, glancing at Millie. They looked blissfully happy, and Russ had the sudden urge to run as far and as fast as he could.

"Janelle—" He shook his head, anger filling him over and over and over. "Her ex came back into town," Russ managed to say. "And she's unsure about us—again." He shook his head and looked down at his phone again. "I don't get it. I feel *so* sure about us."

And he did. So sure. Sure enough to tell the woman he loved her. Everything tangled inside him, and he couldn't believe he'd told her that. He couldn't believe she'd thrown it back in his face only a few days later.

"I'm sorry," Travis said. "What can we do?"

"Nothing." Russ needed to get out of there. Now. "At least she waited until after Christmas, but now I feel like a royal idiot for all the gifts I got her and the girls." He shook his head, pure agony moving through him that not even steak bites could fix. He felt so stupid. So, so stupid. "I'm going to go to bed. Wait. Do we have any of those steak bites left?" He detoured over to the fridge and pulled out the container. "Still a few," he said. "I'm taking these with me."

He left Millie and Travis in the kitchen, their happiness too heavy for him to shoulder. Back in his bedroom, he ate the steak bites and turned something on his tablet. With the volume loud enough, he couldn't think about Janelle. Problem was, he couldn't fall asleep either. But that didn't matter. He didn't want to sleep.

He just wanted to stop thinking.

* * *

Russ had never been as thankful for rain as he was over the next couple of days. The wet, sloppy conditions slowed everything down, from animal care to simply walking out to the equipment shed. The river rose and rose and rose, and Russ and Seth were out morning, noon, and night checking to make sure their embankments weren't going to collapse.

"Lost a bridge," Russ said, stamping his feet as he entered the homestead. He whipped off his cowboy hat and shook the water from it. "Seth?"

"I heard you," he said, appearing in the doorway of the kitchen. "Sorry, I was swallowing."

"Travis said the land is sliding on that south side, the way it always does." Russ shrugged out of his rain jacket and hung it on the hook on the back of the door. It wouldn't dry before he had to go out again, but it would keep Russ dry at least.

Seth shook his head and gestured for Russ to come get something to eat. "Jenna sent over baked potato soup."

The kitchen was warm and dry and smelled like bacon, and Russ's stomach grumbled at him for keeping them out in the rain for so long. He dished up some soup, added bacon, green onions, and another healthy pinch of cheese before joining Seth at the bar.

"How's his house coming?"

"He can't dig," Russ said. "So he's put everything on hold for a little bit." He stirred everything together. "Which is fine. He's not even done designing yet."

"And the dog enclosure?"

"It has a roof," Russ said, glad he and Travis had worked on it in every spare moment they'd had the last three and a half weeks. "And the inside is coming along real well. It should be ready by next weekend."

"I adopted out nine dogs on Saturday," Seth said, and Russ struggled to remember what day it was. The day after Christmas—the day Janelle had broken up with him for the second time—had been Thursday.

He didn't want to ask Seth if that was yesterday or not. All at once, he realized that it was. Today was Sunday, as Darren, Tomas, and Brian didn't work Sundays.

"That's great," he said, perhaps a bit belatedly.

"Do you want me to call Janelle and find out about getting the dogs back?"

Russ flinched, because he hadn't even thought about that. And the care they'd require in all the rain...she was probably going crazy. Part of him wanted to say that he could call Janelle, but he honestly wasn't sure if he could or not.

If he did, and she didn't answer... Russ knew his heart couldn't take any more of her special brand of hurt. *You asked her to tell you if Henry was going to be a problem*, he told himself. *And she did*.

Russ just wished Henry hadn't been a problem. He and Janelle had been divorced for over three years now. This was her fourth Christmas alone, and Russ had been hoping it would be her last—but that she'd be with him, on Chestnut Ranch, next year. And for many years to come.

"I'll call her," Seth said, picking up Russ's phone. "I'm just going to get her number..."

Russ let him do whatever he wanted with his phone. There wasn't anything sensitive on the device anyway, though it buzzed in Seth's hand. "You got a text from Momma."

"I'm sure she's asking me if Janelle will be at dinner tonight," he said.

"That's exactly what she asked." Seth cocked his eyebrows, but Russ didn't want to talk about it.

"I'm not going to dinner tonight," he said, taking his phone. Case closed. He texted his mother back that he wouldn't even be at supper that evening and left it at that.

"You know she's going to ask five million questions," Seth said.

"She's calmed down a little bit since you got married."

"She has?"

"I think she just wanted someone to get married, so good

job." Russ gave his brother a smile. "Has she started asking you about grandbabies yet?"

Seth scoffed and shook his head. "Bless her heart."

"I'll take that as a yes."

"I told her if she brought it up again, I wouldn't come to dinner either," Seth said, starting to chuckle. "I mean, I've been married for what? Five weeks?"

Russ put a smile on his face, but he couldn't bring himself to laugh with Seth. The smile itself felt false, and he let it slip away as Seth stood up. "All right. I have to get home for a minute. Jenna just texted to say she had a surprise."

Russ looked up as Seth put his cowboy hat back on. "Maybe she's pregnant."

Seth stumbled, his gaze flying back to Russ. "Uh, Jenna can't actually get pregnant."

Horror moved through Russ, and his mouth dropped open. "Seth, I'm sorry. I didn't know."

Seth's face darkened, and he nodded. "It's okay. We're talking about other things. Maybe adoption. Maybe doing some foster care."

Foolishness filled Russ, and he nodded. "I'm sorry," he said again.

Seth's smile came back, and he said, "Don't worry about it, Russ," before walking out.

Winner lifted her head and whined, and Russ said, "He'll be back, Winn." The dog sighed, and Russ knew exactly how she felt. "I know," Russ said, imagining his whole existence to be like this. Alone.

With Travis in his new homestead a couple hundred

yards down the lane, and Seth right across the river. But they still wouldn't be *here*, and Russ would be—by himself.

He should find someone else to get to know. But he didn't want to. He'd fallen in love with Janelle Stokes, and he just wanted her.

The furnace kicked on, and Russ got up. He went upstairs to his bedroom to change out of his wet socks, and all three dogs came with him. Even Thunder, who had a hard time with steps.

Russ sat on the end of the bed and scrubbed them all down. "Okay," he said. "You guys stay here. It's nasty out there, and we don't need you to get all wet and muddy and then want to lay on the couch."

Winner looked at him with the saddest puppy dog eyes on the planet, and she came with him downstairs to put on his boots again. Thunder and Cloudy didn't, and Russ hoped they'd keep a spot warm for him for his Sunday afternoon nap.

Chapter 24

Janelle sat by her phone on the twenty-seventh, expecting news from Henry. He'd hired someone at his firm to represent him in the protective order hearing. He could've done it himself, but he'd told her that he just wanted to have a clear head during the hearing.

She wore a pair of leggings, an oversized sweater, and the thickest, warmest socks she could find. The girls were outside, taking care of the dogs, and Janelle could admit that they were being troopers.

The rain hadn't stopped for about twenty-four hours now, but neither girl had complained about feeding the dogs or cleaning out their pens. They didn't let them out in the pouring rain, but kept them in the stable. The pens were open, though, so they had more room to move around, but it wasn't the same as running free through the yard.

Janelle poured herself another cup of coffee and curled

into the couch, checking her phone though it hadn't gone off. She stared out the window at the drizzly rain, feeling absolutely miserable.

"Shouldn't I feel better?" she murmured to herself. She'd broken up with Russ, and she'd thought that would align her thoughts and ease some of her guilt.

But it hadn't.

The agonized, dreadful quality of his voice still echoed in her ears, and the things she imagined him thinking and doing weren't pleasant.

Sometime later, the girls came in, and they were soaked to the bone. "Get in the tub," she told them. "Shed your clothes in the laundry room, and I'll go start the hot water." Though her house wasn't that old, it did take a while for the hot water to reach the bathroom.

Her back cringed as she got off the couch, and she couldn't wait to get back to work. That got her up and out of the house, doing something worthwhile with her time and energy. As it was, she'd closed the firm for two whole weeks, because Christmas was on a Wednesday this year. Some of the lawyers were taking emergency calls, but she didn't have any clients that would need her.

With the steam rising from the faucet, she reached into the tub and put the stopper in. She poured in a healthy dose of bubble bath, and her little girls came in a moment later, big bath towels covering them up.

"In you go," she said, and she held their hands to help them step into the tub without slipping. They giggled and played, and Janelle smiled at them.

Tears sprang to her eyes, and she turned away from her kids. She didn't want them to see her distress, and she stepped out of the bathroom a moment later. Pressing her back into the wall, she drew in a deep breath and tried to find her center.

But she felt so off-balance. Nothing was right in her life, and she couldn't help feeling like she'd made a colossal mistake by breaking up with Russ Johnson.

Her phone chimed, and she swiped at her eyes as she strode down the hall to the living room, where she'd left her phone.

The text was from Libby, not Daniel or Henry, and Janelle couldn't help the slip of disappointment moving through her.

I heard you broke up with Russ. What in the world is going on?

Janelle's breath shuddered in her text, and she planned to ignore her best friend. At least for now.

But Libby texted, *Call me right now* next, and Janelle thought maybe a discussion with Libby was just what she needed.

But was it?

She'd thought talking with her mother would straighten out her thoughts, but all that conversation had done was plant more doubt.

She didn't call Libby, but her phone rang, and Libby's name sat on the screen. Janelle's heart pulsed out extra beats, and she didn't answer the call.

She got two seconds of silence before Libby called again,

and Janelle sighed and answered the call.

"I knew you were there," Libby said. "Not taking my call." She half-scoffed and half-grunted. "Things must be bad."

Janelle opened her mouth to say she was fine, but the words wouldn't come. Her throat narrowed even further, and her chin quivered.

"You're not even speaking," Libby said. "This is so bad. I'm bringing a gallon of hot chocolate and those maple doughnut bites you like." Without waiting for a confirmation, Libby hung up, and Janelle knew she'd be there in half an hour.

Sure enough, Janelle had just finished braiding Kelly's hair when Libby walked through the front door.

"Libby!" Kadence yelled and jumped up from the table, where she'd been painting a picture of a dolphin. Libby received both girls in an embrace, and Janelle was glad she had friends to help her with her kids. With all her problems, really.

Libby zeroed in on Janelle in the next moment, and maybe she wasn't as grateful then. "I brought you girls a movie." She waved the DVD she'd brought, eventually handing it to Kelly, who put it in the player and got the remotes.

Libby joined Janelle in the kitchen, setting a big thermos on the counter. "Hot chocolate," she said. A brown bag joined the beverage. "Doughnut bites from Mabel Maples."

Janelle went for the pastries first, setting three of the

jumbo doughnut holes on a paper plate. She let Libby pour her a mug of sugary hot chocolate.

"How did you hear?" she finally asked once she heard the first song play on the musical Libby had brought for the girls.

"I live next door to Angela Brunner, and she's Millie Hepworth's best friend, and Millie is—"

"Dating Travis Johnson," they said together.

So the whole town knew of her break-up with Russ. She didn't dwell on it, as Janelle knew that the whole town didn't care who she spent her spare time with. They honestly didn't. It simply felt like it.

"What happened?" Libby asked.

Janelle shrugged and filled her mouth with doughnut.

"Oh, come *on*," Libby said. "This is *me*."

Janelle swallowed her treat and hugged her friend. "Henry's back in town, and he wants to be a family again. The girls love him, and…" She couldn't finish, because she didn't want to say she couldn't say no to him.

But that was the real reason. She'd always had a very hard time telling Henry Stokes no.

To Libby's eternal credit, she didn't sigh in exasperation. She didn't remind Janelle that she could barely stand her ex-husband. She didn't tell her that Henry had cheated on her many times—and that he probably would again.

Janelle had all of those thoughts herself, and Libby just let her wallow in it. She sipped her hot chocolate and looked over at the girls as they started belting out one of the songs.

"Where's Henry now?"

Janelle didn't want to tell her, but she couldn't say she didn't know. Janelle might be uncertain about things, but she wasn't a liar. "He's in court."

"Really? I didn't realize he was working right now. Hasn't he been hanging around here?"

"He's not working," Janelle said, and Libby was smart enough to put one and one together.

"Oh, his hearing is today?"

Janelle nodded, and she glanced at her phone as if someone would text her and let her know how things were going in Austin.

"He's not going to have that charge stick," Libby said.

"I know," Janelle said. "I'm not worried about that. I'm scared that this will blow over, and Henry will go home, and I'll have broken up with Russ for no reason."

Libby reached over and covered Janelle's hand with hers. "Maybe you should've waited to talk to Russ."

"I just felt so...inauthentic. Celebrating Christmas with him. Then with my family without him. I should've invited him to that. Why didn't he come? You know why?"

Libby just lifted her eyebrows, and Janelle said, "I know why. Because I was embarrassed to introduce him to my parents and family when I wasn't sure about us. When I was considering getting back together with Henry."

"Honey," Libby said gently. "Is that a real possibility?"

"I don't know."

"The reason he's at this hearing is because he showed up on another woman's doorstep, allegedly intoxicated, and demanded sex."

Janelle looked away, her eyes burning again. "I know."

"Okay, of course you do." Libby patted her hand again and nudged a doughnut bite closer to her. "I just... you and Russ are so good together. I've literally never seen you happier than the few months you were with him."

Janelle wiped her right eye, because she didn't cry, and nodded. "I know." Her phone rang, and she jerked toward it. "It's Daniel." She swiped on the call, her stomach swooping in the strangest way.

She'd spent plenty of time in court before, handling much more stressful cases. "Daniel," she said.

"The protective order was denied," he said.

"Oh, thank heavens," Janelle said, unclear as to why she'd been so worried. "Thanks for handling it."

"Of course," Daniel said. "Well, that's it. No complications."

Janelle nodded and hung up. "Denied."

"As we knew it would be," Libby said. "So what's Henry going to do now?"

Janelle blinked at her, because the answer seemed obvious. She and the girls had the next two weekends and a full week off in between. He'd come spend time with them, and they'd start to rebuild their family.

The thought should've made her insanely happy. But it didn't, and Janelle couldn't deny it forever.

Henry didn't call the way she expected him to, and Libby got up several minutes later and said she needed to get going. Janelle probably should've asked her if Griffin

Johnson had called her, but she didn't think of it until her best friend had left.

Kadence had fallen asleep during the movie, and Kelly came into the kitchen once it was over to ask if she could make grilled cheese sandwiches and tomato soup. "Absolutely," Janelle said, smiling at her. "I think I'm going to go lie down for an hour too. You're okay using the stove alone?"

"Alone?" Kelly asked, her eyes wide as a doe's.

Janelle pressed a kiss to her daughter's forehead and said, "You'll be fine. Come get me if you need me." She went down the hall and into her bedroom and closed the door. She dialed Henry and went toward the window.

"Hey," he said, and music came through the line.

Janelle sighed, as all of her questions had just been answered. She asked, "Where are you?" anyway.

"The protective order got dismissed," he said, as if that answered her question.

"Are you coming today? Kelly wanted to know." She pressed her eyes shut, because that was a lie.

"Not today," Henry hedged, and Janelle saw red behind her closed eyelids.

"Okay," she said, far too brightly. "Talk later." She hung up before he could hear how he affected her.

Foolishness raced through her. Humiliation joined in. Guilt paraded after both of those negative emotions.

And Janelle couldn't hold back the tide this time. She broke, and tears tracked down her face, because she knew only one thing for certain at the moment: she'd broken up with Russ for absolutely no reason.

*　*　*

Henry didn't return to Chestnut Springs until New Year's Eve, and Janelle hadn't seen him in almost a week. He'd texted and called a couple of times, saying he was really busy getting back into the swing of things at his law firm in Austin, and Janelle read between the lines.

He wasn't going to return to Chestnut Springs, at least not permanently. Why she'd thought he would, she wasn't sure. He'd only told her he wanted to have another chance with her; they'd done no talking about the finer details of what that would look like. Where they'd live, and where the girls would go to school, and what Janelle would do with her firm.

How had she been so stupid?

What did her feelings over the holidays mean?

"Daddy, look at that one." Kadence pointed up to the sky, where a brilliant blue and red firework exploded.

Henry held one of the girl's hands in each of his, and Janelle felt like an outsider in her own family. They'd watched a country music concert, and now the fireworks were happening. There was an afterparty at this First Night event, but Janelle wouldn't be keeping the girls up until midnight.

She walked beside Kelly as they went back to Henry's sports car, and they all piled into the tiny thing for the drive back to her house. He collapsed onto her couch while she set about putting the kids to bed, and she wanted to slip into her bedroom and leave Henry to himself.

She came out of the girls' bedroom, and Henry stood at the mouth of the hallway, leaning against the wall. He folded his arms and smiled at her, and Janelle's first reaction was to ask him to leave.

That spoke so much to her heart, and she wondered why she'd let the man back into her house. Back into her life. Back into the fleshy part of her heart, at the most vulnerable time of the year.

"I'm going to bed," she said. "Thanks for spending the evening with us." She shouldn't have to thank him for spending time with his family. A family he claimed to want to have.

"Can we talk for a minute?" he asked.

Janelle padded down the hall toward him, a strange mixture of hope and dread beating through her body with her pulse. They sat on the couch together, and Henry reached over and picked up her hand.

"Sweetheart, I want us to be a family again."

"Yeah, you said that," Janelle said. "But you're obviously going to keep working in Austin."

"And your firm is here."

"Yes."

"Have you thought about relocating?"

"The firm?"

"The family," he said. "Llano is halfway between here and Austin, and—"

"You want to move the girls to Llano?" Janelle would have to commute for forty minutes each way to work. Her already reduced-hours workday would get even slimmer.

They'd have to change schools, and Kadence had just started settling into her second grade class.

"The commute for me from here is impractical," Henry said. "That's why I've been up at my place this past week."

"I need to think about it," Janelle said.

"Really?" Henry asked. "Janelle, what is there to think about? We can't stay here."

"I like living here," Janelle said. It was her safety zone, as she'd established her law firm here sixteen years ago. She and Henry had worked out of jack-and-jill offices until she'd filed for divorce, when he'd left and gotten his own house and a new job in Austin.

She had friends here. She had a support system that had seen her through some very difficult times. She didn't want to move.

"Maybe you could come back to Bird," she said.

He was already shaking his head before she'd even finished the suggestion. "I can't do that," he said. "I make a whole lot more in Austin."

"I don't think we're hurting for money," Janelle said.

"Yeah, but I have a new standard now," Henry said.

"A new standard?" Janelle stood up, her head pounding. "I need to think about it." She walked away, feeling the urge to run.

"Janelle," Henry called after her, but she wouldn't be bullied into discussing something when she wasn't ready.

He'd always given her the space to think, and she wasn't going to agree to move away from her firm and her friends because he was pressuring her to do so.

Not this time.

She made it to her bedroom, closed the door, and locked it behind her. Then she slid down the door and exhaled, because she felt like she'd done the wrong thing.

Again.

Chapter 25

Russ did not leave the homestead for any New Year's celebrations. He woke up on the first at the first light of dawn, the way he always did. "Just another day," he told himself, though he knew it wasn't true.

It was a holiday, and Darren had invited him over for a late breakfast. Russ had finally accepted an invitation to leave the homestead, even though he wouldn't step foot off the property.

His heart wasn't bleeding quite as badly now, but it still felt hollow in both ventricles. He found himself working throughout the day, pausing to text Janelle something funny one of the goats had done. Or to tell her about the litter of abandoned puppies that had been brought to Seth in the middle of the night, just like they'd found on one of their first dates.

He hadn't contacted her, and he was mighty proud of himself because of that. He really didn't want to be the first one to go back to her. And in all honesty, he wasn't sure he'd simply accept her back into his life the way he had a month ago.

Sure, he'd been cautious. At least he'd told himself to be careful, go slow. But he knew in his heart of hearts that he'd simply welcomed her back into his life, his heart, and onto his ranch with open arms.

Flashes of Kelly and Kadence moved through his mind, and he wondered if they ever asked about him. "Not if their daddy is back," he muttered.

He stepped into the bathroom and looked at himself in the mirror. Russ was very good at operating on six hours of sleep without looking tired, but today, he looked absolutely exhausted. He had a long-standing tradition with himself to set goals for the year, and he always sat down first thing in the morning on New Year's Day to do it.

Today, though, he had zero motivation to make a list of any kind, let alone goals to improve himself or things to accomplish that year.

He brushed his teeth and got in the shower. He got dressed and sat down at the desk in his bedroom. Just as he suspected, nothing came to mind as he stared at the blank page in front of him. He couldn't write down something like *get married*, as that was completely out of his control. And Russ only set goals or listed accomplishments he could actively work toward and at least semi-control.

Get over Janelle Stokes.

He watched himself write the words, and he wondered if

he'd be able to do that in a twelve-month timespan. At the moment, it didn't feel like it.

Expand the goatherd to twenty.

That, he could do.

Finish the dog enclosure.

Maybe that one was a cop-out, as it would be done in a week, but he didn't care. Constructing a huge building like that in only five weeks was impressive, and he wanted to start the New Year out right.

Remodel the back porch.

Now that he'd been to Jenna's house, he knew the homestead needed a serious upgrade, and he didn't mind the work. In fact, Russ craved having something to do to keep his hands and mind busy.

Hire another ranch hand.

He needed someone to replace Travis, who'd already pulled way back. If it hadn't been for Darren and the rain, they'd be behind already.

Satisfied with his list for now, Russ got up and went to make coffee. He was surprised his mind could function as well as it had pre-caffeine. He cracked eggs into a hot pan, and they started sizzling right away.

He paused for a moment, looking around the kitchen. All he had to look forward to the next morning was this exact same scenario. Coffee for one. Eggs for one.

Travis's footsteps sounded on the steps, and Russ actually turned toward the sound in surprise. "Do you want some eggs?" he asked, ready to serve his brother his own eggs and make some more.

"Sure," he said. "But aren't we going to Darren's for breakfast?" He opened the cupboard and got down a mug. "You have to go, Russ. You haven't left this house in too long."

"I'm going," Russ said, automatically annoyed. "It's not until ten, and that's hours from now."

"Just a few," Travis said, sugaring up his coffee and leaving hardly any in the pot for Russ. He didn't care. He slid the eggs out of the pan and handed the plate to Travis.

"If you don't want them, give them to the dogs. They're begging." Russ nodded to the three dogs that sat on the edge of the kitchen.

"I'm surprised Jenna and Seth didn't take at least Cloudy. Jenna loves that dog." Travis opened a drawer and pulled out a fork.

"They're still getting settled in," Russ said. "I'm sure I'll lose Cloudy soon enough. Probably Winner too. She loves Seth."

"She loves the closest person with food," Travis said with a chuckle. He fed the dog part of the egg white, and Winner practically caught his finger in her jaws.

Russ put four eggs in the pan this time and noticed the coffee had dripped enough for him to have a cup.

"Are you going to try to talk to Janelle this year?" Travis didn't even look at him, and Russ wasted one of his best death glares on the side of his brother's face.

He turned back to the stove, his brain bubbling like the edges of his fried eggs. He put them on a plate for himself, and instead of sitting at the counter, he went over to the table.

"Come on," Travis said.

"I'm not talking about her," Russ said. "I never pressed you for a single detail about Millie. I never suggested you call her or do anything you didn't want to do." His chest heaved, and the thought of eating made his stomach turn.

"I know, I'm sorry." Travis brought his plate over, accompanied by all three dogs. "I just know—I can tell you really like her."

"I don't just like her," Russ said darkly. "But what can I do? She chose her ex-husband over me. I can't compete with that." He didn't even know how to compete for a woman. He shook his head. "It's fine. I don't want to talk about it."

"All right," Travis said. "I just know you make goals on the first."

"I wrote down a few things," Russ said, slightly on the defensive.

Travis's phone rang, and he turned his attention to it instead of hounding Russ with more questions. Thankfully. He wolfed down his eggs while Travis talked to a wood supplier out of Bourne and poured his coffee into a to-go cup so he could take it out onto the ranch with him.

He left through the back door without saying goodbye to Travis, and he went out to the goats and horses, leaving the chickens for Travis. He worked and fed and watered and fixed a fence in the dog yard before letting them out. At ten, he started toward Darren's cabin, heading up the back steps like he'd done many times before.

He opened the door just as he heard someone say, "He's coming in now. Move."

Move?

Russ automatically paused, cocking his head toward the kitchen. People were definitely moving, and they'd stopped talking. Sheer annoyance filled him, and he turned back toward the door, ready to leave. The last thing he needed was people talking about him. And not just people. These cowboys he'd thought he knew and trusted.

As far as he knew, this breakfast was just for the men who worked the ranch, and those were his brothers and Darren, Tomas, and Brian.

"Russ?" Darren said, peering around the corner. "I thought I heard you come in. Hurry up, the French toast is hot right now."

Russ couldn't leave now, and he sighed as he followed Darren around the corner and into the kitchen. These cabins had one large room that served as kitchen, dining, and living room. Russ saw all the expected guests, but they were clustered oddly. As he scanned them, it became obvious that they were hiding someone.

His heart dropped to the soles of his boots, and he said, "I'm leaving."

"Russ," Travis said, stepping forward. Sure enough, Janelle's dark hair peeked out from behind someone's back, and Russ experienced a rush of panic unlike he'd ever felt before. He had to get out. Now.

"Give her a chance," Travis said. "She came out here."

"No," Russ said, shaking his head as he backed away. He spun around as Janelle said, "It's okay, guys. Let him go."

Just her voice made every wound he carried on his heart open up, and he barely made it outside before he sucked in a breath that sounded like a sob. He couldn't get the right air no matter how he tried, but he hurried down the back steps and away from the cabin.

He simply couldn't face Janelle right now, even if she had come all this way.

Chapter 26

Surprisingly, Janelle did not cry on the way home from Chestnut Ranch. Sharp disappointment cut through her, and she'd paid Audrey to stay with the girls until noon, so she drove to the diner and got a table in the corner to eat her bacon and egg special, with a cinnamon roll drenched in maple syrup.

She ate the dessert first, hoping the sugar would kick in and get her brain to work. Maybe she just needed some time to sort through things. But she was tired of thinking so much. For some people, they needed to slow down before making decisions.

For Janelle, she needed to get out of her head and act. As a lawyer, she was very good at this. The law made sense. She could look up a point of law, a subsection, an obscure subparagraph, interpret it, and make a quick decision, sometimes in front of a judge and jury.

But feelings of the heart?

She was completely lost.

What she knew was that Henry hadn't changed hardly at all. He wanted to push her to make decisions she wasn't ready to make, and he started to veil threats soon after that. Janelle hadn't even gone to bed yet before Henry had said, *We won't make it if we stay in Chestnut Springs.*

Janelle had slept on it, and she'd awakened in the morning with worry and panic deep in her soul. She didn't want to move from Chestnut Springs. She loved this town, all the customs, and her short commute.

She'd questioned herself through her shower and makeup routine about her selfishness. Then she reminded herself that Henry had always thought of himself first. Almost always. Janelle hated absolutes, but she could say with absolute certainty that she was miserable.

And now Russ had practically run away from her. "No," she said. "He *did* run away from you."

Humiliation filled her, and she couldn't get Travis's mournful eyes out of her mind. Not only that, but she'd embarrassed herself—and Russ—in front of all of his brothers and friends. Everyone would think of that every time they saw her, even if Russ did take her back.

"He's not going to take you back," she muttered to her plate of bacon, and the tears came then. She sucked them back, because she was in public and the last thing she needed was a witness to her sobbing in the corner of the diner.

She took a bite of her bacon and let her hair fall down between her and the rest of the diner. She focused on her phone as if the Queen of England had messaged her.

* * *

THE NEXT MORNING, Janelle woke but didn't get out of bed right away. She didn't hear anything down the hall or in the kitchen, and she was sure the girls were still in bed.

Keeping her eyes closed, she tried to identify how she felt.

She felt like she was in the right place, and her conviction to stay in Chestnut Springs solidified. Her phone buzzed, and she turned and picked it up from her nightstand.

Libby had texted a single picture. A screenshot, it looked like.

Janelle's pulse pounded as she tapped on it and zoomed in, as her eyes weren't as good as they used to be. It was a picture of Henry's status, and it listed him as "in a relationship" with a woman named Tiffany Whitehead.

The life left her body, and she knew in that moment she'd been played. Again.

And she'd acted too soon with Russ. She never acted too soon, and yet she'd broken up with him out of guilt.

"Momma?"

"Yeah." She flipped her phone upside down and turned toward the door. "Come on, baby."

Kadence skipped across the room and climbed into bed with Janelle.

"What should we do today?" she asked her daughter.

"Aren't we takin' the dogs back to the ranch?"

Janelle's stomach clenched. "I forgot about that," she murmured. Seth had called last week, and Janelle had said she'd bring the dogs back today. Seth had dropped off a truck last night and everything.

She knew Russ fed the dogs in the morning, and she wanted to jump out of bed right now and get everyone rounded up and ready for the trip. At the same time, the man clearly needed time and space, and Janelle wanted to honor that.

So maybe she should start with a text. Maybe she'd taken too many steps yesterday, showing up to breakfast at his friend's house.

She picked up her phone as Kadence started singing a nursery rhyme and typed out two texts.

One to Henry: *We're over. Please contact my lawyer for visitation arrangements.*

Sent.

One to Russ: *Would love to talk when you're ready.*

She read over it a couple of times, trying to decide if it was too pushy. In the end, she sent it and got out of bed with a sigh. "All right, baby. I'm going to shower, and then we have to get the dogs ready. Will you go wake up your sister?"

"All right, Momma." Kadence slipped off the bed and ran out of the room, calling Kelly's name. Janelle smiled at the thought of them, beyond grateful that she had these two little girls in her life. She wished Henry would choose them over whatever his flavor of the day was, but she couldn't change Henry.

She couldn't make Russ talk to her or respond to her texts either.

All she could do about that was pray.

A couple of hours later, she pulled up to the ranch in the truck Seth had left for her, glancing around as if Russ would come out the front door with that trademark smile on his face. She took a moment to imagine the scenario, but no one appeared.

She eventually got out and told the girls to get all the leashes. After dialing Seth, she waited while the line rang.

"Hey, you here?" he asked, and he sounded out of breath.

"Yes," she said as one of the dogs started barking. "We have the leashes and stuff, but I'm a bit worried about getting the dogs in the right place."

"We're heading your way," he said, and the call ended.

Her chest vibrated in a strange way, because "we" could include Russ. Surely it wouldn't though. Seth had been a witness to yesterday's humiliation.

Winner came tearing toward her, barking every other second. She slowed and wagged her tail around all three of them as Kelly and Kadence giggled and squealed. Janelle just tried not to get knocked down as Winner looped around and around them.

The dogs in the back of the truck definitely got riled up, and Janelle was very happy to see four cowboys walking toward her, a couple more dogs with them. The girls passed over the leashes, and Seth took charge of the dogs as his three ranch hands got everyone secured.

"Thanks so much, Janelle." Seth grinned at her and opened the tailgate. He handed his leash to Darren, and the ranch hands took the six dogs with them. "You kept King?"

"Yeah," Janelle said. "The girls and I love him."

"I'm glad." Seth re-secured the tail gate and met her eye again. "Russ is inside."

"Oh, I'm not doing that again," she said.

"He asked me to send you in when you got here."

Janelle frowned at Seth. Russ hadn't responded to her text from only a couple of hours ago, and she didn't believe him. "Uh, I..." She seized onto Kelly's hand. "I have the girls with me."

And she wasn't ready with her apology like she'd been yesterday. Her entire explanation had fled completely.

"Come on, girls," Seth said. "Pile in. My wife has fresh chocolate chip cookies at our house."

"Momma?" Kelly looked up at her, and Janelle didn't know what to say.

Seth swung Kadence into his arms, and she squealed as she laughed. "They'll be fine," he said. "Although, she might try teaching them the piano if you stay too long."

"I want to play the piano," Kelly said, much to Janelle's surprise.

Before she knew it, Seth had the girls loaded up and was backing out of the driveway. Without a way to leave, Janelle faced the homestead. Had Russ really asked Seth to send Janelle inside?

The Christmas tree in the window and the wreath from the door were both gone now. The Christmas lights had been taken down, but the ranch and house still held a magic that Janelle really wanted in her life.

"You want Russ," she told herself, and that gave her the courage to take the first step toward the house. She thought she saw the blinds flutter in the living room window, but she didn't pause.

When she reached the top of the steps, the front door opened. Russ stood there, wearing the sexiest jeans on the planet, a brown leather jacket over a blue button-up shirt, his cowboy boots, and that delicious cowboy hat.

Janelle froze, because he stole her breath, just the way he had at the speed dating event where they'd first met. She'd had her eye on him for a solid half-hour before she'd been able to sit down in front of him and introduce herself.

He said nothing, and he filled the doorway so spectacularly. Janelle's stomach quivered, and she imagined she was standing in front of the toughest judge in the county.

"Hello, Russ," she said. "I want to start with a plea for understanding. I know you've never seen me argue in a courtroom or know much about me as a lawyer. In that, I always know what I'm doing. In that world, things make sense." She drew in a breath, trying to remember her arguments.

She couldn't.

It was time to go with her heart.

"But when it comes to men, I'm really bad at knowing what to do. I'm bad and slow at making decisions. But I know that I've been brilliantly happy with you when we're together, and I'm nothing but miserable when I do this stupid thing and break-up with you."

She lifted up her hands as if she could call down Texas magic from the sky. "I hope you can forgive me for a second time. You can take as much time as you need, obviously. But

I want that hot tub installed, and I want you to come sit in it with me, and I want to find all the different ways I can to tell you I love you."

Russ finally moved, and it was to take four strong steps toward her to sweep her into his arms. He still said nothing, but his actions had always been more powerful than his words. Janelle melted right into his strong embrace, her emotions shaking as they streamed from her.

"I'm sorry," she whispered. "I'm so sorry."

"I know you are, baby," he said, his voice husky. He pulled back as suddenly as he'd come forward. "Is that true? You love me?"

Janelle exhaled as she nodded, her smile instant and finally feeling like it belonged on her face. "Yes, Russ. I'm in love with you. Please forgive me."

Please, please, she thought, clenching her arms around her middle as she waited for him to say something.

Chapter 27

Russ hadn't slept hardly at all last night. Neither had any of his brothers, as they'd all sat in the living room while they talked Russ through every possible scenario with Janelle.

And no matter what the thread was, no matter where the path went, in the end, Russ wanted to be with Janelle.

"So you have to talk to her," Rex had said.

"She's coming over tomorrow," Seth had said. "To bring the dogs back."

Russ had wanted to help her with that. He should make sure she didn't have a ton of clean-up to do afterward. But he'd needed a couple of hours of sleep, and then he had chores to do.

When Janelle had texted that morning, Russ had shown it to Seth, who'd been standing beside him as they watched Griffin work the horses. "When she brings the dogs," he'd said. "You should tell her to come talk to me."

"All right," Seth had said, and that was that. He'd even taken the girls without specific instructions to do so.

"Russ?" Janelle reached up and cradled his face in one hand.

He leaned into her touch and sighed. "I love you, Janelle. And part of that is forgiveness. I'm sure I'll do stupid things in our relationship."

"I just need you to love me," she said.

"I already do."

"And I need you to put me and the girls first."

"I can do that."

"And I need you to be faithful to me."

"You're the only woman I've ever wanted," he said, taking a step toward her and leaning his forehead against hers. "Will you tell me what happened with Henry?"

She sighed and leaned into his body. "I will, but does it have to be right now?"

"No," he said, his heart hammering. "Right now, I want to kiss you." He pressed his lips to hers, glad when she melted into him. Russ definitely felt something new in her touch, and it certainly felt like she loved him.

He wasn't going to rush into anything though—at least that was what he told himself. And right now, it didn't matter, because Janelle loved him and he loved her and the rest would come as they worked to merge their lives.

* * *

January passed in a blur of ranch work, rain, and driving to town to see Janelle, Kelly, and Kadence. Russ had learned how to make the "best pizza ever," as Kelly had taught him the proper kneading technique. He'd helped clean up Janelle's stables and backyard. He'd hung more of Kadence's paintings on the fridge at the homestead than it could hold.

But the little girl loved seeing them when she came out to the ranch. Janelle brought the girls out often, as they loved the horses and dogs and goats. All the same things Russ loved.

Travis's house started to come together, and he and Millie were getting married in March. *Next month*, Russ told himself as he listened to Travis nailing something together down the lane.

Janelle's firm had bought thirty tickets to Chestnut Springs's Valentine's Day dinner and dance, and she gave them away to clients and employees. But she'd reserved two for her and Russ, and Russ had thought perhaps Valentine's Day would be a great day for a proposal.

So maybe he hadn't slowed down any. Maybe he'd been thinking about getting married before Momma and Daddy left for their service mission at the end of May.

He and Janelle had talked about marriage, and she claimed to want something simple. "Simple" worked for Russ, who thought a wedding on the ranch would be beautiful. Janelle had said that would be fine with her, surrounded by friends, family, and co-workers, and Russ had started shopping for diamonds.

The engagement wouldn't be a surprise for anyone. He and Janelle had even spent one of their date nights at the mall, looking at rings. He'd gotten a good idea of what she liked, and he maybe just needed a couple of hours to himself to get to town and find something she would like.

That didn't happen until the following week, and Russ walked into a jewelry store in the mall after consuming the best cinnamon roll on the planet from the front seat of his truck.

"Good afternoon, sir," a man said, and Russ met his eye.

"Afternoon."

"What can I help you with?"

"I'm looking for an engagement ring," he said, his voice catching on the last word. He was really doing this. And it felt right. Janelle would say yes. There wasn't anything in between them anymore. Henry hadn't contacted her about his visitation, and she'd told Russ that he'd disappeared before after one of their break-ups.

"Do you know what you're looking for?" the salesman asked.

"Uh, let's see." Russ swiped to get his phone open. "She likes a round diamond. Something bigger in the middle. White gold band." He read through his notes. "And something unique." That was one of his requirements. "Do you have anything like that?"

"I'm sure we do." The man led him to another counter, where literally dozens of engagement rings waited. "Here are some of our round-cut diamonds," he said, lifting out a case of ten rings. "And you might consider a brilliance cut.

They're beautiful. That's what we have here." He set another tray next to the first.

Russ started looking at them, eliminating some instantly. In the end, he said, "I think these are all boring." He looked up at the man. "No offense."

The man smiled. "Of course not. Unique. Let's see." He moved down the case and pulled out another tray. "These are different. They have a classic white diamond for the center, which signals the purity. But diamonds come in other colors as well, and these all have colored settings with the white diamond."

Russ looked at those, immediately seeing Janelle in them. "I like these."

"The pink and yellow are highly popular," the man said. "Red and blue are the most rare."

Russ looked through the tray, finding one with a large white diamond in the center, in the cut Janelle liked. Several colored stones rounded it, like flower petals, in a variety of colors. "I like this one," he said.

"All right," the man said, taking the ring from him. "Do you know her size?"

"Yes." Russ went back to his phone to check it. "Seven."

"Sir, this ring is one of our signature pieces." The man met Russ's eye, seriousness in his.

"What does that mean?"

"It means our master jeweler hand-crafted it. It's truly one-of-a-kind." He looked a bit apologetic. "That means it's quite pricey."

"How much?" Russ asked, though it didn't matter. His bank account could handle whatever this man threw at it.

"Fifteen thousand dollars," the man said. "It's one of our most expensive pieces in the store." He studied Russ. "Do you still want it?"

"Yes," Russ said, wondering if Janelle would be upset by the price tag. *She doesn't need to know it*, Russ reasoned with himself. She'd accepted the hot tub, and they'd enjoyed several evenings together on her back patio.

The man said it would take an hour to size the ring, and Russ said he'd be back. He had no other reason to be in the mall, so he went to the food court and ordered a basket of fried chicken and biscuits. As he ate, he thought about how he could propose to Janelle.

In the end, he decided he couldn't wait until Valentine's Day, and he drove straight from the mall with the properly sized ring to her house.

She wasn't there, and he called her as he sat in her driveway. "Where you at?" he asked after she'd picked up.

"The girls have Boys and Girls Club today," she said. "We'll be home in ten minutes."

"Great," he said. "I'm in your driveway."

He almost drove away several times as he waited for her to pull in. But he held his ground, glancing at the ring box as her sedan came to a stop beside his truck. He grabbed it and got out before any of them could.

Kadence was the fastest getting out, and Russ had to dart in front of her and say, "Hold on a second, tiny tot," to get her to stay.

In response, Kadence threw her arms around Russ and held him tight. "Are you staying for dinner? Momma ordered pizza."

"I never say no to pizza." He smiled down at the little girl. "I wanted to ask you guys something." He waited until Kelly came around from the passenger side of the car. He faced the three of them and pulled out the ring box, his throat sudden as dry as sand.

"Russ," Janelle said at the same time Kadence said, "What's that?"

"This, little lady," Russ said. "Is an engagement ring." He cracked the box. "The center stone is a big white diamond. These other ones are colored diamonds, and I liked this one because it's colorful and pretty and it reminded me of your momma."

He showed it to Kadence and Kelly and then Janelle. "Janelle," he said. "I love you. I want to be your husband, and Kelly and Kadence, I want to be your daddy. What do you think? Do you think your mom should marry me?"

"Yes, yes, yes!" Kadence shrieked, and she started to dance around.

Kelly wore a big smile, and she nodded emphatically. "Yes, Momma. You should marry him."

Russ looked at her and cocked his head. "Well?"

Her eyes looked like polished glass as she nodded. "Yes," she said. "Yes, I'll marry you." She threw herself into Russ's arms as her daughters cheered, and he kissed her. Relief and love filled him, and Russ took the girls into a big embrace too.

"Do you guys think you can come live with me at the homestead? That place is so big, and I'm so lonely."

"Yes," Kelly said. "But I want that bedroom at the end of the hall."

"Kelly," Janelle said, but Russ only laughed. "You can have any room you want, Kelly. There's plenty to choose from." He beamed down at the girls, who headed into the house as they discussed which bedroom they'd each get.

"You know they'll end up in the same room," Janelle said. "Right?"

"Yeah," Russ said. "I know." He kissed her properly, right there in her driveway, and slid the ring on her finger. "Do you like it?"

"I love it," she said. "Just like I love you."

"I love you too," Russ said, in awe that this was his reality. But it was, and he'd never been happier or more hopeful for his future.

"We should hire Millie," Janelle said.

"And get married at the ranch," Russ added.

"Deal," Janelle said. She gazed up at him, and Russ wanted to be the best man he could be—for her. "I can't wait to marry you."

"I can't wait for that either, baby. Are we still thinking the end of May?"

"Yes," she said. "The end of May should work out just fine."

Russ thought everything between them would work out just fine too, and he couldn't wait to live his life with this woman at his side.

* * *

Keep reading for Travis and Millie's wedding, as told by Travis's brother, Rex! Then go read **A COWBOY AND HIS DAUGHTER - available in paperback!**

Sneak Peek! Chapter One of A Cowboy and his Daughter

Rex Johnson liked weddings, because there was always a lot of available women clamoring for the bouquet. They had their hair done up, their makeup perfect, and those high heels he liked a whole lot.

He sat in the front row with the rest of his family, his mother already weeping and Travis hadn't even come out to the altar yet. As the baby brother, Rex had a special relationship with his momma, and he reached over and took her hand in his.

She squeezed his hand, and he knew she wanted this marital bliss for all of her sons, including him. He didn't want to disappoint her, but he wasn't going to get married. That was why he kept the women he dated at arm's length, why he only went out with them for a maximum of two months, whether he liked them or not. And most of the time, he knew after the first or second date if a woman would even get that long on his arm.

His brothers thought he was a player. Even Griffin, the next oldest brother and the one Rex lived with full time in town, thought Rex was a bit cruel to women. What they didn't know was that Rex had given his heart away six years ago. He couldn't give away what he didn't have, but he didn't want to stay home every weekend either.

Most of the women he went out with knew what they were getting, and those that didn't, Rex told them the rules.

Yes, he had rules, and he wasn't sorry about them.

The twittering in the crowd increased, and Rex looked to his right to see Travis had come outside. Finally. The sooner this wedding got started, the sooner it would end. His brother took his spot at the altar, shook hands with the preacher, and nodded as the other man said something.

Rex hadn't gotten the fancy ranch wedding, with miles of flowers and lace and the rich, black tuxedo with the matching cowboy hat. He hadn't had people rushing around to make sure all the chairs were perfectly aligned or that the guest book sat at a perfect forty-five-degree angle from the five-tier cake.

He'd dressed in the nicest clothes he had and met the woman of his dreams at City Hall in downtown Bourne. Her sister and her husband had been there as witnesses, and Rex had smiled through the whole thing.

He'd smiled when Holly told him she was pregnant. Smiled at her parents when they'd gone to tell them. Smiled, smiled, smiled.

Rex was tired of smiling.

He hadn't been smiling when Holly had lost their baby.

Or when she'd said she'd made a mistake and then filed for divorce only two months after they'd said I-do. Or when she'd left for work one morning and never came home.

He'd packed up everything they'd owned and put it in storage, where it still remained in a facility on the outskirts of Chestnut Springs. He wasn't sure why he'd chosen to store it so close, as he hadn't heard from Holly in the five years since all of that had happened, and he wasn't living in his hometown at the time.

Maybe for distance. In the end, he'd returned to Chestnut Springs, and he'd been living with Griffin in the downtown home they'd gone in on together for four years now.

The music started, and a hush fell over the crowd as they stood. Rex did too, going through all the motions. He was happy for Travis and Millie. He was. They made the perfect couple, and Travis had always been a bit quiet when it came to women.

Rex, on the other hand, was the complete opposite. He smiled at Millie as she came down the aisle with his father. Hers apparently lived somewhere else, and they didn't have a great relationship.

Every step his father took over the white river rock was slow and looked painful. Rex really didn't know how he was going to leave in a few short months to work a service mission in the Dominican Republic, but Mom insisted they were going, that the doctors said it was okay.

Daddy kissed Millie's cheek and passed her to Travis, who hugged him. Rex's heart—the little he had left—

swelled, and he felt a brief flash of the perfect family love he shared with his parents and brothers.

He did love them, and he enjoyed the Thursday night dinners at his parents' house and the Sunday afternoon meals and activities that still took place at the ranch. Seth and Jenna came every week, and with Travis and Millie living in the front corner of the ranch, Rex assumed they'd keep coming too.

"Sit down," Griffin hissed, pulling on Rex's sleeve. He practically fell backward into his seat, and his face heated.

"Pay attention, baby," his mom whispered to him, and Rex tried to focus on what was happening in front of him. The pastor spoke about nice things, about keeping the lines of communication open, of working through problems instead of letting them fester into bigger things.

Mille and Travis each read vows while the gentle spring breeze blew under the tent, and then the pastor pronounced them husband and wife. Travis grinned at his new wife, dipped her though she squealed, and kissed her.

Rex cheered and clapped the loudest, as always. He knew he had a loud voice, and he didn't even try to quiet it. The new bride and groom went down the aisle to the applause, and everyone stood up.

It seemed like a whole lot of work for a ten-minute ceremony. At least to Rex, and he once again found himself thinking about the simplicity of his marriage. He'd known it wasn't what Holly wanted, but with the time and money constraints they'd had, it was all Rex could give her.

Now that his bank account was considerably bigger, he wondered what kind of wedding they'd have now.

You've got to stop, he told himself sternly. Most days, he did just fine not thinking about Holly and the baby that wasn't meant to be. He'd kept the secret from everyone he knew for six long years, and if he didn't think about it, the burden was easier to carry.

But weddings—especially his brother's—had really brought back the memories in full force. He followed his parents down the path toward the butterfly gardens at Serendipity, thinking he'd probably like an outdoor wedding now too.

That so wasn't banishing the thoughts of marriage and weddings and Holly from his mind, but Rex couldn't help it. He stayed quiet, his cowboy boots making the most noise as they walked through the gardens and out to the parking lot.

Jenna had a sprawling patio that was heated and cooled, and the wedding dinner would take place over there. After that, Millie and Travis had decided to forgo any type of formal dance, and instead, they'd rented a couple of hot air balloons for guests to enjoy as they celebrated with an ice cream bar for anyone who hadn't been invited to the family dinner.

Rex hadn't had a reception either, and his frustration with himself grew.

"See you over there," his mother said, and Rex looked up from the ground to find Griffin helping her behind the wheel of the minivan she drove now. Daddy couldn't drive with his leg, and most of the time, Rex thought his mother shouldn't be driving either.

"Ready?" Griffin asked as he closed the door behind their mother.

Rex handed him the keys in response. "You drive."

"What's goin' on with you?" he asked. "You've been real quiet during all of this."

Rex shrugged, because he didn't want to say what was going on with him. Maybe he should just try calling Holly again. He'd done that for the first few months after she'd left, and she hadn't answered once. He hadn't known if her number was the same, and he was certain it wasn't now.

He didn't know if she was still in the state, though he suspected she was. She'd been born and raised in the Texas Hill Country, and she'd told him once during their year-long relationship that she couldn't imagine living anywhere else.

"Not even Dallas or San Antonio?" he'd asked.

"Definitely not," she said. "I'm a country girl, Rex."

He'd laughed, because he was a country boy too, and he sure had loved Holly Roberts. With effort, he pushed her out of his mind and focused on the radio station Griffin had set.

He liked country music as much as the next red-blooded cowboy, but Rex's tastes were more on the modern side than Griffin's. He didn't reach over to change the station, though, something he'd done in the past. He and his brother could argue the whole way to the ranch about what to listen to.

"I'm going to apply for that camp counselorship again," Griffin said, and Rex looked over at his brother.

"Is it that time already?"

"Yeah," he said. "Applications are due by April fifteenth. Do you want to do it with me?"

"Maybe," Rex said. He and Griffin had both gone to Camp Clear Creek out near Lake Marble Falls and Horseshoe Bay in the Hill Country. It was beautiful country, and Rex liked being outside. He'd had a group of six boys every two weeks for three months, and he loved boating, hiking, fishing, and hunting.

"Just fill out an application with me," Griffin said. "You can change your mind later."

"You don't need to fill out an application," Rex said. "You can just email Toni." He swung his gaze to his brother and found Griffin's face turning bright red. He burst out laughing, connecting all the dots in an instant.

"What?" Griffin asked, obviously not amused.

"You still have a thing for Toni."

"I do not," Griffin said. "First of all, the word *still* is all wrong. It implies I had a thing before and now I *still* do, which is totally not true."

"Mm hm," Rex said, because he knew Griffin better than anyone. And whether or not Griffin admitted that he'd had a cowboy crush on their boss last summer didn't mean he didn't. Because he totally did. "Well, I'm sure she's always looking for good counselors."

"So maybe you shouldn't apply," Griffin quipped, and Rex laughed again. "Besides, I heard she left Clear Creek, which is why I do need to apply."

"All right," Rex said. "Apply then."

"You don't want to?"

Rex watched the last of the town go by before Griffin started down the curvy road that led to the ranch. "You know what? I'm going to stick closer to home this summer. I'll handle all of your chores at the ranch."

Griffin snorted. "Right. You'll hire someone the moment you can. You can't even get out of bed before nine-thirty."

"I can," Rex said. "I just don't like to."

"You're not even a real cowboy," Griffin said with a chuckle.

"Getting up at the crack of dawn isn't a characteristic of a cowboy," Rex said, reaching up and settling his hat on his head. He had all the proper attire to make him a cowboy, and that was good enough for him.

Griffin eased up on the gas pedal, and Rex looked over at him. "What?"

"I don't know where my phone is."

"Are you kidding me right now?" Rex started lifting up the sunglasses cases in the console between them. "It's not here."

Griffin was notorious for losing his phone. Leaving it places. Not knowing where it was. Another round of annoyance pulled through Rex, especially when Griffin slowed and pulled over. "I know where it is. I left it in the groom's dressing room. On the windowsill."

"Do you need it right now?" he asked

"Yes," Griffin said, no room for negotiation.

"We're going to be late," Rex said.

"Text Seth with your phone," he said. "It'll be fine."

"Fine." Rex scoffed and pulled out his phone and texted their oldest brother. He was so changing the radio station while Griffin ran back inside the fancy building at Serendipity Seeds to get his device.

Several minutes later, Griffin pulled up to the curb and dashed off without even closing the driver's side door. Rex promptly leaned over and changed the radio station to something that played more of the country rock he liked and sighed as he settled back into his seat, reaching to put his window down so the breeze would blow through the cab of the truck.

"Come on, baby doll." The woman's voice stirred something in Rex, and he turned to look out his window.

A little girl had crouched down on the path, her dark hair curly and wispy as she examined something on the ground.

Rex couldn't see her mother, but he heard her say, "Sarah, come on. We're going to be late."

That voice.

Rex got out of the truck and looked further down the path to find a dark-haired woman standing there, wearing a pair of jeans and a T-shirt with a lightning bolt on the front.

"Holly?" he asked, his voice barely meeting his own ears. But it couldn't be Holly. Not his Holly.

She sure did look like her, though, and Rex took another step toward the little girl. "Hey," he said, making his voice as gentle as he could. The girl, who'd ignored her mother completely, looked up at him. She was beautiful, with deep, dark eyes and the same olive skin Holly had possessed. She couldn't be older than four or five, as her face still carried some of the roundness that chubby babies had.

"What're you lookin' at?" He crouched next to her, the sound of the gravel crunching as the woman came closer.

"Sarah," she said, her voice almost a bark.

Rex straightened, and now that Holly was closer, he totally knew it was her. Number one, his wounded heart was thrashing inside his chest, screaming about how this woman held the missing bits of it.

"Holly," he said, and it wasn't a question this time.

Pure panic crossed her face, and she fell back a step, one hand coming up to cover her mouth. He still heard her when she said, "Rex."

He looked back and forth between her and the little girl, beyond desperate to know what in the world was going on. But for maybe the first time in his life, he stayed quiet, giving his ex-wife the opportunity to explain.

Sneak Peek! Chapter Two of A Cowboy and his Daughter

Holly Rasmussen stared at the tall, dark, deliciously handsome cowboy in front of her. Rex Johnson, the man who'd been haunting her for five long years. The man she saw every time she looked into her daughter's eyes. The man she'd hoped to never see again.

"Well?" he prompted, and Holly blinked her way out of the trance she'd fallen into.

"How are you?" she asked, but he shook his head.

"Try again."

She reached for Sarah's hand, the tears coming more easily than her daughter did. Thankfully, the little girl slipped her dirty hand into Holly's, and she glanced down at her. She'd just turned five, and if Holly's memory was right, Rex was very good at math.

And her memory was right.

"Baby doll," she said, her voice tight, scared. She hated

that seeing him made her feel this way. He'd once made her feel loved and cherished, like nothing in the world could go wrong.

She'd showed him, though. With her, disaster always struck.

"This is Rex Johnson," she said, and the little girl looked up at her father. "Rex." She cleared her throat, cursing herself for agreeing to come to Chestnut Springs. She knew Rex was from this town, but she'd reasoned that she'd be here for less than a day, and surely she wouldn't run into him.

"Holly," her mother called, and Holly pressed her eyes closed. Wow, she didn't want her mom to see Rex. Everything started crashing around her, every half-truth she'd told. Every lie. Every secret. Every day for the past five years.

She turned around and said, "Go tell Gramma I need a minute," to Sarah. She gave her a quick kiss, glad when the little girl did what she'd asked.

"Gramma," Rex said. "She's your daughter." He took a step closer to her, those dark-as-midnight eyes sparking and catching hers. "Is she *my* daughter?"

Holly couldn't lie about this. She also couldn't vocalize it, so she just nodded.

Rex searched her face, more and more anger entering his expression than Holly liked. She'd expected it, of course. Or had she? She'd never imagined seeing Rex again, and she honestly didn't know what to expect next.

"You didn't lose the baby?" he asked, his voice hoarse and cut to shreds.

"No," she whispered.

He stepped back and blew out his breath. "You just didn't tell me. You disappeared in the middle of the night. You hated me that much?" He shook his head, his fists clenching and unclenching. "You know what? I don't care." He leaned closer and closer, his fury a scent in the air. "You're a terrible, terrible person. I can't believe I've wasted six years of my life thinking about you."

Footsteps sounded behind her, but she couldn't move. *You're a terrible, terrible person,* rang through her entire soul.

He wasn't wrong.

She just hadn't expected to hear him say such things. Her mother certainly had. Her grandmother. Everyone. But Holly couldn't explain herself to them, because she didn't understand why she'd done certain things either.

"Ready?" a man asked, and he joined Rex's side. He definitely belonged to Rex, and Holly guessed he was one of his four brothers. She'd never met any of them, and Rex had basically given up everything to be with her.

"Who's this?" he asked, and Rex shook his head, his jaw clenched.

"No one. Let's go." He turned away from her, and Holly flinched. Wow, that hurt. *No one.*

You started it, she thought, and she felt like she'd gone backward five years in only five minutes.

The two cowboys walked away from her, Rex's brother casting a worried look over his shoulder as he went. Rex got in the truck, almost immediately opening the door and coming back toward her.

"Is she really mine?" he asked in a loud voice from several paces away.

"Yes," Hollly said.

"Then I want to see her," he said. "What's your number?"

"I'm only in town for a wedding today," she said.

He laughed, the sound high and cruel. "Get a hotel, then, Holly. Because if she's my kid, I'm suing you for custody."

"There's no if, Rex," she said, finally finding her voice. "You're the only man I've ever been with."

"Not comforting," he said, holding his phone out. "I'm serious. Give me your number."

Holly looked helplessly at the other brother, who'd come closer too. "What's going on?"

"She's my ex-wife," Rex practically bellowed. "And she told me she'd lost our baby. But I just met her." He glared at her. "I want your number, and if you leave town, I'm filing kidnapping charges."

Tears streamed down Holly's face, but she nodded. She recited her number, and Rex tapped it into his phone. Her device in her back pocket buzzed, and he said, "I just texted you. Text me where you're staying, and I'll come pick her up in the morning."

"What are you going to do?" she asked.

"My brother got married today," Rex said. "So I'm going to keep everything real quiet for right now. And then I'm going to make sure I get to see my daughter whenever I want." He took one menacing step toward her. "You stole five years from me. I gave you *everything*." He broke then, and Holly's heart wailed and wailed.

She watched him cover his emotions with that furious mask again, and he said, "If you don't text me, I'll call the police."

"I'll text you," she said, wondering how she was going to explain having to stay in town to her mother.

He turned back to his brother, who wore a look of complete shock on his face. So Rex had kept their secret this whole time. Rex marched past the brother and got in the fancy pickup truck parked at the curb. The brother stared at her, so many questions in his eyes.

Then he turned and got behind the wheel, driving away in the next moment.

Holly watched the truck go, and then she collapsed onto the nearest bench and sobbed.

* * *

"I don't know, Momma," she said later that night, after the wedding. "But I'm staying for a bit. I have a place for me and Sarah." She glanced around at the tiny studio room she'd gotten for the next week.

"Who's going to take care of Sarah?" Momma asked. "You're really going to get a job up there? Why?"

Holly drew in a deep breath. "I ran into Rex today."

For maybe the first time in her life, Momma had nothing to say. When Holly had taken Rex to meet her parents and tell them she was pregnant, her mother had had plenty to say. A born-and-raised Texan, she didn't hold back her opinions.

"He knows about Sarah," Holly continued.

"Dear Lord in Heaven," her mother said, her voice breathless.

"I'm ready, Momma," she said. "I've been telling you that for months."

"I know," Momma said. "But I thought you'd start easy. Get a job, and I'd take care of Sarah during the day."

"Well, I'm going to get a job up here," she said. "They have daycares and stuff here."

"You can't afford that," her mother said. "Where are you even staying? You can't afford anything in Chestnut Springs."

Holly pressed her eyes closed against the questions. Her momma had fired them at her like this when she'd shown up five years ago, divorced and six months pregnant. She'd been living with her parents ever since, fading in and out of depressive episodes that didn't leave her much time to learn how to be a mother.

But she'd been doing really well for a long time now. Over a year. Once her father had passed away and Holly had seen her mother start to slide, she'd pulled herself together and gotten help. She still talked to a therapist every day through an app, with weekly video appointments.

And she was ready to be the mother Sarah needed. Her mother had been resistant, because she loved playing the hero. And if Holly got back on her own feet and started taking care of herself and her daughter, Momma couldn't give herself a medal at the end of every day.

"Momma," she said, when she realized her mother was still talking. "I'm thirty-one years old."

You're a terrible, terrible person.

"I can do this," she said. "It's time to come clean. Tell the truth. Move on."

"In Chestnut Springs?"

"I owe Rex a proper apology and explanation," she said quietly, powerful guilt moving through her. "Aren't you the one who always says that?"

"Yes, but—"

"Momma," she said over her mother, and it felt good to stand up to Momma. "I'll call you tomorrow, okay?"

A long silence came through the line, and Holly knew her mother was working through a lot of her own issues. "Okay," she finally said, and Holly nodded. She hung up and looked over to the sleeping form of Sarah.

A pretty little girl, Sarah had brought more joy and light into Holly's life than anything else.

"Except Rex," she murmured, because that man had been her whole world.

You're a terrible, terrible person.

She knew an apology wouldn't go far with Rex. The man loved deeply, and she heard his angry voice as he accused her of stealing six years of his life. As he threatened to call the police. She reached over and stroked Sarah's hair, the soft, silky quality of it helping her feel a tiny pinprick of hope.

"You're better now," she whispered to herself. "Maybe you can fix things with Rex, too."

She'd texted him the name of the motel she'd found, and he said he'd be there at nine o'clock in the morning. Holly hadn't brought clothes to Chestnut Springs, because she'd planned to stay for just one day.

Momma was right; she didn't have much money. But she had a credit card, and she could get a few things for the week she'd be here.

"Might be longer," she said to herself, because she remembered Rex being the kind of man that fought for what he wanted. He'd called her for six straight months after she'd vanished from his life. He'd gone to her parents' house. He'd called her friends. Gone to talk to her boss.

And when he found out where she'd been, maybe he'd understand.

Maybe.

Hopefully.

"Please," she prayed, because she was ready to move forward, and she couldn't if Rex didn't come with her.

***

Oh, dear, I sure hope Rex and Holly can figure things out! Find out if they can in **A COWBOY AND HIS DAUGHTER - available in paperback!**

Chestnut Ranch Romance

Book 1: A Cowboy and his Neighbor: Best friends and neighbors shouldn't share a kiss...

Book 2: A Cowboy and his Mistletoe Kiss: He wasn't supposed to kiss her. Can Travis and Millie find a way to turn their mistletoe kiss into true love?

Book 3: A Cowboy and his Christmas Crush: Can a Christmas crush and their mutual love of rescuing dogs bring them back together?

Book 4: A Cowboy and his Daughter: They were married for a few months. She lost their baby...or so he thought.

Book 5: A Cowboy and his Boss: She's his boss. He's had a crush on her for a couple of summers now. Can Toni and Griffin mix business and pleasure while making sure the teens they're in charge of stay in line?

Book 6: A Cowboy and his Fake Marriage: She needs a husband to keep her ranch...can she convince the cowboy next-door to marry her?

Book 7: A Cowboy and his Secret Kiss: He likes the pretty adventure guide next door, but she wants to keep their relationship off the grid. Can he kiss her in secret and keep his heart intact?

Book 8: A Cowboy and his Skipped Christmas: He's been in love with her forever. She's told him no more times than either of them can count. Can Theo and Sorrell find their way through past pain to a happy future together?

Bluegrass Ranch Romance

Book 1: Winning the Cowboy Billionaire: She'll do anything to secure the funding she needs to take her perfumery to the next level…even date the boy next door.

Book 2: Roping the Cowboy Billionaire: She'll do anything to show her ex she's not still hung up on him…even date her best friend.

Book 3: Training the Cowboy Billionaire: She'll do anything to save her ranch…even marry a cowboy just so they can enter a race together.

Book 4: Parading the Cowboy Billionaire: She'll do anything to spite her mother and find her own happiness…even keep her cowboy billionaire boyfriend a secret.

Book 5: Promoting the Cowboy Billionaire: She'll do anything to keep her job…even date a client to stay on her boss's good side.

Book 6: Acquiring the Cowboy Billionaire: She'll do anything to keep her father's stud farm in the family…even marry the maddening cowboy billionaire she's never gotten along with.

Book 7: Saving the Cowboy Billionaire: She'll do anything to prove to her friends that she's over her ex…even date the cowboy she once went with in high school.

Book 8: Convincing the Cowboy Billionaire: She'll do anything to keep her dignity...even convincing the saltiest cowboy billionaire at the ranch to be her boyfriend.

Texas Longhorn Ranch Romance

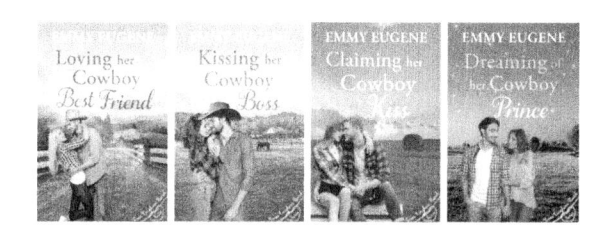

Book 1: Loving Her Cowboy Best Friend: She's a city girl returning to her hometown. He's a country boy through and through. When these two former best friends (and ex-lovers) start working together, romantic sparks fly that could ignite a wildfire... Will Regina and Blake get burned or can they tame the flames into true love?

Book 2: Kissing Her Cowboy Boss: She's a veterinarian with a secret past. He's her new boss. When Todd hires Laura, it's because she's willing to live on-site and work full-time for the ranch. But when their feelings turn personal, will Laura put up walls between them to keep them apart?

Book 3: Claiming Her Cowboy Kiss: He's tried and failed in country music - and women - before. She wasn't supposed to be at the ranch that summer. When Maddy shows up unexpectedly, will she and Kyle have their second chance romance? Or will the call of the stage lure him away?

About Emmy

Emmy is a Midwest mom who loves dogs, cowboys, and Texas. She's been writing for years and loves weaving stories of love, hope, and second chances. Find out more at www.emmyeugene.com.